FOOL'S FOLLY:
THE COMPLETE ADVENTURES
OF THE MAJOR, VOLUME 5

FOOL'S FOLLY
The Complete Adventures of the
Major
VOLUME 5

BY

L. PATRICK GREENE

ILLUSTRATED BY

WILLIAM M. ALLISON

ALTUS
PRESS

2023

TABLE OF CONTENTS

BLUE MONGRELS

THE RAIN storm had burst with the suddenness that is Africa. In a very few minutes its devastating floods had made a desolate ocean of mud of the dreary waste of land which fringed the diamond town, and men hastily sought the shelter of their ragged tents or weather beaten shacks.

Outside one of the huts a man crouched, an ear pressed against the wall, on his face the strained look of one who is endeavoring to overhear a conversation.

Presently he cursed and relaxed somewhat. Evidently the pattering of the rain on the tin roof completely drowned the murmur of voices within the hut.

From the roof the rain ran down in a steady stream on to the man's helmet, and from thence a khaki colored cataract trickled on to his face, dripped from the point of his enormous nose on to his mustache, causing that once waxed and bristling hirsute adornment to droop dispiritedly.

Trooper Harry Short cursed again. His thin khaki uniform was saturated, his feet had sunk out of sight in red, stinking mud.

"Oh, hell!" he groaned as he shifted his position slightly. His curse was echoed by two loud soughing noises as he raised his feet from the clinging mud. "An' ter think I jined the police fer this! Wot chance 'as a man got of makin' any money on a beat like this 'un? Not a dog's chance! Been on it now fer a week an' this is the first time anyfing's come my way. Only a lousy quid at that."

He spat viciously and stared dull-eyed through the thick curtain of rain. Men hurried by, sliding awkwardly in the mud, heads bent, sheltering their faces with upraised arms from the driving force of the storm.

One of them shouted a mocking invitation to, "Come along and have a drink. It's damn' dry."

Another admonished him to keep a close watch on his, the speaker's, claim, yelling, "I was just about to wash out a big stone, but the rain washed me out. I'll hold you responsible if anybody takes it!"

The gurgle of the rain blended with the miner's chuckle at his feeble joke and Short's rumbling curse, echoing against the tin roof of his shelter, was comparable to a peal of thunder presaging the greater flow of words which followed.

"Think you're blarsted funny, don't yer?" he shouted at the retreating miner after he had exhausted his stock of blasphemy. "I hopes yer get pinched fer illicit diamond buyin' and sent to the breakwater for the rest of yer dirty life. That's what I hopes!

"The blaggard!" he continued to himself, looking and feeling as if the rain had dissolved his back-bone. "I ought ter have turned my hand ter diamond digging or—or illicit diamond buying, instead of joining the police. But 'ow was I ter know they'd stick me in a 'ole like this? Besides, they all told me there was plenty o' money to be picked up easy, an' without risk, in the police. The liars! I've been done proper."

He lapsed into a moody silence, thinking of the events leading up to his enlisting in the force which was entrusted

with the safeguarding of the property and morals of South
Africa's Diamondapolis.

Born in a Sydney slum—and such Australians out-cock-
ney the cockneys, and their language would make a
Billingsgate porter blush with envy—his early life had
been spent in the gutter, learning the life and language of
the gutter. As a sneak thief he had prospered until, fearing the vengeance of the pals of a man he had betrayed to
the police, he had fled to the gold fields at Ballarat. Three
years of that life had improved him out of all recognition
physically; but morally—!

Morally he was still a gutter sneak and possessed of
all the vices that implies. Finally, getting implicated in
a cowardly stabbing affray, he had fled to South Africa
to avoid arrest, confident of hiding himself amongst the
multitude of men who had come from the four corners of
the earth in search of vast wealth easily acquired.

Once in Africa it occurred to him that if he only could
join one of the police forces he would be absolutely safe, for
who would think of looking for a wanted man in the ranks
of the police? And of the several detachments, that of the
diamond town most strongly appealed to him.

The stories he'd heard of troopers keeping large racing
establishments, of men retiring after a few years' service,
multi-millionaires and respected members of the commu-

nity! And all saved on a miserly pay of five, more or less, bloomin' shillings a day! It was to laugh! It was also a mark for Short to shoot at.

So he had joined up. There had been little difficulty about that. He could ride and shoot. Physically he was fit; morally—well, he had good letters of commendation, forged, of course, and anyway the recruiting officer didn't seem to be overconcerned about morals. Hadn't he said, with a wink at that, that the police force offered unlimited opportunities for advancement?

The recruiting officer had meant that it was possible to get a commission from the ranks; the wink was intended to convey to the sergeant escorting Short the impossibility of that man ever achieving commissioned rank.

But Short, taking it to refer to wealth easily acquired, had been well satisfied and had applied himself industriously to his recruit's drill, thus hastening the day when he was annointed a full duty man with the road to wealth before him.

Instead of which, here he was posted on the very outside fringe of things, where the claims were petering out, where nothing ever happened and no one had ever tried to bribe him to look the other way whilst they conducted an illicit piece of business.

He had protested to his immediate superiors, applying for a more remunerative beat. And they had laughed at him and when he still protested, said that he would have to stay where he was until he had earned promotion. First he must prove his mettle.

Short cursed again. Possessing a single-track mind and intelligence, he still was convinced that all policemen were criminals, that all of them battened on the bribes of men they were supposed to arrest. He did not realize that the majority of his comrades were above suspicion; that only a small minority, their numbers continually lessening, accepted hush money from evil doers.

A horseman cantered by, splattering mud into Short's face.

"You blarsted fool!" he shouted, and then once again was overcome by the unkindness of Fate.

He was marooned, that's what he was. He visualized himself plodding around here in the mud, drenched to the skin, until he rotted.

"Nothing ever 'appens 'ere," he growled.

He was conscious presently that the murmur of voices inside the hut was getting louder, the voices of three men raised in acrimonious dispute.

Short smiled sardonically as he listened. They were going to need him after all.

The door opened suddenly and an undersized, crafty-looking individual peered out, winked broadly at Short and then raised his voice in a shrill cry of, "Officer! Mister Policeman! Here!"

Short tipped his helmet rakishly over one eye, pulled down his tunic, and after a slight wait advanced ponderously.

"Well, what is it?" he asked gruffly. "What d'yer want, Johnson?"

"Come in here a minute, officer. Me an' my partners want to consult with you."

The speaker stood aside so that Short could enter, then bolted the door again.

"Well, wot is it?" Short growled again and scowled forbiddingly at a fair haired youth who was backed up against the wall, his hands high above his head.

"Just a little business dispute, officer," said the third man. He looked like a boozing prizefighter, but there was that indefinable something about his speech and carriage which tradition ascribes to be the hall-marks of a public school boy. "You know Johnson. I'm Saunders. And this chap," he jabbed his revolver into the youth's ribs, "is Moore, the third member of our partnership."

"All right. Get on with it," Short said uncertainly. He apparently was not sure of his lines.

"The matter is very simple," Saunders continued. "We— that is Johnson and myself—discovered that Moore has been holding back 'stones.' It was my intention to have him arrested, but Johnson's very soft-hearted—"

"I'm afraid I am," that man murmured with a hypocritical sigh. "But Moore's so young, and it would break his mother's heart."

"Oh! Get on with it," Short interrupted roughly. "Cut out the preaching."

Saunders laughed harshly. "Well! To make a long story short, I agreed to Johnson's plan. That is: On condition Moore releases to us his share in the claim and mining property, we will drop all talk of prosecution. Moore's agreed to our terms and we just want you to witness the agreement. That's all."

He turned to the white-faced youth. "You can take your hands down now, Moore. I don't think you'll be such a fool as to try and shoot me in the presence of a police official. There's the agreement on the table, and pen and ink. Sign, and you can go to hell, for all I care."

Moore lowered his arms and advanced toward the table. He picked up the pen, dipped it in the ink, and—

"I'm damned if I do," he cried hotly. "It's all a put-up job. You know I didn't take the diamonds. You, or Johnson—the sneaking rat!—put them in my pocket."

"And to think we befriended him," Johnson sighed, "when he didn't have a penny in the world. And now he's biting the hand which fed him."

Moore looked at him wrathfully. "You're a damned liar, Johnson," he said scathingly. "It was my money which bought the claim, it was my money which outfitted us and kept us going. And I've done most of the work. I took you and Saunders in as partners because you professed to know the country and the diamond business, and because Saunders was in the same Form as my brother at school. I thought I could trust him; I never trusted you. And now, when my money's gone and we were just beginning to strike it rich, you try to pull this game off. But I'm damned if I'll sign that agreement. Prove your charge if you can!"

"That will be easy," Saunders said smoothly.

"All right. Prove it. Send me to the breakwater. But I intend to hold on to my third share, and when I get out I'll make you divide up."

"Get your handcuffs, officer," Saunders interrupted. "I charge this man with stealing diamonds."

Short advanced slowly, handcuffs jangling harshly together.

"Oh, his poor mother!" Johnson moaned. "Ten years on the breakwater, he'll get. He won't be young and pretty when he gets out, and his mother'll have died with the shame of it."

"Come on, hold out your hands," Short said heavily. "I arrest you—"

Moore impatiently waved him aside. "I'll sign," he announced in a dull voice, and picking up the pen he wrote his name at the foot of the agreement. "There! Now are you satisfied, you damned robbers?"

"Quite," Saunders answered with a mocking bow as he opened the door. "This way out."

Moore glared at him, looked as if he were about to risk a hand encounter, then passed dolefully out into the pelting rain.

"Be a good boy and don't steal no more," Johnson shouted, then the door closed and the three were left alone.

"Your signature here, officer," Saunders said briskly, "and we won't need to trouble you any further."

Short wrote his name laboriously. "I ought ter get more than a quid fer what I've done," he grumbled.

"Yes? And what have you done save sign your name as a witness to a business document? A pound is very good pay if you ask me."

"If it 'adn't 'a' been fer me," Short protested, "you couldn't 'ave bluffed that youngster out o' his share of the claim."

"Oh, I think so, officer. But you mustn't say things like that. You mustn't talk of bluffing. It was a straightforward business dealing as one glance at the agreement will prove. See, it says here, 'In return for value received I, Thomas Moore, sell my share in the Peg 24 Claim to Messrs. Saunders and Johnson.' Quite businesslike, you see. No talk of bluffing or stolen diamonds, you see. Moore sells for 'value received'—and that's that. Actually we've done our late partner a good turn, a very good turn indeed. We had to do it this way, we had to save him in spite of himself. He would have been ruined completely if he'd been sent to prison."

"Aw, hell! Tell that to the marines. You've diddled him out of a rich claim an' I helped you, an' I ought ter get part of the profits."

"How big a part, Officer?"

"A thousand quid, say."

Saunders and Johnson laughed derisively. "We'll sell you the claim and the outfit for that."

"Well," uneasily, "I ought ter get more. If I don't, I'll—" He stopped short, intimidated by the meaning expressions the two men exchanged.

"You'll what?" Saunders prompted gently.

"I'll blow the gaff. I'll give the game away."

"Don't be a fool," Saunders exclaimed irritably.

"An' think, Officer," Johnson's tones were very suave, "how could you show up? What could you say? There's two of us, our word against yours, and of your signature on a business agreement, you can't go back on that, can you? Well, then?"

"Here's your quid," Saunders took up the conversation. "Take it or leave it, it's all you'll get. And damned good pay for a signature if you ask me."

He threw a sovereign down on the table.

Short scowled at it and at the two sneeringly triumphant faces of the two men. "Aw, hell!" he exploded wrathfully, picked up the coin and left the hut.

The two men stood in the doorway, watching his progress through the mud, shouting sarcastic farewells. Then when the curtain of rain hid him completely from sight they closed the door and, opening a bottle of Dop, drank to the success of their knavery.

"At that," Saunders confessed with a laugh, "young Moore had me going for a while. We'd have been done if he'd held out. We couldn't have made good our charge. It isn't as easy to frame a man as it used to be."

"Well, the bluff worked," Johnson said complacently. "So why worry? He was too much concerned with thoughts of his de-ah Moth-ah to dare take a chance. Pass the bottle, will yer?"

MEANWHILE TROOPER Harry Short, having located an empty deserted shelter, was seated on a rickety stool, gazing vacantly out through gaping holes in the walls and cursing the rain, his folly in joining the police, the miserliness of Messrs. Saunders and Johnson—cursing everything!

"A lousy quid," he muttered. "That's all I get. I ought ter 'ave held 'em up fer more. But wot chance did I have? A lousy quid, not enough fer one good blindo. Oh, hell! If only somethin' 'ud 'appen!"

As he spoke a white man was murdering a half-caste woman in a shack not a hundred feet distant; a native limped by, and the cause of his limp was a deep cut in his thigh, and in that cut a good sized diamond was embedded. A white man rode by on his way to keep an appointment with the limping native, planning as he rode to take the diamond and pay for it with half-pennies gilded to look like gold. A group of natives, helplessly drunk on rot-gut gin, reeled by on the way to their *kraals*, having completed a long term of service at the mines; and dodging their footsteps were three ruffianly white men who intended to rob the helpless natives of their hard-earned wealth. Farther on a coolie fruit seller squabbled violently with a Chinese laundryman, a squabble which was to end in an exchange of knife thrusts.

But Short saw or heard nothing of all this. He was only conscious of the rain, the stinking mud and the chill which, penetrating to his marrow, added to his abject misery.

"If only somethin' 'ud 'appen," he whined his complaint, "so's I could arrest somebody an 'ave a good case! Then they'd move me to a proper beat where the pickings is easy. But 'ere— Aw, hell!"

He took the coin Saunders had given him from his pocket, and holding it out on the palm of his hand looked at it resentfully. Presently the feeling of resentment passed and he thawed inwardly as he thought of the drinks the little coin would buy. He would go that night to the Royal Bar where all the big men of the diamond field congregated. Maybe one would tip him off to something good. Maybe—

He closed his eyes in order to visualize better the life he would lead once he had acquired wealth.

After a little while he slept, snoring hoggishly.

WHEN TROOPER Short awoke two hours later, the rain had ceased and the gray clouds had dissolved into a vivid blue sky in which floated a molten sun.

Men in white ducks, dirty flannels, ragged khaki, red shirts, blue shirts and shirts improvised from sacking, hurried back to their claims, eager to continue the feverish search for wealth in the oozy mud.

Already the mud was hardening; soon it would be fine powdered dust again. Even now, over the veld beyond, dust devils were madly gyrating. The rainstorm had been purely a local one, its bounds as clearly defined as if they had been plotted with rule and compass.

Short rose sluggishly to his feet and went out into the sunshine. Almost immediately he was enveloped in the thin mist of steam which rose from his clothing. He put his hand in his pocket, seeking the coin which was to reimburse him for his trouble. It was not there. With a frantic haste he searched his other pockets fruitlessly. He cursed volubly, scowling at sundry passers-by who jokingly questioned him anent his loss. Remembering suddenly that he had been holding the coin in his hand when sleep overtook him, he re-entered the hut. But he found no coin, only the naked footprints of a man. The evidence was clear. While he slept a native had crept in and taken the coin from him.

Further embittered by his discovery, Short decided to throw all caution to the winds, and acting on a sudden impulse set out for the claim of Messrs. Saunders and Johnson, determined to make them shell out again, and shell out heavily.

"There ain't another claim within shoutin' distance of ther'n," he muttered as he significantly patted the butt of his revolver. "That makes it easier. I'll 'old 'em up."

But once beyond the fringe of huts his pace slackened, came finally to a halt and he sat down moodily on a rock outcrop.

"There's two o' them," he said aloud as if in answer to an inward voice that was urging him on. "There's two of 'em, an' that Saunders knows 'ow to 'andle a gun. I don't like it. They might shoot me. It 'ud be easy fer them to trump up some damned lie to clear themselves. It ain't no use tryin' ter get anything out o' them. Hell!"

The loud cracking of a whip roused him from the sullen reverie into which he had fallen.

Looking up he saw a wagon, drawn by sixteen oxen, coming slowly over the veldt toward him. The driver, he saw, was a squat, powerfully built Hottentot who walked at the side of the near-side wheeler, flourishing a long whip and talking in endearing tones to his animals. No one else appeared to be with the wagon.

Short jumped to his feet and went to meet them, licking his lips in evil anticipation of the game he was going to have with the nigger. And maybe there would be something in the wagon worth looting.

As he approached, the Hottentot shouted a shrill order and the wagon came to a groaning, protesting halt.

"Whose wagon an' oxen are these, nigger?" Short asked roughly.

"Baas?" the Hottentot questioned, shaking his head, indicating that he did not understand the other's speech.

Short swore irritably. "You're lying," he shouted. Then slowly, at the top of his voice as if by shouting he could make his words understandable, "Your boss? Where the hell is 'e?"

"Baas?" the Hottentot said again, and shrugged his shoulders.

"Think yer smart, eh?" Short snarled. "Pretending yer don't understand white man's talk. Well then, that'll larn yer!"

He struck out viciously, hitting the Hottentot on the point of the jaw, knocking him off his feet.

"You black fool!" he growled his wrath somewhat appeased by this exhibition of senseless brutality. Turning from the prostrate Hottentot he critically examined the span of oxen.

"They're good beasts," he said admiringly; he understood animals. "Them two black bulls, now, they'd pull a mountain if they was 'itched to one."

He scowled at the Hottentot who had not moved since the blow which sent him headlong.

"There must be a white man with this outfit," Short continued. "A nigger, left alone, wouldn't look after 'is beasts as well as this." And therein Short proved that his knowledge of natives was infinitely inferior to his knowledge of cattle.

He climbed up into the wagon and quickly surveyed its interior. It was almost empty, there was nothing in sight worthy of looting. A few tins of bully-beef, half a sack of flour, cooking utensils and some blankets; that was all.

Sitting down on the front seat he grinned malevolently at the Hottentot who now had risen to his feet and was tenderly fingering his swollen jaw.

"I'll learn yer," muttered Short, then turned his attention to the oxen again. Suddenly his muscles tensed and a gleam of cupidity shone in his eyes as he remembered a case which had been the chief topic of conversation among the police when he first had joined up. An old transport driver had been brutally murdered, his oxen and wagon stolen, and the murdering thieves had left no clues. As he looked again at the oxen before him, Short recalled the description of the stolen cattle which had been posted on the notice board.

If these were the stolen cattle, as he was almost sure they were, life would be very much brighter. He would wait here until the nigger's boss came along and hold him up for a big bribe. Or it might be a good plan to play an honest game. He'd be sure of promotion if he arrested the murderer.

But first he must make sure that these were the cattle.

Jumping down from the wagon he passed slowly along the line of oxen, feeling their off-side ears. Each one was nicked with two V-shaped notches.

Elated at his discovery he drew his revolver and yelled "Hands up!" to the Hottentot. The native obeyed with a promptitude which suggested a contemptuous familiarity with at least two words of the English language.

"Wish I could speak yer lingo," Short said. "Howsomever, I don't know as that matters much; you'd only lie. Well, we'll see. You an' me, my beauty, are a-goin' ter wait 'ere, inside the wagon, until yer boss comes along. And then, there'll be doings."

Getting behind the Hottentot, he jabbed the muzzle of his revolver with brutal force into the small of the native's back, then pushed and kicked him toward the wagon.

So intent was he on this operation that he did not notice the approach of a horse carrying two riders, one of whom was a tall man in crude, ill-fitting garments. The other was the youth, Tom Moore.

"Up into the wagon, you nigger," Short fumed and drew back his fist in threat at the Hottentot.

"Oh, really now," a suave, musical voice drawled behind him, "I wouldn't do that. Really I wouldn't."

Short turned quickly, and the Hottentot clambering quickly into the wagon sat down on the seat, grinning happily.

"An' who the 'ell may you be, ducky?" Short growled. "An' wot's that blighter Moore doin' with yer?"

"Ah!" breathed the tall man softly as he slid from his flea-bitten gray horse, and then turned to help the other dismount. Moore was bleeding from a deep cut over the eye, and his clothing was torn and dusty.

"Ah," said the tall man again. He was even taller than Short had first imagined, and broader, and more muscular. "Ah! Thereby hangs a tale." He fished a monocle from a pocket in his ragged coat and fixed it in his eye.

Short laughed boisterously. The newcomer looked like a back-country clodhopper aping a stage-door Johnny. His round, smooth shaven face seemed flabby to Short's unobservant mind, his soft smooth voice and the innocent blue of his eyes caused Short to forget the thrill of fear he had felt when he first had turned to face him. The policeman now was sure that he could insult this soft apology for a man with impunity, and the thought filled him with a delusion of strength and great courage.

So he laughed again.

"Yes," the monocled one continued and sighed profoundly, "I suppose I do look like a bally scarecrow. These clothes don't fit me awfully well, although they do fit me—er—awfully, if you catch the distinction."

"Aw, 'ell! Come off yer bleedin' perch, ducky," Short growled. "Wot's yer bleedin' game?"

"Yes, yes," the other replied with nervous haste. "You wanted to know about friend Moore, eh? Shortly, Short—I understand your name is Short; short of temper, short of brains, short of— Yes, of course. Rude of me to be so— er—verbose. I'll proceed. In short, Short, I was riding over the rolling veld, heading for yonder great hive of industry, diamonds an' all that, an' thinking of all the comforts of civilization which awaited me there. A bath, Short; a hair-cut; a, maybe, manicure; new clothes and a—bally important this—a new monocle. And so—where was I? Oh! Riding over the veld. Ah, yes. And I passed, Short, quite close to Claim Peg 24 and there I saw this young man Moore being most brutally maltreated by a gentleman named Saunders, aided and abetted by one Johnson. You, dear old arm of the law, know them both I believe? Of course I intervened; that's understood, eh, and fair play's a jewel, if you get my meaning?"

" 'Ell! Cut it short," the policeman interrupted.

"Eh? Oh, yes, Short, certainly. I intervened and, my word, I do wish you could see Mr. Saunders! You know the old song, of course? 'Two lovely black—'but I see you do. Well, that done, and seeing that young Moore was the instigator of all the trouble I brought him along with me. He's a frightful young firebrand. Imagine the colossal nerve of him, too. How dare he resent the theft of his claim. I believe, Short, that you had a hand in that little matter. But of that anon. I think I have explained Moore's presence with me here. As for the rest, we ride on here and I find you manhandling my servant, Jim. Why?"

The last word came with a snap. The flabbiness seemed to have left the speaker's face, his eyes flashed a cold, steel gray, and once again Short felt fear.

"An' so you're the nigger's boss, are yer?" he said slowly. "An' wot might yer name be?"

"It might be most anything, but Aubrey St. John will do for you."

"Pretty name, Aubrey," Short commented with a grin.

"Very. But you haven't answered my question, and I'm afraid I must insist on an answer."

"When I'm ready I'll give it to yer, Mister Audrey St. John." He covered the other with his revolver. "But first you're a-goin' ter answer my questions, see? Then, if I like it, I'll answer yourn."

"Your hand's shaking, dear man, and I'm sure you would miss me if you pressed the trigger. However," the ill-clad stranger shrugged his shoulders, "let me hear your questions."

"If," said Short deliberately, "this is your nigger, then I supposes this is your wagon?"

"You supposes most correctly."

"An' these are your cattle?"

"Oh, wise judge! A Daniel come to judgment. A—"

"Stow it. Answer my question. Is these your cattle?"

"Oh, quite."

"Then," Short exclaimed triumphantly, "you're under arrest. Get up into that wagon with the nigger."

"But why?" the other protested as he meekly obeyed the policeman's commands.

"These cattle an' wagon," Short said slowly as he handcuffed the Hottentot and the white man together, "belonged to a old transport rider 'oo was murdered. An' you say they're yourn, so you're under arrest, charged with murder an' 'ighway robbery. An'," he gabbled in conclusion, "I warn yer that anything yer say may be used as evidence against yer."

"Splendid!" Aubrey St. John exclaimed enthusiastically. "An' now what?"

"Now I'm goin' ter take yer to the Charge and Inquiry office. Unless—unless—" He winked broadly.

"Go on, dear lad," his prisoner prompted encouragingly. "Unless what? Don't be so beastly mysterious."

"I'm a-willin' ter sell yer the key to the handcuffs an' ferget I saw yer—fer a thousand quid."

"That's sportin' of you, old top. But I haven't the price. 'Pon my word of honor, I haven't as much as a silver sixpence on me."

Short scowled. "You mean that?"

"Oh, absolutely."

"All right then, we'll trek into the *dorp*. Unless," he seemed very reluctant to give up all thought of blackmailing a bribe from his prisoner— "Unless you're a-goin' ter change yer mind an' fork out. Fer the matter of that I reckon I'll search yer. And," he leered triumphantly, "findings keepings."

He made as if he would carry out his threat when a shout from Moore made him draw back.

That youth who had been listening to the conversation between the policeman and the man who had befriended him had come to a sudden decision that this man who posed as a dude fool was no murderer. And hard on that he resolved to attempt a rescue.

Mounting the horse he covered the policeman with a revolver and, "Take those handcuffs off," he ordered tersely.

"Damn yer! Short shouted as he fished the key out of his pocket. "You'll pay for this, yer young fool!"

"Maybe," Moore taunted. "In the meantime, do as I say."

"You mustn't interfere, Moore," the monocled one said gayly. "But thanks all the same, old top. I'm under arrest and it's a criminal offence—oh, very—to interfere between an officer of the law and his prisoner. No, really," he continued earnestly as Moore commenced a violent protest. "I'm quite all right. I'll go, er, quietly with the policeman, and you ride on to the Royal bar and wait for me there. You will? That's priceless of you. And remember: There's not a thing you can do to Messrs. Johnson an' Saunders. Not a thing. Legally their position is absolutely unassailable. You'll remember that, won't you? Now trot along. I'll see you later. Or, as Jim is so fond of saying, 'If I don't see you, s'long, hullo.' "

Moore hesitated, then reassured by the merry twinkle in the speakers' eyes spurred his horse and cantered away toward the town.

With a rush of courage, Short said truculently, "I'll give you one more chance, you idiot. Pay up, an' you may save yer neck from bein' stretched."

"Not a cent for tribute, dear lad," the other laughed. "I appeal to Caesar and to Caesar I must go, eh? I'm getting a trifle mixed. But on, Stanley, on!"

"You fool!" Short snarled. He suspected he was being laughed at and, like all puny-brained men, murderously resented it. "You fool!" he repeated, and struck his prisoner in the face.

"That was foolish of you, very," the monocled man said softly. Short quailed and, picking up the driving whip shouted, "Get hup!" as he lashed the oxen mercilessly.

The wagon moved ponderously forward, and then inside the Hottentot quietly said to his master, "Where does this game end, *Baas?*"

"Who knows, Jim?" The white man's vernacular was as pure as the native's. "But it is only a game."

The Hottentot grinned; evidently he was greatly relieved. "I thought," he commented, "that the *Baas* suffered himself to be taken very easily. And that fool," he nodded toward the policeman, "forgot to take the *Baas'* revolver from him. So we can go when and where we please."

The white man nodded absently as he looked at their manacled wrists. Blood was oozing from the Hottentot's.

"The iron is biting into your wrist, Jim."

"It is nothing, *Baas*. He tore the flesh a little as he fastened the iron. He is very clumsy, and a great fool."

"And also he kicked you, Jim."

"Aye, *Baas*. And struck me with his fist. But I laughed at the kicks and the blow, thinking of their recoil upon his own head. It has always been the *Baas'* custom to pay for value received."

"*Bai* Jove, yes," the white man murmured in English. "That's very well put indeed, Jim. Payment for, er, value received."

AN HOUR later Constable Harry Short ushered his two prisoners into the presence of the officer on duty at the Charge and Inquiry Office.

That official's back was turned and Short, greatly embarrassed, waited patiently for him to speak.

Somewhat Short didn't like the way things were turning out: Failing to extract a bribe from his prisoner, he had comforted himself with thoughts of the promotion this arrest was sure to bring him. And with promotion went chances for big money. Of that he was well convinced. But during the trip into the township his prisoner, it seemed to him, had not acted as a man threatened with an uncomfortable stretching of the neck ought to act. And he seemed to have a host of friends, white men and black; men who offered him their services, who shouted advice and offers to release him if that was what he desired. A few, a very few, jeered at him and were greatly elated at his predicament. These men—and the fact puzzled Short—were men of ill-repute, men whose crimes were as base as their filthy lives.

According to Short's idea it was they and not the law-abiding, who should have shown sympathy with his prisoner. And no one called him Aubrey St. John. Not that that was so very extraordinary. Short had not for one moment supposed that that was his prisoner's right name. But everyone called him "Major," and that had an uncomfortable, military sound.

Had he, he wondered, arrested one of his superior officers?

He cleared his throat nervously.

Lieutenant Murray, the Charge and Inquiry officer, turned around with a start, and at the broad grin of
welcome which swiftly passed over his face Short's low
spirits sank even lower.

"Why, hullo, Major," the officer cried jovially. "Didn't
expect to see you so soon. And Jim, too! The grinning old
ape!" He added a few words of greeting in the vernacular.
Then, to Short, "And what in the name of God have you
got these men handcuffed together for?"

"They're under arrest, sir, an'—"

"What for? I.D.B.?" Murray looked reproachfully at the
man he had greeted as "Major," smiling with relief when
that man shook his head.

"Worse than that, old bean. Murder." The prisoner
dropped his voice to a hoarse whisper. "Murder most foul."

Murray cocked his eyebrows skeptically, and turned
back to his constable. "Explain, Short. But first remove the
handcuffs. I'll be responsible for your prisoners."

Short obeyed, gulped painfully and reported: "Sir, these
men were driving the oxen and wagon of the transport
driver who was murdered three weeks ago. This 'un—
Aubrey St. John, he told me his name was, said the outfit
was hisn. An' so I arrested 'im."

"Oh, get out!" Murray exclaimed impatiently. "If you
were up to your work and read the police circulars you'd
have known that that matter was cleared up weeks ago.
Get out."

Short saluted sulkily, and got out.

"Just the same, Major," the lieutenant said reprovingly,
"you might have told the blankety fool what it was all
about and cleared yourself without making an ass of him
and bringing him off his beat."

The Major nodded. "I would have," he replied, "but the bounder wouldn't have believed me. And after the way he had treated Jim, he needed a lesson. Besides, he was so beastly officious; aching for a case, you know. And so I humored him, 'specially as he was, in a sense, so accommodating. He actually offered to let me go for a price. Took it quite hard when I refused. And I had to—I'm quite bankrupt. But about Short. He's newly joined, isn't he? How did he get on the force? Thought you'd reorganized and were accepting only the most moral minded young men."

"That's right, Major."

"Then how did that, er, bally mongrel of a fellow get in?"

Murray laughed. "Oh, a black sheep slips by once in a while. However, we know all about Short and he's being watched very closely. He hasn't any brains, only a little cunning of a degenerate sort. He's easy to watch so we're giving him plenty of rope, hoping thereby to get our hooks on to some of the outside men."

The Major nodded understandingly.

"And now," the lieutenant continued in a more official voice, "you want to know just where you stand. On the receipt of your letter we made full investigations and checked up your statements pretty thoroughly. In consequence the High Powers are planning to give a banquet in your honor."

The Major held up his hand in protest. "But I did nothing except, er, my duty. I believe that's the correct thing to say."

Murray laughed. "Quite! And I reply: 'My brave fellow, do you call saving the white race from the consequences of a black rebellion nothing?" But, seriously, Major, that was a good piece of work. But for you those two gun-running murderers would have succeeded in arming the warriors of a white renegade, and hell would have been loosed. Instead of which, the three men are dead, the guns smashed and peace forever reigneth. And all because you were Mister Johnny-on-the-Spot."

"All credit should go to Jim," said the Major with a bow.

"I understand Jim is to be suitably rewarded," the Lieutenant said. "What would you like most, Jim?"

"I am very thirsty, *Baas,* and if there is good beer in the *dorp,* and plenty of it—maybe I could get drunk? I would like that."

The two white men laughed.

"And about the oxen and wagon?" the Major questioned.

"They are yours, Major. They belonged originally to Seemster, the man Hans and Pete murdered. Seemster left no relatives and so—" He waved his hands eloquently.

"Splendid. I must auction them off at once; ought to get a good price for them. Jim's trained them well and'll hate to part with them. But we're without funds, and anyway oxen are too slow for my profession."

"Just what is your profession, Major?"

"I'm hanged if I know, dear lad. But I must be on my way. I must shop. These clothes, now! Bally rotten fitting, eh, what?"

"If I can lend you—"

"Not a penny, dear boy. S'long! Come, Jim."

He paused with his hand on the door knob. "I say— know anything about two chappies named Saunders and Johnson?"

"Quite a lot. Better not have any dealings with them."

"Alas! That I have already," the Major murmured and smiled reminiscently as he blew softly on the knuckles of his right hand. "But what do you know about them?"

"They're both swindlers. I feel sorry for the youngster they've got in tow now. He seems a clean—"

"He's cut loose," the Major interposed.

"Glad of that. They're a rotten pair. Johnson knows the diamond game and has brains. Saunders is the bully of the outfit."

The Major nodded. "Thanks for the information. S'long!"

"Major, just a minute. You won't do any, er, diamond business while you're in town, will you?"

The Major took his monocle from his eye and polished it carefully. "What a question! Really now, I—er— Why I'm looking forward to this banquet you mentioned. I suppose the diamond-mining magnates will be there? Of course, yes. And I'm so anxious to meet my fellow craftsmen. But as to diamonds. I never—oh, well, hardly ever—touch the bally things. Toodle-oo! *Hamba*, Jim!"

MEANWHILE, IN one of the barrack huts, Short was being ironically congratulated by his messmates on his clever capture of the Major.

"Damn it!" he exploded irritably, "who the bleedin' 'ell is this clod-'oppin' dude 'oo calls himself the Major?"

"Thought everybody knew the Major," one of the men answered, winking covertly at the others. "He's given us police more to laugh at than any other ten men in the country. You said it right. He's a damned fool monocled dude. But you ought to see him when he's dressed up! And he likes to make people think he's a clever I.D.B. Of course he isn't; we don't even bother to watch him. He's an easy mark, that's what he is. I can't begin to tell you how many times he's bought lumps of alum sucked to look like diamonds. Yah! And paid a good price for them, too.

Don't believe he'd know a diamond if he saw one. He an' his nigger, Jim, are just damned fools. Everybody knows that."

"Murray treated him as if he were somebody," Short objected.

"An' why wouldn't he? The Major's a remittance man—gets a big check every month—and you can bet your life the lieutenant gets some of it."

"Well, if this Major is so well known as you say, 'ow is it this is the first time I've 'eard of him?" Short queried. He had a vague feeling that his leg was being pulled. And yet, this Major looked like the brainless nit-wit, the scoffers were declaring him to be.

"Oh," said the other airily. "You haven't been with us long, an' the Major's been away. Some clever devil sold him a plan to get rich at ivory poaching without risk. All he had to do was, to lassoo the elephants—you ought to have seen him practicing throwing a rope—tie 'em to a big tree, cut their tusks off an' let 'em go free again. So the Major borrowed on a year's remittance, outfitted an' went out to catch elephants. He's just come back broke, of course. I'd like to hear him explain why he failed. It's sure to be funny!"

"Yer mean to say he swallowed a yarn like that?"

"Yah! An' paid money for it, too."

"But 'ow about this wagon an' oxen? 'Ow did he come ter get 'old o' them?"

The other looked nonplussed for a moment then, quickly, "Oh, he bought them all fair and proper. You ought to read the circulars, Short."

Short slowly digested this piece of information. Then, cunningly, "An' you say he likes people to think 'e's a I.D.B.? Well, maybe he is. An', if he is, 'e ought to be caught in the act an' arrested."

"Lord!" The exclamation was one of admiration. "Why didn't some of us think of that!"

"Well," Short waved his hand with a grand flourish, "I thought of it. You leave 'im to me. 'E's my meat."

And with that he stalked out of the hut.

The faces of the men who remained were red with suppressed merriment.

"You spun him a wonderful yarn," one chortled. "He'll try to frame the Major now. See if he don't."

The others howled with laughter at the thought. "The Major's his meat, is he? He'll get indigestion if he tries to eat it."

"Do you remember," said another, "the time Detective Jenner tried to trap the Major to buy some 'stones' from him, and the Major wasn't having any? But later Jenner found that pieces of glass had been substituted for the diamonds he'd used as bait."

"And," chimed in another, "there was the time he loaded shot-gun cartridges with diamonds he'd helped himself to and fired 'em into a buck, and then sent a piece of the meat, well-peppered with stones it was, to Sergeant Burke. That was white of him, if them stones hadn't been recovered the sergeant and a few others would have been demoted and nearly everybody in the force would have suffered."

"Yeh! That was white of him. But the Major's always acted white. Remember when he—"

And so for a time they exchanged memories of the Major and Jim, the Hottentot. Memories which took them up and down the Black Continent on the trail of a man who masked his wit, his strength, his knowledge of the ways of man and beast, with a pose of vacuous inanity; tales of a man whose career of illicit diamond buying was regarded as a political offence, an active protest against the ill-considered, autocratically-enforced diamond buying laws: tales of a man who had never failed to ally himself on the side of justice against injustice, championing the cause of the underdog, merciless in his dealings with evil-doers.

There was silence after a while, but not because the men's knowledge of the Major had come to an end.

"I wonder if he'll do any dealing while he's in town?" someone said presently.

"I heard he'd sworn off. He and the Big Man came to an understanding. The I.D.B. law was to be changed and—"

"Yah! We've all heard about that. But the Big Man's in Europe an' the law'—as it was. An' so—watch the Major. That's my tip."

"It'ud be worth a commission to catch him."

"Well, get him square. No dirty traps. He's royal game and protected"

"Sure, I know it. As if me, or anybody else for that matter, *could* trap him. Come to think of it, I'm going to warn him to be on guard against that blighter Short. He's equal to putting a diamond in the Major's pocket and then arresting him for I.D.B. Any of you got any objections to me warning the Major?" The speaker looked challengingly at the others.

They laughed good humoredly. "No, not a bit. He won't need the warning, but he'll thank you damned politely all the same."

APPARENTLY THINGS were not going well with the partners, Saunders and Johnson. Short found this out when he called one morning at their hut a week after his first introduction to the Major.

Entering their small and disgustingly dirty shack, he found the two men seated on empty crates, ruefully eyeing a small heap of bluish colored stones which were strewn on the third crate between them.

"Well, what do you want?" Saunders asked curtly.

Short looked at him and leered with a contemptuous familiarity. "My Gord!" he exclaimed. "Did the monocled dude give yer them pair o' peepers? They're beauties. They're just lively, they are."

"Shut up, will you," Saunders snarled as he tenderly fingered his still rainbow-tinted eyelids. "What do you want here?"

"Not so much, guv-nor," Short smiled meaningly, "an' don't get on yer high 'orse with me, see? First of all, I wants a bigger share o' the profits. Yer ought ter be ashamed of yerselves fer givin' me only a quid. Yer got ter give me more or I blow the gaff. Wot do I care wot they do to me at 'eadquarters? They've already got their 'ooks into me. Confined to barracks, I been, fer a week, an' fined a month's bleedin' pay. An' all because that blaggard of a Major told 'em I'd tried to bribe 'im."

He paused, wondering why they had let him say so much without an interruption.

"Anyways," he concluded boldly, "I wants more money."

They both smiled at him, Saunders wrathfully, the little man Johnson fawning.

"The claim's no good, Mister Officer," the latter whined. "We've been had. Young Moore—and I treated the brat as if he were an only son—got away with all the stones, an' there's nothing left but them." He indicated the pile of stones on the upturned crate and shook his head sorrowfully.

"Well," Short exclaimed wonderingly, "wot are yer crying abart? If I 'ad one of them stones I'd be more than satisfied."

"You can take the lot," Johnson said smoothly.

Short started greedily. "Yer mean it?" he questioned, looking at Saunders who nodded irritably.

He swept the stones up then in his big paw and rattled them exultantly.

"Bli'me," he cried, "I won't 'arf cut a splurge! I—" He paused and looked at the stones suspiciously. "But wot's yer game? Why are yer givin' me these with no more trouble than if they was worth no more than dirty bits o' glass."

"They're not," Johnson said with a sigh. "You tell him, Saunders."

"Johnson's telling the truth," that man said heavily. "They are 'blue mongrels,' and they've pinched the 'pipe.' When you find 'blue mongrels' on a claim, you might as well get out."

"Blue mongrels? Pinched the pipe?" Short exclaimed in bewilderment. "But they're diamonds, ain't they?"

"Of a sort, yes. But worthless. I didn't believe it at first, although I'd always heard that it was a bad sign to find blue mongrels on your claim; had always heard that they pinched the pipe. But I thought Johnson was trying to double cross me, trying to get the claim for himself. But he offered to sell me his share for a tin of tobacco and actually drew up this agreement—" he indicated a piece of paper sticking out of the breast pocket of his shirt—"and signed it. Not that I want the damn' claim now. But it was enough to show me Johnson was on the level."

"Aw, 'ell!" Short groaned. "I might 'a' known you two blokes wouldn't give anyfing away as easy as that." With a disgruntled air he replaced the stones on the crate, secretly retaining one, however. He had a need for that. "Bli'me," he muttered again, "ain't that just my luck! Oh, well—" He moved toward the door.

"Here," Johnson said suddenly. "Where are you going and what are you going to do with that stone you held back?"

"I'm goin' ter trap the blasted Major wiv it. I reckon it's good enough fer that!"

THE SUN was very hot that afternoon and the stifling breeze which blew was laden with minute particles of burning dust.

But that was no excuse for Short's desertion of his beat and, fully aware of the consequences if caught, he sat at a remote table in the Royal Hotel bar, quietly sipping his beer, his helmet pulled down over his eyes.

He looked up whenever someone entered the bar. Evidently he was waiting for some one.

Once the door opened slightly and a white helmeted, monocled man peered into the room and quickly withdrew, his blue eyes twinkling with merriment.

But Short missed White Helmet's entrance and departure and that, for Short, was a pity.

A little later the door opened again and the Major entered. With him was the youngster, Tom Moore.

Short gaped and with difficulty checked a loud outburst of ribald laughter. A dude, a man dressed as the Major was dressed, seemed so ludicrously out of place in the Diamondapolis, the town of hard living and harder livers.

He was immaculate from head to foot. The small brass buckle on the patent leather chin strap of his sun helmet shone like gold; his white duck tunic coat fitted him snugly, tapering at the waist and flaring full over the hips. His riding breeches were of an exaggerated cut, over full here, skin tight there; his brown polo boots were wonderfully polished and, crowning glory, the rowels of his box spurs were two gold coins which jingled musically as he walked. And as the clothes fitted the man, so did the man fit the clothes. His slightly slouching carriage, which detracted from his height, prepared people for his affected, drawling speech; his round beaming face was innocent of guile, and whatever intelligence it might have betrayed was completely blotted out by the glistening monocle he wore.

He leaned against the bar, first wiping it carefully with a gayly colored silk handkerchief, and doffed his helmet with elaborate courtesy to Aggie, the elderly, hard-visaged barmaid who came for his order.

Short gaped again, at the lemon-colored gloves on the Major's well-shaped hands, at the way his jet-black hair, graying slightly at the temples, was brushed back in an immaculate pompadour. But mostly Short wondered at the happy smile of welcome which softened Aggie's sin-tired face.

"But that," Short told himself, "is because she knew she'll worm a big tip out of the blitherin' dude."

Short rose from his chair, his half empty glass in his right hand, the fingers of his left closed over the blue mongrel. Edging his way cautiously through the men crowded about the Major, drinking his health, laughing at his drawling description of an adventure he had experienced. Winning to a position directly behind the Major, Short waited patiently for his opportunity.

It came very soon. The Major turned slightly, thrusting a hand deep into the right hand pocket of his tunic, leaving his left hand pocket gaping open almost under Short's nose.

Short could have dropped the diamond in, could have tossed it in, but there was a chance that he might be seen, or that someone might joggle his arm, spoiling his aim.

And Short did not want to take any chances. He wanted to make sure that the diamond really got in his victim's pocket. He anticipated the triumph that would be his when he arrested the dude for being in possession of an illicitly procured diamond.

He leaned forward, his right arm outstretched, in order to place his glass on the counter. At that same moment, as he brushed against the Major, his left hand entered the Major's gaping pocket.

He withdrew it with the haste of a badly frightened man, and hanging to the skin on the back of his hand was a scorpion. Its pincer claws dug tightly into his flesh, its tail, with its poisonous sting, whipping over its back and injecting its venom into the policeman's hand.

Events followed too quickly then for Short.

Cursing loudly, surrounded by a crowd of mocking, jeering men, he shook the scorpion off his hand and jumped on it in a frenzy of fear. The diamond, which he had been too startled to leave in the Major's pocket, dropped from his nerveless hand. But no one seemed to see that. The heel of a brown polo boot in which jingled a gold roweled spur covered the stone.

Above the policeman's curses and the laughter of the men, the Major's voice could be heard raised in bitter complaint. "Oh! The bounder's killed little Archie. My pet scorpion is dead. For years I trained the little fellow to guard the, er, honor of my pocket. An' now—" His voice ended in a choked sob, or it may have been a gurgle of laughter.

The bar-room door opened and a corporal of the police with two men entered. They forced their way through the hilarious crowd and ranged themselves beside Short.

"You're under arrest," the corporal said.

"What for?" Short asked wearily, ruefully eyeing his swollen hand, further embittered by the knowledge that the dude was not the fool he looked.

"Deserting your beat an'—come on, the C.O.'ll tell you all about it. He's just received a little billet doux from Sydney about you."

"And that's that," exclaimed the Major with a sigh of relief as the door closed behind the policemen. "But I feel sorry for little Archie Scorpion. He was a pure blooded little beast and, even if Short hadn't killed him, I suppose he would have died of shame for having, for a while, been so closely attached to a mongrel. But let's drink, dear lads. Name your, er, poison. Our young friend Moore will pay the bill, eh, what? I hear he's struck it rich on his new claim."

"AND THEREIN," said the Major a little later as he sat down with Moore at a table in a far corner of the room, "we have taken one trick and stacked the cards for a second. I do wish that Jim could have seen Short with little Archie clinging lovingly to his hand. But I'm afraid that Jim, the old heathen, for the moment is too gloriously drunk to have appreciated such a, er, subtle and humorous revenge. Oh, well. We must be on the *qui vive* now, laddie. I imagine Messrs. Johnson and Saunders will be very interested in your new claim."

"But I haven't one, Major," Moore protested.

"Ssh! But you have. I pegged one in your name this morning. And, wait a minute—"

He stooped as if to adjust the spur of his right boot. From the heel of that boot—it was filled with wax—he pried out the diamond with which Short had attempted to frame him.

"Take it," he said softly as Moore was about to protest. "It is quite, er, an open and aboveboard piece of business. Really. That stone came from your claim, or at least a third of it was yours until Messrs. Johnson and Saunders swindled you. We are only, as it were, spoiling the spoilers. So take it and register it at once. It's not very valuable—almost worthless, in fact—but it will serve. Register it and, when you do, act as if a jolly old uncle had died and left you an enormous fortune.

"Toddle along, now, and then come to my room at the hotel. I fancy we'll have a visitor before the day is over."

THAT EVENING when Saunders left the hut he shared with his partner, he was greatly dejected. When he returned, an hour later, he was full of confidence that a suddenly inspired plan would recoup the partnership for the disappointment they had just incurred.

During his short trip to the *dorp* he had discovered several things: That their erstwhile partner had located a rich claim; that the monocled dude was Moore's partner: that the strike was all fool's luck, for neither man knew the first thing about diamonds. And, finally, Saunders had gathered that Moore wished to regain his holding in his first claim, the holding that had been swindled from him.

Saunders whistled gayly. He and Johnson would let Moore have his share back, at a price. Better still, they would sell Moore all the shares *and* the mongrel diamonds. It would be a smart play, perfectly legal, and called for no elaborate preparations.

As he neared the hut Saunders' gait slowed, his whistle died away. After all, why should he share with Johnson?

Entering the hut he discovered Johnson fast asleep, snoring hoggishly, his right hand clutching the neck of an empty whisky bottle.

Saunders smiled grimly. That settled it. He would carry his little scheme through single handed, and there would be no division of the profits.

He felt in his pocket for the agreement Johnson had signed. It was still there. Then, with great caution, he took from under Johnson's pillow a small tobacco bag. It contained the diamonds, blue yellow, green and red mongrels, that Johnson had kept, he said, as a curiosity.

Saunders grinned, glanced casually at his sleeping partner, then quietly left the hut, heading for the Major's headquarters at the Royal Hotel.

"Look here, you fellows," he said later, when he was ushered into the Major's room. The Major and Moore had been playing Double Canfield. "Look here, you fellows, I've just discovered that I owe you an apology, Moore."

"Yes?" questioned Moore uncommittally.

"Really!" murmured the Major.

"Yes," Saunders continued. "I've only just discovered the whole thing from Johnson—he's drunk and I couldn't thrash him as I'd like. I'm sorry I accused you unjustly, and—and I want to make amends."

Moore made no reply. He was watching the Major.

"That's most awfully sportin' of you, Saunders," the Major drawled. "And just how do you propose to, er, make amends?"

"This way," Saunders said, and sighed with relief. It was going to be much easier than he had dared hope. But then, they were both fools, the Major the biggest of the two. Moore, alone would have been difficult to handle. He had a nasty gleam in his eye. "This way," Saunders repeated, and he put the agreement Johnson had signed on the table. "I made Johnson sell me his share of the claim, and now I'm going to endorse it over to you, Moore. I don't suppose," he contrived to get a very wistful note into his voice, "you'd care to take me as a partner again?"

"No," Moore answered curtly. "I wouldn't!"

"Oh, tut-tut!" the Major reproved. "We must let bygones be bygones, what? Mr. Saunters is bein' very generous. He made a mistake and he honestly admits it. He's acting extraordinary white. Yes. Mr. Saunders, your whiteness completely wipes out the black eyes I, er, inflicted upon you. It is, you see, my turn to apologize."

"That's all right, Major," Saunders said easily, but he could scarcely control the scowl which clouded his face and he wondered, vaguely, how this soft-sneaking, soft-looking dude could have thrashed him so easily. The Major's clothes covered a multitude of splendidly developed muscles.

"Now then," Saunders continued briskly, "have you pen and ink? Right. Now I'll endorse this—and I'll feel an honest man once again." He signed the document and handed it to the Major to read and witness.

"There's one thing more," he added as Moore moved impatiently. "There's one thing more."

"There always is," the Major agreed with a chuckle. "And that is?"

"These!" Saunders emptied out on to the table a little heap of diamonds.

"Oh, they're perfectly priceless!" the Major exclaimed, his eyes sparkling.

"Yes," Saunders agreed with a smirk. "That just describes them. And this is my proposition, and I hope you will agree to it for I had to pay Johnson heavily for his share of the claim. I want you to buy these from me."

"I have no money," Moore began slowly.

"I'll lend you two hundred," the Major said eagerly. "I insist, old chap. Why those diamonds—" He turned to Saunders. "You understand, of course, why I don't offer to buy them myself, don't you? I, er, have the reputation— quite undeserved, of course—of being an I.D.B. It's a fact! So, whilse I don't mind handling a solitary stone occasion- ally—who doesn't?—a lot like this is too much for me.

"So, Moore, old laddie, if you won't accept the loan you must act as my agent and buy them for me. That would be most open an' aboveboard. You have a bally dealer's license an' all that. So you'll be my agent, won't you?"

"If you insist, Major, of course," Moore assented readily, and took the notes the Major handed him.

To Saunders he said, "I'll give you two hundred for them."

Saunders laughed ironically. "They're worth two thou- sand at least."

Moore looked at the Major.

"I haven't another penny. But if you'll wait, Saunders—?"

"I'd rather not wait," Saunders said slowly. "I can get a good price from any one of the registered buyers. I gave you first chance, Moore, because—well, because I thought I owed you something."

The Major looked disappointed, then he beamed as a sudden thought struck him. "I'll tell you what," he cried. "I authorize Moore to offer you two hundred pounds and my share in this new claim. Will that do?"

"But, Major," Moore started to protest.

"No, I insist," the Major said firmly. "These stones are priceless, Moore, I tell you. Of course I'll be sorry to dissolve partnership with you. But Saunders—he's acted bally white—will be a much better partner for you."

Moore turned away as if to hide his disappointment. "You heard what the Major tells me to offer you, Saunders," he said in a queer, choked voice. "Will you accept?"

Saunders hesitated, cleverly. "Yes, I'll take his offer. I'd made up my mind to give up diamond mining, I'm so sick of the rottenness of it. But if you're willing to let bygones be bygones and for us to be partners again, we'll call it a deal. Let's draw up the agreement."

The Major rubbed his hands briskly together. "That's priceless, old dears," he drawled. "We'll have a case of fiz sent up, and then we'll celebrate properly."

IT WAS very late that night when Saunders' staggering gait carried him to his hut. He found the place in great disorder; chairs and tables overturned, bedding strewn all over the floor.

Johnson was down on his hands and knees, searching feverishly.

"Wha'cha lookin' for?" Saunders hiccupped.

The other rose to his feet and looked suspiciously at his partner.

"My bag with the mongrels in it. It's gone. Did you take it?"

Saunders giggled.

"Hell, no. Why should I? Mongrels no good to me. Pure blood, that's me."

He sat down heavily on the edge of his bed, and Johnson with a snort of impatience continued his search.

Saunders, heavy lidded, watched him Sleepily until a vague suspicion formed cloudily in his mind.

"An' what," he asked truculently, "you making so much fuss about a mess of mongrels for? You said they were worthless. You said—" He rose threateningly to his feet.

There was a loud knock at the door.

Johnson went to it and opened it. Someone put a note into his hand, then vanished swiftly into the darkness.

Closing the door, Johnson held the envelope so that the light of the guttering candles fell on it. It was addressed to Saunders and himself.

"A letter from a girl," Saunders tittered. "An' it's for both of us. Open it." He rose, as Johnson obeyed, and stood behind the little man, so that he, too, could read the note.

Dear old tops (it said.)

I suppose I ought to address you as mongrel dealers, but I imagine your senses will twirl most toppishly by the time you have read my little letter.

It's not much I have to say, but most important. In short, I desire to beg of you to be, in the future, square with each other even if you are crooked to the well-known world at large. Of course I don't know the whole sad story but the little I do know is most amusing. Oh, most!

I will make no mention of the way you swindled young Moore except to say, in passing as it were, that swindlers must expect to be swindled. But taking up the story from there, let's see what happened.

You found mongrels on your claim—red, blue, yellow and green mongrels. "Alas!" moans Johnson, "they're no good. They're worth nothing at all. And the blue mongrels have pinched the claim. We'll get no more diamonds here."

And you, dear Saunders, believed him. There are so many silly superstitions about mongrel diamonds, and Johnson has a very persuasive way with him. I wouldn't be a bit surprised to learn that he offered to give you his share of the claim as proof that his statements were true; I imagine that's how you got hold of that agreement. And I don't suppose he took any special care of the mongrels he'd found. Probably keeping them as keepsakes, or something like that. And all the time, Saunders, dear lad, your loyal little partner was planning to leave you in the lurch, planning to bolt with the diamonds at the first opportunity. And he probably had some way of getting hold of the claim for himself. You thought it worthless, didn't you?

Well, now, dear old chappie, you know what sort of a man your partner was. Cheerful little mongrel, isn't he?

But let's be fair. What, dearly beloved Johnson, do you know about Saunders! He's a fool, of course. He doesn't know anything about diamonds and your plan for bilking him was going ahead very nicely. But—dear old Saunders, of the Public School spirit, fair play's a jewel, an' all that, took your bag of mongrel diamonds, of which two or three are worthless, and the agreement you signed and exchanged them for two hundred pounds and a half share in a most worthless piece of ground. It was most noble of him. He said he was doing it in order to make amends to Moore. I wonder, don't you?

And so, Moore now has his old claim back—all of it, not merely one third. And I fancy it will really prove to be quite rich. Even if it's not he'll realise thousands from the sale of the mongrels. One of them alone—perhaps you will recall it, Johnson—a red mongrel, I judge to be worth at least two thousand pounds. That, Moore insists on selling for me. It is my commission and, really, I think I deserve it. Don't you?

And the glorious thing about this little affair—I hope you appreciate it—is this: Everything is most businesslike. Quite legal and aboveboard, you know. Moore has in his possession signed and witnessed documents giving him for value received, a parcel of mongrels and a claim.

You have—well, 'pon my soul, I'm not quite sure what you have, but I fancy you'll be snapping at each other like a pair of mongrel curs by the time you have come, to the signature of,

Yours for pure breeding,
The Major.

For a little while there was a hate-filled silence, and then, as if acting on a common impulse, the two men closed.

A HOTTENTOT'S GOD

ONCE, MANY years ago, when he was a golden-haired, blue-eyed soloist in the church choir, a good lady, happily unconscious of the vice which even then was hidden by a fair exterior, called Baines a cherub. The name stuck to him through all the ensuing years—years in which he had given rein to his grosser passions; years which had seen him sink slowly in the social scale until now he was numbered with the lowest of the low, a white *kaffir* and a manufacturer of rotgut liquor which he sold to native laborers of the South African diamond fields at an enormous profit.

He was grossly fat, his duck trousers—the only garment he wore—filthily dirty. But his hair—when clean—still clustered in crisp, golden curls about his peculiar shaped head and he looked out upon the world through bright blue eyes which were unclouded by the vice he had lived through or the moral slime with which he now surrounded himself. His voice was still a clear, fluting, almost sexless, treble. But as he now decanted a green, poisonous looking liquid into a number of bottles labeled "PURE HOLLANDS," he still justified his nickname; he was still "Cherub" Baines.

There was a knock at one of the outer doors of his large tin-shanty; a shanty of many narrow passageways, of false doors and hidden traps; a building which sprawled over the veld like some unclean fungous growth.

Again the knocking sounded: *Tap*—a pause. Then, *tap tap.*

Cherub Baines paused from his labors, and listened intently. He could hear one of his women interrogating the visitor and smiled as the latter replied in the vernacular with a harsh, guttural intonation.

Doors opened and closed; footsteps sounded in the passageway outside. A door behind him, opened, and a woman—an expression of fear in her yellow eyes—announced furtively:

"The big Dutchman Nessor is here, boss. He wants to talk with you."

Cherub turned slowly.

"How many times must I tell you to knock before you come into this room?" he demanded shrilly. "Let him come in—then go. Quick! Before I kick your ribs in."

He resumed his interrupted task and the woman withdrew to make way for a ponderously built Dutchman who closed the door behind him and sat down with a stolid deliberation on an upturned packing case.

"Well?" Cherub questioned, his back to his visitor. He showed a certain cunning in that; he always judged the truth of a man's statement to him by the intonation. Knowing his own eyes lied, he distrusted other people's.

"Well?" he questioned again, a little louder.

The Dutchman coughed and spat noisily. He did not like this talking to a man's back.

"That trip, Cherub," he began clumsily. "That trip I was to take with you and the man Anders—I can no longer go."

Cherub carefully corked a bottle.

"Why not?" he asked gently.

"Because I no longer have a mule team or wagon. I sold all my outfit. A monocled dude of an Englisher offered me a good price and so—I sold. Yah! I sold. I came to tell you because," he stumbled over his words, uncertain of their reception, "I promised you I would take you. In a way I was contracted to you. But it was a long trip and dangerous. There was little money in it for me. I would not have listened to you only—only I no transport could get to carry. But this dude—*Ach*, he is one big fool!—offered a good price and so I sold."

He made a nervous gesture with his hands.

"Who was this monocled dude?"

"He called himself 'the Major' but—" Nessor's face expressed the bland bewilderment of a child—"he is not of the police. But he is a fool." He laughed heartily; sure of his ground on this point. "I would have cut my price in half if he had bargained. But no; without words he paid the price I at first asked. And so, Cherub—" he rose, evidently anxious to depart—"I cannot take you in the morning."

"No!" Cherub agreed smoothly. It would seem that way. But sit down, sit down, I tell you, Nessor."

His voice was still clear, friendly, carrying no suggestion of threat, but Nessor quickly resumed his seat and removing his hat nervously played with its battered brim.

"You gave your word, Nessor," Cherub continued, "and you will keep it. There are other wagons, other mules."

"Almighty, yes!" the Dutchman agreed promptly.

"Then you will get them. You will go with us—though I could get another man for the job—because you know the veld and I can trust you." He might have added, "And because you are a fool, and will obey orders, asking no questions."

"Then I will go now and ask questions where I can buy an outfit. Four mules—they will be plenty—and a small wagon. If I am careful I will have much money left over. And that, with what you will pay me, will be enough to buy the farm I have for so long wanted. A farm and cattle with which to stock it."

Again he rose, again he sat down, sighing profoundly, at Cherub's voice.

"Sit down, Nessor. There is plenty of time. First we will talk a little."

"To me it is all one," the Dutchman replied. "But I am not fond of talking. Words trip me up."

"Don't talk, then," Cherub advised dryly. "Listen, you big, hulking, clodhopper of a Dutchman. We—Anders and me—contracted with you to take us over the Portuguese border in *your* wagon and *your* mules. And I'm going to keep you to the bargain, see? There's style to your outfit; style and comfort. And that's the way I'm going to travel. Sixteen mules and your wagon. See? And that's the end of it. You go and buy your outfit back from the dude."

"But listen, *ma-an*," the Dutchman protested tearfully, "he may not want to sell them back."

"Then you'd better find a way to make him. I've heard you boast you can kill an ox with your fist—"

"It was no idle boast," Nessor muttered proudly.

"Well, then, the dude's no ox, is he?"

With that, Cherub gave all his attention to his bottling. Save for the gurgle of the liquid, the Dutchman's stertorous breathing and Cherub's hissing intake of breath, there was silence for a little while.

"It is true," Nessor then said heavily. "I gave you my word, so now I will go and find a way of getting back my outfit."

He rose to his feet but instead of going to the door, went over and stood by Cherub, watching, with a childlike curiosity, the other's labors.

"Is that the stuff you sell to the *verdoemte* niggers?" he asked presently.

Cherub nodded and looked up into his visitor's face for the first time since he had entered the room.

"Yes—want a drink?"

Nessor nodded thirstily.

Cherub poured out a tumbler full of the stuff and handed it to Nessor, laughing merrily at the wry face the other made as he sniffed it gingerly, almost doubling up with laughter when the Dutchman, having taken a mouthful, gagged violently and demanded water, swearing that hot flames had seared his mouth.

Nessor then made his way slowly toward the door, stopping in his tracks when it suddenly burst open and a slim, guttersnipe of a man rushed into the room, slamming the door violently behind him, his thin, hatchet face white with fury. His stiff hat was badly dented; his tight fitting, ornately checked suit was torn and covered with the red dust of the veldt.

He swore violently as he sat down on a rickety chair, removed his hat and ran his long, skinny fingers through his greasy hair.

Cherub looked up at him, then quickly turned away, smiling covertly.

"Well! What ails you, Toad? You look as if you'd been running up against something tough."

"I have," the other snarled, and yellow lights flickered in his beady, black eyes.

"Yes? Well tell us about it."

"It was like this—" Toad Anders began, then, suddenly conscious of Nessor's presence stopped. "What's Dutchy doing here?" he asked.

"Come to say he'd sold his outfit and can't take us tomorrow."

"Hell. 'S that so? Well, he can go an' buy his damned outfit back again."

"That's what I told him, but he's afraid the buyer won't sell back again."

Anders turned wrathfully on Nessor.

"You'll make him sell, Dutchy."

"I told him that, too," Cherub interposed with a chuckle. "But I think he's doubtful about his power of persuasion."

"I'll go with him an' see he puts it through," Toad said. "Who'd you sell to, Dutchy? Anybody that I can persuade with this?" He tapped the butt of his revolver.

"There will be no need of that," Nessor answered slowly. "It was a monocled dude I sold to. He—"

"What was his name," Anders interrupted fiercely.

"He called himself the Major an'—"

"That's enough!" Anders waved his hands wildly. "The swine!"

"You'd better tell me what it's all about," Cherub said. "Nessor can wait. So tell us; an' if you tell a good yarn, we'll all curse together. Hell yes!"

"Give me a drink, first; and not that nigger wash, either."

Cherub laughed lightly as he poured out a drink for his partner; laughed louder at the wistful expression on the Dutchman's face.

"Well, look here," Anders began alter he had finished his drink. "It's all the fault of your rot-gut booze. Here's me, thinking I'd pick up a few quid doing business with some niggers who, I'd heard, was going back to their *kraals;* full of money, they was, too. Well, I had all my pockets loaded down with bottles of booze and—"

"Ah!" Cherub interposed. "I wondered where those bottles had gone to. I gave one of my women a thrashing—thought she'd given them to her pals. She'll laugh when she hears it was you who'd taken 'em. But I thought I'd warned you not to do any booze peddling? It's too damned dangerous. Let the niggers come here for what they want. I'll talk to you later about that."

"You'll do nothing of the kind, Cherub. I ain't one of your Totty women. I go my own way an' please myself what I do—See?"

Cherub waved his hands in an airy gesture; Anders looked uneasily at the Dutchman as if seeking support and, finding none, cursed viciously.

"Well, anyway," he continued, "I sold the bottles—some of them—at a damned good price, and the niggers are getting the corks out, getting ready for a blindo. Me? I'm hanging around in the bushes, waiting for the sleep to get them so's I could help myself to the rest of their money. An' then a monocled dude comes up, swinging a cane an' all."

"Give us another drink," Anders interrupted himself to say, then drank avidly and went on.

"Well! This dude comes up an' talks to the niggers, talked like he was one of them, he did, so's I could get the drift of what he was saying, an' they listened as meek as Moses. When he was all through, damned if they didn't hand their bottles over to him an' he dives down into the pockets of his white duck riding breeches, paying them niggers just what they'd paid me for the booze and then *shoos* 'em away, just like they was a bunch of school kids. Blimey!"

"Then me—I've been lying doggo all this time, too taken aback to do anything—I got to my feet, meaning to go after them niggers. You see, I've still got some more bottles left. And—

" 'Here, young feller me lad,' the dude says; as if he had a hot pertato in his mouth. 'Hi!' he says, 'I want to have a talk to you—what. You must be the chappie who sold those black laddies this beastly stuff.'" Toad Anders' feeble imitation of the affected drawl of a certain type of Englishman was oddly incongruous with his appearance. "And while he was speaking he smashed the bottles on a rock—all but one, he smashed. And how the stuff did stink, Cherub. Must have been one of your strongest brews. S'elp me! It burned up the grass."

Cherub laughed.

"Nessor, here, thought it was a bit too strong. But go on: You're long winded."

Anders grunted. " 'Yes,' says the dude. 'I'm now going to persuade you not to sell any more of this frightful stuff to natives—'

" 'Oh! Are yer?' I asks. 'An' who the hell may you be?'

" 'They call me Major,' he says, holding up the bottle he hadn't smashed, 'and I'm going to take those other bottles from you. Then I'm going to make you drink this.' And he smiled, Cherub, when he said it, just as if he was asking me to have awfternoon tea.

" 'Like hell, I will,' I says, getting ready to kick him in the shins because, now I look at him closer he ain't so fat as I thought he was, an' he seemed to have grown taller, an wider, an' harder; an' his eyes don't seem like the baby blue they was.

" 'I'm very much afraid you'll have to,' he says with a sigh and then, somehow, suddenly, he didn't look such a blasted fool and I turned an' ran. But he caught me, Cherub, before I'd done a hundred feet. Course I tried to get away, but he held me as easy as if I was a kid. He—don't laugh, damn you—put me across his knee and smacked me. And he was a-laughin' all the time. Then he got me down on me back an' pinched me nose so's I had to open me mouth to breathe, and poured some of that blamed poison you make down my throat.

"It burned like hell an' I was sicker than a dog. Damn you! Don't laugh. Near to dying I was. And then, when I was laying there helpless, he took my other bottles and broke them, an' fished the money out of my pockets what I'd got from the niggers an' walked away.

"An' that's all—only it ain't the end., I'm going to get even with that monocled dude if I have to swing for it."

Cherub Baines laughed softly and continuously.

"I wasn't laughing at you," he gasped, "but at the thought that this monocled dude is the same chap Nessor sold his outfit to and I was planning to get it back so's we could travel in style. An' you needn't feel so bad about the way you've been treated. Better men than you have come up against the Major and failed."

"Who the hell is he?"

"He's a monocled dude who has the reputation of being one of the slickest Illicit Diamond Buyer's in the country. He's been away from the *dorp* on some expedition up north for a long time; otherwise you'd have heard of him before. He's a popular character; he knows niggers, and hunting, and all there is to know about the I.D.B. game. There's a big reward out for anybody who can catch him dealing in diamonds, and a lot of people have tried to collect it.

"Up to now he hasn't run across my path and I've left him alone. But now, partly because I want Nessor's outfit back again, but mostly, Toad, to avenge your wrongs, I'm going to get him."

"How are you going to do it if he's so bleedin' smart?"

Cherub smiled and sitting down facing Anders, the tips of his fingers pressed together—he looked particularly angelic at that moment—expounded his plan to Anders and Nessor.

"It'll work, I tell you," he concluded. "All these other people who've tried to beat him have failed because they haven't taken into account Jim—his Hottentot servant. I'm willing to gamble that Jim's the brains of the outfit. No; not that. I'll put it this way: Get the nigger and you'll get his boss."

"I don't see how we can lose," Anders cried with vicious enthusiasm. "An', when we've got him, I'll make him drink a vat full of your rot-gut."

Cherub smiled and turning suddenly on Nessor, asked, "You'll go through with it?"

The Dutchman scratched his head doubtfully.

"Almighty! I do not like it. To take you and Anders with a parcel of stones is dangerous. But that I would risk. It is no sin to take the stones. They were put into the earth for any man to take. But this other business; that I do not like. To kidnap the man—that is nothing. He is full grown, he should be able to look after himself. But the taking of his wagon and team—that and the killing of the nigger, I do not like."

"Oh, listen, Nessor," Cherub said smoothly. "We do not kill the Hottentot. We only give him a chance to get as much drink as he wants. If he takes too much and dies— that is not our fault. And as to stealing the outfit—we do not steal it. You shall give the dude the money you think it is worth and—"

The Dutchman took up that point very quickly.

"Almighty!" he cried with a chuckle of delight. "That will be a *slim* trick. That, truly, is not stealing—to sell a thing one day and buy it back the next for but half of what was received is honest business. So I go now to make ready. If you have done your part, we will trek tomorrow at moon-rise."

"And now," said Cherub as the door closed behind Nessor, "we will put up the stones."

From a cupboard he took several tins of bully beef; from a locked and padlocked drawer he took a chamois bag containing a quantity of uncut diamonds. Anders, mean-while, had taken from a carpenter's chest a blow-torch, tools, solder and soldering-iron.

Then, for a while, the two men worked in silence. First, they carefully removed the labels from the tins; then they made a neat V shaped cut into the containers and carefully pulled out the point of the V. The diamonds they inserted into the hole, pushing them as far into the centre of the meat as they could. That done the V shaped piece of tin was pushed back into place, the cuts neatly closed with solder and the label pasted on again.

"I don't see why you want to come on this trip—I can handle it alone," Toad Anders grumbled, breaking the silence. "Anybody 'ud think you didn't trust me. As if I'd go back on a pal!"

"I don't intend to give you the chance," Cherub replied.

TROOPER JENNINGS, of the Mounted, was deeply apologetic.

"I'm sorry, Major," he said. "The boys must have been having a game with me. But I don't see why you couldn't have given me your word you had no diamonds. I'd have accepted it, you know."

"Yes," the other drawled affectedly, a disarming smile on his bland, innocent-looking face. The gold-rimmed monocle he wore effectively masked any expression of intelligence his eyes—otherwise—might have contained. "Yes," he said again, passing his hand languidly over his black hair, "I suppose you would have accepted my word and, 'pon my soul, I would have given it only I don't like to encourage the police in lazy habits. Always search an I.D.B. suspect and everything that is his."

Jennings looked around the disordered bell-tent. Tin uniform cases were open, their contents—silk shirts and underwear, pajamas; expensive, well-cut suits; boots of all sorts—were strewn all over the place.

"At least, Major," he grinned, "you'll have to admit I did a good job once I did start."

"Oh, ripping!" The Major's even white teeth showed in a pleasing smile. "Only—you—if I may say so—delayed your search too long. I am speaking now, you understand, most pedantically. You see, supposing I had had a diamond secreted on my—er—person when you first came to my camp—an' I wouldn't be such a bally ass as to hide it among my kit—you lost so much time with your preliminary chatter that I had ample opportunity of getting rid of it. You will remember, for instance, that in my haste to do the hospitable I knocked my helmet off. Well, supposing I had hidden the diamond in my helmet, it would have been so easy for Jim—he picked the helmet up for me—to have removed the bally stone to a safer hiding place and— Eh, what? Where *are* you going, dear boy?"

"To search Jim, confound you, Major. Why didn't I tumble onto that helmet trick. It's obvious—"

"Tut, tut! Likewise not at all. Don't blame yourself. The dear old brain isn't capable of grasping everything. And, really, I wouldn't take the trouble of searching Jim. You must have forgotten, I think, that I was only supposin'. Carrying our little study in suppositions a little further; supposin' the diamond to have been hidden in my helmet and that Jim—the dear old heathen Hottentot—had taken it. Why, dear and honored policeman, he's had nearly an hour in which to hide it where you'll never find it. Search him if you wish, of course; it'll be a bally good experience for you. Hope you don't object to my looking on. I might be able to offer a few valuable suggestions—"

Chagrin and mirth struggled for the mastery, then Jennings laughed wholeheartedly.

"I give it up, Major," he cried. "Don't believe you had a diamond, anyway. If you're going into the town, let's get along. It's damned hot and a drink at the Royal is in order."

"Oh, absolutely. Just a minute while I give Jim a few instructions, then we'll trot along.

"*O-he*, Jim!"

A Hottentot came running in answer to the call.

"Yah, *Baas?*" He grinned in reply to Jennings' good-natured nod of greeting.

"The *Baas* Jennings and I have been looking for something which wasn't here and—"

"Did you find it, *Baas?*"

Jennings, laughing heartily, went to the tent's opening and gazed over the rolling veldt toward the distance-blued hills.

"No!" he heard the Major answer and wished he could speak the vernacular with as pure an accent. "No! So you will repack everything. My brush, Jim!"

Jennings, looking back over his shoulder, saw the Major grooming back his hair with the palm of his hand and a silver-backed stiff bristled brush. A wild thought came into the policeman's mind; a half-formed doubt. Never before in his knowledge had the Major used pomade on his hair. Maybe— And then, with a shrug of his shoulders, he dismissed the thought as a foolish flight of fancy.

"There," said the Major with a sigh of satisfaction. "I think that bally lock will stay in place now." He handed Jim the brush and carefully adjusted his white helmet. "I'm going to the *dorp* now, Jim, to buy more provisions. Tomorrow we trek."

"Where, *Baas?*"

The Major waved his hands.

"North, south, east, west—what does it matter so long as we trek."

"We might," Jim suggested, "make for the *kraal* of Bomva where the *baas* left his horse so many moons ago."

The Major nodded.

"I, too, had thought of that, Jim. It would be good to see Satan again. Yes, I think we will head for Bomva's place and—

"Coming, Jennings."

Together the two white men left the tent, heading for the town, the trooper's horse following close at their heels.

When they had disappeared from view the Hottentot turned to his task of bringing order to the disordered tent. But first he carefully examined the Major's hairbrush and found, securely embedded in the bristles, a small, rose-tinted diamond.

"What a man!" Jim chuckled. "Even whilst the policeman searched him, this was hidden in my *baas'* hair. *Tchat!* What a man. And I—I am his servant."

And having paid his customary tribute to his *baas,* the Hottentot applied himself with zeal to his task, working so efficiently that, in a very little while, the tent presented a neat, well-ordered appearance. He remade the bed, smoothing the wrinkles out of the white, linen sheets; he adjusted the pillow to a nicety and on the top of it placed a pair of gaily striped pajamas.

That done he went outside and walked for a while amongst the sixteen mules which, securely hobbled, were grazing nearby. And, so great was his knowledge and understanding of these freakish, contrary beasts, that, although he had known these particular ones less than twenty-four hours, he was already familiar with each one's worth and pet idiosyncrasies.

"They are good beasts," he said with a contented, satisfied grin. "A little thin, but well trained and veldt wise."

He examined, for the hundredth time that day, the light wagon and all the newly acquired trek outfit.

"My *baas* paid a big price," he muttered, "bigger than he needed to. The Dutchman would have taken half what was offered. And my *baas* knew that. But he does not bargain about small things. And the outfit is good. I can find no fault with it. And so, after many lean months, my *baas* once again treks in a manner fitting to him."

He climbed up into the wagon and sitting on the driver's seat, his abnormally long, powerful arms clasped about his up-drawn knees, mused for a while on the glorious adventures which had befallen them—white master and black servant; man and man; proved comrades during the years they had followed Africa's trails. Each had faced death many times that the other might live; both had suffered that others might go unharmed. They had always thrown into the scale of justice the wealth of their wit and sinew, quitting themselves at all times like men.

And so Jim grinned happily as he thought of the morrow's trek and sang, in a harsh, guttural voice, one of the hunting songs of his people, clapping his hands together in time to its barbaric rhythm, losing himself in joyful anticipation of the hunting days which were to come. The creatures of the wild had no sin-warped code of ethics; they played the game—kill or be killed.

He was suddenly recalled to the present by the appearance of a native dressed in the castoff clothing of a white man. The suit he wore was a loud checked plaid, his socks, a billious green, his shoes—holes had been cut in them to give his toes greater freedom—abnormally long and pointed.

"Greetings Hottentot," he said with a conceited smirk, pulling up his trousers that Jim might view the full glory of his socks. "And how are the mules, your brothers?"

Jim looked at him contemptuously.

"Do not go near them," he warned, "or they may mistake you for a painted lizard and tread on you."

The other laughed and pulling a bottle from his pocket, uncorked it and drank noisily.

Jim licked his lips. His one weakness was an inordinate liking for spirits, and the more caustic the better. When he was with his *baas,* or on the trail, or with some definite task to perform, the craving never exhibited itself. It was only at times, when, as now, he had no task and time hung heavily on his hands that he was tempted—and fell.

"I, too, am thirsty," he insinuated.

"Your water bags are full," the other mocked. "Drink, Hottentot!"

"Water!" Jim spat in disgust. "I need a man's drink." He jumped down from the wagon and walking toward his visitor, held out his hand imploringly.

The other squatted down on his haunches in the shade of the tent, motioned Jim to sit opposite and then held the bottle to the Hottentot's mouth, only to snatch it away suddenly.

"Pig! Would you drink all and leave none for me?" he cried.

"It is as mild as milk," Jim grumbled, his eyes on the bottle, forgetting everything but his overpowering thirst.

"It is not a good thing to spit upon a gift," the other remarked sententiously.

Jim made a grunting, noncommittal answer and then the two conversed of divers things, exchanging names and reminiscences, boasting of their prowess.

Eventually, Jim was not conscious of how this came about, the two played a gambling game and Jim was the possessor of the garments and wealth of the other man.

"I can play no more, Hottentot. I am naked, I have no more money and you have emptied the bottle. I am thirsty."

Jim gazed at him dull-eyed.

"There is water," he began thickly.

"I throw back to you your own words, Hottentot," the other interposed scornfully. "I need a man's drink. Go and get another bottle—or two. You are rich. Or—" he added— "if you do not wish to go, give me the money and I will go and get the drink."

Jim laid his fingers alongside his squat, broad-based nose.

"If I gave you money," he leered craftily, "you would not come back." He rose to his feet swaying slightly. "And so, tell me where to go and I will get the drink."

"You go to that place—" the other pointed to a rambling building standing on a rise of the veldt about two miles distant—"and knock thus on the door: *Tap—tap-tap*. A woman—her skin is black—will come to the door. Tell her that I, Matiswa, the servant of the Dutchman Nessor, sent you. Tell her you are Cherbim—be sure to say that, Cherbim; it is a magic charm—and thirsty. Then she will take you to a room where a white man will give you as many bottles of *puza* as you wish to buy. It is strong *puza*—not like this other—and the price is small."

"*Wo-we!*" Jim exclaimed. "I will go now." He walked off a few paces, then halted and glared threateningly at the other. "If you dare to move," he threatened, "from the place where you now are, or dare to touch anything whilst I have gone, I will suffer you to live only to pray for death."

"Why should I move Hottentot? The sun is as warm here as any other place—and I am thirsty. Make haste."

Jim hesitated another minute or two, evidently endeavoring to justify to himself a desertion of the camp. Eventually his thirst won and he set off for the place of Cherub Baines at a dignified walk; a pace which quickly passed through successive gaits until, before he had gone fifty paces, he was running over the veldt at the top of his speed.

CHERUB BAINES smiled triumphantly at Toad Anders and the Dutchman, Nessor, when they had played with Jim, the Hottentot, long enough and had finally given him a drink which was even more potent than their usual rot-gut.

Everything was going as the three white men had planned. They could, of course, have overpowered the Hottentot without having recourse to the poisonous concoction sold by Baines; but Jim, they knew, was a powerful man and there was some slight risk of themselves being hurt in the process of overcoming him. This way, once he had deserted camp to buy the liquor, he defeated himself; besides, it was part of their plan that he should be helplessly drunk.

Jim's eyes were glazed now; he muttered to himself; he broke into snatches of war chants, beating the rhythm on the floor with an empty bottle.

Presently, it smashed to pieces in his hand.

He looked at it owlishly, blinked, then reached for another bottle.

As he did so a queer, stick-like insect, looking very much like a frail, dried twig, alighted on his hand.

Jim's fingers tightened convulsively about the neck of the bottle; apart from that he did not move but watched, with awe-stricken eyes, scarcely venturing to breathe, the insect pose itself as if it were engaged in prayer.

He was so still that Toad Anders came softly up to him, curious to see what held his attention. Realizing then that it was only an insect, he knocked it off Jim's hand and crushed it under his foot with a sneering laugh and a shout of boisterous good humor.

"Drink, Hottentot, you—"

But that was as far as he got for, with a hoarse cry of rage Jim sprang at him, battering him with his fists, sending him down to the ground in a huddled heap. Nor would the matter have ended there, for Jim was like one possessed, had not the Dutchman, Nessor, coming up from behind, struck the Hottentot on the back of the head with the butt of his revolver.

The blow instantly silenced Jim's bloodthirsty shouts and paralyzed his muscles. At a second blow, swiftly following the first, he pitched face forward to the ground, groaned once, rolled over and was very still.

"What got into the nigger?" Anders exclaimed as he rose unsteadily to his feet. "I only knocked a bloomin' Praying Mantis off his hand and—"

"Almighty!" the Dutchman interposed, a look of superstitious awe on his face. "If that I had known I think, *ma-an,* I should have let him kill you. I tell you, *ma-an,* you have killed our luck."

"Don't be a fool, Dutchy," Anders growled, kicking the prostrate Jim savagely in the ribs. "I tell you it was only a bloomin' mantis and—"

"And I tell you, *ma-an,*" Nessor interrupted savagely, "that you have killed our luck. Almighty! Nothing do you know. Only a mantis you say you killed. I tell you that you have killed a Hottentot God. Truly. *Ach!* The things I could tell you. Did you not yourself see what happened to this nigger? Peacefully he was drinking and then— I tell you, *ma-an,* I would flay a nigger alive before all the warriors of his tribe—and fear nothing. But I would not kill a mantis, a Hottentot god, in the presence of one—only one, look you—Hottentot."

"You talk too much, Nessor, and talk like a fool, at that," Cherub Baines broke in impatiently. "Both of you give me a hand and we'll take this nigger into the drinking room. I don't think you've done any harm, Anders. He looks drunk enough to deceive anybody and I'm ready to gamble that those two clouts Nessor gave him—what with the booze he'd already put away—will keep him sleeping for quite a while."

"WHO ARE you? And what make you here?"

The Major looked keenly at the half-naked native he had found sleeping under the wagon on his return from the *dorp*.

The native grinned impudently at the white man then quickly turned away, and shivered; there was something which reminded him of assegai points in the steely gaze of the Major's eyes.

"My name is Thuso, *Baas*," he said humbly. "I am the driver of the Dutchman, *Baas* Nessor. I wait here until the Hottentot returns. I was to watch the camp for him. He—"

"And where is the Hottentot?"

"We played a game, *Baas*, and he won all that I had—my clothes and my money. He has gone with the money to buy drink, for we were both very thirsty."

"Where did he go? Answer quickly!"

"He should have been back long ere this, *Baas*. It is not a very long way to the place there—" Thuso pointed to the buildings of Cherub Baines—"but maybe he has stayed to drink. Maybe he—"

The Major did not stop to hear more; he was walking swiftly over the veldt toward the shanties of the illicit liquor dealer. His monocle no longer gleamed in his eye and his face had lost the vacuous, inane look which he was wont to don. His lips were set in a stern line; his strong, square jaw had a pugnacious tilt to it.

Knowing full well the evil potency of brews sold to natives by men like Baines; knowing, too, the savage conscienceless manner in which such men treated natives once they had them rendered helpless by drink, the Major had real fears of the Hottentot's safety. And his fears increased his speed so that he was presently running, with the ease and grace of a trained athlete, at full speed over the veldt.

Arrived at the booze hell he knocked loudly on the door with the butt of his revolver. A native woman opened it and timidly asked his business.

"I come for one Jim, a Hottentot," he answered and then glared wrathfully at Baines who suddenly appeared in the gloom of the passageway beyond the door.

"If you're the Hottentot's *baas,*" Cherub said smoothly, in his clear, passionless treble, "let me tell you it's about time you came. He's been raving mad; broke my furniture and half killed my partner, Anders."

"Pity he didn't finish the job," the Major retorted coldly. "Pity he didn't kill you both."

"That's no way for a white man to talk to a white man," Cherub protested. "I will—"

"Get out of the way! I'll deal with you and your precious partner later on. Now take me to the Hottentot—quick!"

Cherub cringed as the Major menaced him with his revolver and with many apologetic expostulations led the way down the narrow passageway.

The Major, his revolver pressed into the small of the liquor dealer's back, every nerve on the alert for traps, followed close on his heels.

At the end of the passage was a doorway, so cleverly concealed that it would have eluded all but the most searching scrutiny.

Cherub Baines flung it open and, with a grandiloquent gesture, motioned to the Major to enter. Coming forward a few paces the Major looked into the room and saw that the floor of it was littered with the bodies of natives in diverse stages of intoxication. Directly opposite the door, lying prostrate on a pile of filthy blankets, was Jim. He was moving uneasily, muttering incoherently.

The Major's face hardened.

"You'll have to pay heavily for all this, my friend," he said to Cherub Baines and then, all thought of caution forgotten, ran forward to the Hottentot.

A heavy weight crashed on his head; a myriad dancing lights confused his vision. Total darkness followed and the floor shook as his big frame pitched heavily to the ground with a jarring thud.

IT WANTED an hour to noon the following day when Jim awoke to full possession of his senses; awoke from the stupor induced by the gin he had drunk and the Dutchman's blows.

Ignoring the taunts of the other victims of Cherub Baines' dear hospitality, angrily refusing the invitation of the women to stop and drink more, he reeled out of the room to the water-tank at the rear of the building. Here he stripped and washed thoroughly. Dressing again he started across the veldt for his *baas'* camp.

His head throbbed painfully, his eyes were bloodshot and he walked with head bent, pondering on what excuse he could offer his *baas,* wondering what had caused the big lump at the back of his head.

"I must have been very drunk," he muttered, "not to remember how I came by that. *Wo-we!* And the *baas* will be very angry—but not so angry as he will pretend. He will say that I have played the part of a monkey—not of a man. And then, maybe, he will talk to me no more until two suns have risen and set. *Au-a!* Worse yet! In the days to come, when I have forgotten all this, he will remember. Yah! He will remember and go a-hunting and not take me with him. He will—he has done it before—walk where danger is and close his eyes in order, he will say, to teach me a lesson.

"*Tchat!* But first, I think, he will teach those white men who gave me the *puza* a lesson. Truly! And that man who killed the mantis—*Au-a,* now I remember' how came this bump!—he will be given good cause to remember the evil of his deed."

Jim's eyes glowed with anger as he ruefully fingered the bump.

"*Au-a!*" he exclaimed. "It was an evil thing—that killing of the mantis. For that there must be an accounting. And that is work for me to do—not for the *baas.*"

And so, musing on his own folly, and on the revenge he would take on the man who had killed the mantis, the Hottentot god, Jim came in time to the place where his *baas* had made camp, halting beside the gray ashes of a dead fire.

He stood there motionless, his head still bent, his eyes fixed on the ground, waiting for his *baas'* reproaches. When none came and becoming, of a sudden, panic-stricken because of the unnatural silence and emptiness of the place, he slowly raised his head.

"*Baas!*" he cried then, and in that one, pregnant word was expressed misery and loneliness, bewilderment and reproach.

The tent had gone, the wagon and mules vanished. Nothing remained to show that there had been in this place a white man's camp save the cold ashes of a fire.

Stunned, Jim squatted on his haunches and stared blankly across the undulating veldt. He felt utterly alone in an empty world—alone, friendless and afraid.

After a long hour spent in angry, self-recriminations and in formulating vague, tormenting explanations of his *baas'* departure, a happy thought came to him.

"Yah! That is it," he exclaimed after he had carefully weighed all its pros and cons. "To punish me, to make me remember my folly, the *Baas* has trekked on ahead. To the *kraal* of Bomva he has gone intending to take to himself the horse he left there so many moons ago. That is it. Now what must I do?"

He scratched the thick, woolly mop of his head then, closing his eyes, conjured up a vision of all the veldt which was between him and the *kraal* of Bomva. In his mind's eye he could see the winding, poorly defined dirt road his *baas* would have to follow. Here it made a sweeping detour to avoid quaking bog-land, and there it almost doubled on its course in order to cross a swift flowing river at the ford. Here, fetching a wide circle, it circled about the base of a line of precipitous *kopjes,* and there, and there, in order to avoid impassable thorn scrub and lava rock—

And then Jim saw another trail; at present a trail which existed only in his imagination. It was the trail which he now planned to take. It stretched out in a beeline from the place where he sat to the *kraal* of Bomva. It led over marsh and *kopje;* across deep, swiftly flowing rivers; through swamps which reeked with the uncleanly musk-like stench of crocodiles; across a waterless plain of desolation.

An occasional *kraal* dotted this trail of Jim's, and from those *kraals* he planned to win—by the laws of hospitality, or wit, or exhibition of his abnormal strength and fighting prowess—sustenance for his travels. Even so—

But Jim gave no conscious thought to the perils which would beset his path. Other things were far more important. By thus trekking across country he could reach Bomva's *kraal* several days in advance of his *baas*. He would get the horse, groom him—as only he knew how to groom—clean the saddlery, and then ride back along the trail to meet his *baas*.

Yes, that was it.

And, having made his plan, Jim lost no time in putting it into execution.

Jumping to his feet he set off at an easy gait, heading north. Fifteen miles distant was a *kraal* where he was sure of a welcome; there he would get food and weapons.

JIM, THE Hottentot, mounted on a coal black stallion—an Arab with a leavening of *Basutu*—waved a light hearted farewell to the people of Bomva's *kraal* and rode back along the trail, singing lustily.

He was little more than a shadow of the man who had set out from the deserted-camp near the diamond town three weeks ago. The trials of the difficult trail had taken their toil of him. He had faced death in many guises, and only his great strength, his inexhaustible knowledge of the bush and its ways, and his indomitable will had carried him through.

But with the perils past and overcome Jim did not concern himself. He had gained his objective and now was riding to meet his *baas*. All that day he rode, on the alert, expecting to sight the Major at every turn in the trail, at the top of every rise.

Sundown and darkness found him still unrewarded and he was obliged to camp alone. Sunrise next morning found him once again on the trail; sunset, and he was making camp again—still alone.

Another day, a day in which vague fears began to clamor for attention in Jim's mind, and then, when the sun was at its setting, he saw in a clearing down by a river's bank, the white bell tent, the wagon and mules of his *baas*.

A wild shout of joy rose to his lips, but he did not give it utterance, neither did he act on his impulse to ride forward at breakneck speed. Instead, a look of puzzled indecision on his face, he tethered the horse amidst a clump of elephant grass, then crept forward on his belly, worming his way to a point of vantage where he could overlook the camp, unseen.

And then his powers of self-restraint were put to a severe test for he saw his *baas* performing menial tasks at the order of two white men—the fat white man with the woman's voice, and the white man who had killed the mantis. Another white man—"The sickness has him," Jim muttered—was sitting listlessly on the driver's seat of the wagon, and, lolling nearby, laughing loudly at the white man—Jim's *baas*—was the native Thuso.

"*Au-a!*" Jim muttered wrathfully. "See what evil comes from a little thing. I was thirsty, a mantis was killed, and now this. Truly—the punishment shall be great."

In his passionate wrath he was almost at the point of madly charging the camp, then a cold, reasoning anger took possession of him. He made his way back to his horse, mounted and rode back along the trail to Bomva's *kraal*.

Meanwhile Cherub Baines and Toad Anders were making vicious sport of the Major; a sport which the Dutchman viewed with dull, lethargic eyes.

The Major—he was singing the chorus Of a song and dancing clumsily to its lilting measure—looked like a disreputable scarecrow. His clothes hung on him in rags; his feet were bare; his hair long and matted; his face covered with a black, stubbled growth. His cheeks were sunken and his eyes dulled. Looking at him one would have said that he was a man whose spirit had been utterly broken by harsh treatment and insufficient food.

"That's enough of that squalling," Cherub announced suddenly.

"You've said it," Anders agreed thickly—he had been drinking—punctuating his remark with a shot from his revolver, the bullet entering the ground perilously close to the Major's naked toes.

Both men laughed at their victim's yell of fear and wild leap, which was almost instantly followed by a plea for food.

Cherub smiled. "Something to eat? Of course, if you can pay for it."

"I have no money left but—" hopefully—"I'll give you an I.O.U."

"No," Cherub said. "Cash transactions only. Besides, you ought to have some money. What have you done with all the cash Nessor gave you for this outfit?"

"You ought to know." The Major's tone was very bitter. "You've made me pay a ridiculous price for everything I've had since you started on this trip. I've paid you every penny I had and now—"

"You can go to hell and starve for all of us, Ducky," Anders interposed.

"We've treated you fair," Cherub added. "Everything has been done businesslike. We didn't ask you to come with us—"

"No, you knocked me on the head, bound me hand and foot and brought me along with you."

"That's as may be," Cherub rejoined equably. "But seeing as you came, it was only right you should pay your way."

"You stole my wagon and mules," the Major continued dully.

"No. That's wrong. Nessor—he's such a honest devil—put the money for the outfit in your pocket. He bought it in an open businesslike way. And we sold you the grub you've had. And now you've got no money left, I don't see that we're obliged to keep you. So get to hell away from us—we're not stopping you."

The Major looked about him with an expression of fear.

"But," he expostulated, "I've got no shoes, no helmet, no weapons. I'd be helpless in the bush like this. I'd get sunstroke, lions 'ud get me. At least, give me some food to take with me."

Cherub shook his head.

"You ain't so badly off. The Dutchy says there's a niggers' *kraal* three or four days' trek ahead. You head for there; maybe you'll be able to make it all right. Sleep up in the daytime an' you won't get sunstroke; and there's roots and things you can eat. Course it will be hard traveling without shoes, but that's your lookout. We're ready to sell you a pair if you're willing to pay for them. Anyway, I'm damned if we'll give you a thing. I'd have given you some grub at that if you hadn't been so nosey the other day, trying to help yourself to some of our tinned beef."

"You're too long winded," Anders cut in savagely. "Let the fool go.

"Get out of here, d'yer hear, Major. Go on, on yer way before I let daylight into you."

He aimed his revolver at the Major's head and that man, with a squeal of dismay, turned and ran at top speed toward the river; Anders, laughing loudly, and firing his revolver into the air, close at his heels; Cherub following at a slower gait.

He paused for a moment on the edge of the river, then dived in—and disappeared.

"The fool has drowned himself," Anders swore, turning to Cherub, after a close scrutiny of the river failed to reveal the Major. "What did he want to do that for? I wanted to play with him a little longer. We needn't have driven him away so soon."

Cherub shrugged his shoulders.

"We've done enough, Anders. He's out of the way and—" he made a mock pious gesture—"our hands are not stained with his blood. He's done for himself, and Nessor'll be satisfied. He wouldn't have stood for much more of the treatment we were giving the Major. Nessor's softhearted, blast his funny conscience. And we can't afford to have a row with Nessor—not until this job's done. We don't know the country or the niggers, he does. Come on, let's get to bed. No use looking for the Major. He's gone. There ain't a man living who could swim in that current."

They returned to the wagon and announced the Major's fate to the Dutchman.

"*Ach sis!*" he exclaimed dolefully. "I do not like it; nothing about this trip do I like. Now the Major he has drowned himself and fever is coming to me, and all because you, Anders, put your dirty paws on a Hottentot's god."

"Aw, don't be a fool, Dutchy," Anders growled. "You take a stiff peg of whisky and you'll be all right in the morning. Hottentot god—hell!"

"Maybe you're right, *ma-an*," Nessor said dolefully. "But it is bad luck, I tell you, to play tricks with things like that. Now I will see that Thuso has properly tethered the mules, you go to bed. We will trek early in the morning. But me, I will not sleep. Almighty no! I will keep watch. Maybe the Major's spirit will return."

THE NEXT day's trek was a painful experience for Baines and Anders. Nessor had succumbed to fever and, helpless as a child, could do nothing but toss restlessly in his blankets, muttering vaguely of Hottentot gods and evil spirits.

And Thuso, making the most of his own importance now that his *baas* was unable to supervise him and the other two white men were ignorant of the bush ways, did pretty much as he liked.

He inspanned the mules carelessly with the result that they got dangerously entangled with the harness, almost upsetting the wagon. That fault rectified, he drove so recklessly that both Cherub and Anders, greatly frightened, threatened to shoot him if he did not drive at a lower speed.

At the noonday outspan he allowed the mules to graze too far and hours were wasted before they were all caught and further time was lost, when, later in the day, the near wheels of the wagon—Thuso had driven off the trail—sank hub deep in mire. Both Cherub and Anders had to do a lot of digging before they were clear of that mess.

And so, when they finally made camp for the night they—too tired, even, to find open fault with the food Thuso so slovenly prepared for them—lost no time in getting to sleep.

And Thuso, chuckling to himself at the way he had made merry at the expense of the two white fools, half determined to desert on the morrow if his *baas* were not recovered, built up a huge fire and sat by it, drinking luxuriously from the bottle of whisky he had stolen from the wagon.

Presently he slept, snoring hoggishly.

The fire died down, the bush rustled, shadows moved stealthily.

At the time of the great darkness which presaged the break of day, Cherub and Anders were awakened by a violent crashing amongst the bush surrounding the camp; the mules brayed vacuously and Thuso's voice was raised shrilly in an endeavor to calm them.

"Come quickly," he shouted. "Come help me, or these misbegotten fools will stampede." Then, *"O-he!* They have gone."

Grumbling many curses the two white men lighted a lantern, and joined Thuso.

"If we go now," that man assured in reply to their expostulations that there was no hurry, that they could wait until break of day before trying to recapture the runaways, "we will get them before they have gone far. In the darkness they will keep together. When the sun rises they will scatter."

"The nigger's right," Cherub said, "so it's no use cursing him now. But I'll let him feel the weight of my *sjambok* later. What do we do, Thuso?"

"It is best that we separate and get behind them. Then we will drive them slowly back to the wagon. They will give no trouble, I think. All mules are fools. Listen! You can hear them in the bush. I will go this way; you, *Baas* Baines, that; and you, *Baas* Anders, that."

As he concluded his instructions Thuso silently left the white men and lost himself in the bush shadows. He was not a little puzzled at the strangeness of the stampede, convinced that it was due to some external cause and not their own foolishness. But he quickly put the matter out of his mind and sitting down amongst some bushes gave himself over to inward merriment at the white men's incredulity in believing that he needed their help in recapturing the runaway mules.

"I suppose we'd better do as he says," Baines grumbled and crashed his way through the thickets in the direction Thuso had indicated he should go.

Anders watched him depart, a look of indecision on his face. Then the light of the lantern he was carrying fell upon one of Thuso's knobkerries. He grinned evilly as he picked it up and tested its balance. Nodding presently, as a man will who has suddenly conceived a plan of action, he put out the light and followed silently in the direction taken by Baines.

Darkness slowly gave place to a cold gray gloom; the grayness, and that swiftly, disappeared as the sun shot above the horizon.

About the wagon the mules huddled closely together. Anders, *sjambok* in hand, looked angrily at the native.

"We will inspan and trek now," he ordered.

"But, *Baas*, there are two other mules we have not found; and *Baas* Baines, he is not here. We must wait for him."

"We have waited too long. He is lost, or lions have taken him. As for the lost mules, we have sufficient. No more talk. Inspan."

Shrugging his shoulders, fearing that further procrastination would cause the biting lash of the *sjambok* to fall again about his shoulders, Thuso obeyed and, five minutes later, drove rapidly away. Anders, sitting on the driver's seat beside Thuso, looked straight ahead, a leering grin of triumph on his face.

And so he did not see Baines stagger out from the bushes and stand swaying weakly to and fro, shaking his fists and mouthing inarticulate curses.

"Stop! Stop, blast you!" Baines yelled and ran after the wagon. The rattle of wheels and the rifle-like reports of Thuso's long whip mocked his cries.

"Wait!" he cried with a sob of despair and, suddenly remembering his revolver, pulled it from its holster and fired all the chambers in a burst of inane rage.

The revolver drooped from his nerveless hand; he ran a few more paces and then, tripping over a tiny ant heap, pitched heavily to the ground. For a while he did not move, stunned by the hopelessness of his position, abandoning himself to a flood of self pity.

Red hot needle-like pricks aroused him and he jumped to his feet, frantically brushing a black swarm of ants from his legs. Then, of a sudden, he was conscious that he was not alone. Looking up he saw the Major standing before him, a mocking light in his eyes. His hand leaped to his holster, then he cursed again, remembering that he had dropped his revolver.

"Oh, quite," the Major drawled and laughed.

Baines looked at him with an expression in which fear, curiosity and relief were intermingled.

"Then you weren't drowned?" he said.

"Oh, rather not."

The Major waved his hand airily. There was nothing cringing about him now, yet—two days ago—Baines would have been prepared to take oath that his spirit had been completely broken. This puzzled the angel-faced scoundrel. And the Major had boots, and a helmet! He had a cartridge belt buckled about his waist, a rifle hung over his shoulder.

"Where'd you get them boots an' things?" Baines asked dully; his head ached from the blow Anders had given him with the knobkerry.

"I got them, and other things, from the wagon this morning whilst you chappies were searching for the mules. That was very funny! Of course, you understood this, I'm sure. I caused the mules to stampede. Quite clever of me, wasn't it?"

Baines slowly digested this piece of news. "So you were having a game with us all along, eh? You weren't as scared of us as you made out?"

"Oh, but I was, dear lad, frightfully so. Specially of Anders. I never knew when he would get out of hand and shoot me. Of course Nessor—funny, honest yokel, isn't he?—kept you both from going too far. I knew eventually you would have to pass close by Bomva's *kraal* and Bomva is a great friend of mine. A word to him and he would have set all his warriors on you—really! Then, too, there was always dear old Jim—my Hottentot servant, you know. He's sure to be somewhere on my trail unless—" the Major's face became very stern, the vacuous light departed from his eyes—"unless you have killed him. Did you?"

"No!" Cherub gasped, frightened by the Major's expression. "I take oath we didn't. Nessor wouldn't stand for killing."

"Ah!" The Major sighed with relief after a searching scrutiny of Cherub's face. He became the silly-ass dude again. "I'm glad of that—very. You see I'm very fond of Jim and, had you killed him, I'm afraid I should have had to send you to chirp in hell. Yes."

Baines swallowed painfully. "Look here, what's the game. Are you and Anders playing against me, or—?"

"No, no," the Major broke in hastily. "You misjudge me. I did all this by myself. You see, when I saw that dear old Nessor was going down with fever I came to the conclusion that the time had come for me to depart. I didn't know what you other two Johnnies would be up to without his restraining influence. Otherwise, of course, I should have waited until you got to Bomva's.

"As it was, I planned to have such merry games with you on the way. The first night I left you alone because Nessor had still enough strength to keep watch. And it's easier to catch a weasel asleep than a Boer hunter. But the next night—I knew Nessor was down because your travels were so erratic—I played my first card.

"It would all have been very amusin', oh, very. But now—" he shook his head dubiously—"I'm dashed if I know what to do. You see, I never thought you precious pair of thieves would fall out. Most careless of me to have overlooked that probability. And now I have you on my hands. That complicates matters, rather. But you look quite pale. Anders must have given you a fearful crack on the old bean. What?"

"Blast him!" Cherub sat down on a rock outcrop and endeavored to collect his reeling senses. "He ambushed me, he went back on me and— But I'll get even with him!"

He collapsed suddenly, rolled over and was horribly nauseated.

The Major looked down at him then, with a shrug of his shoulders, turned away and disappeared in the bush.

He returned presently leading two mules, one carrying an improvised pack, two bulging sacks tied together. From one of them came the noise of clinking tins.

Cherub Baines looked up imploringly.

"You won't leave me here, alone, will you, Major," he pleaded. "You couldn't leave a white man—"

"No!" the Major interrupted coldly. "I couldn't leave a white man; neither can I leave you."

He bent down, picked up Baines without undue effort, and put him on the unburdened mule.

"Better hold on tight," he said. "I'm going to trek fast across country. With luck we'll be at the noonday outspan in time to receive your precious partner. And," he added grimly, "he'll get a warm reception. Oh, very!"

TOAD ANDERS was in a killing mood. Having arrived at the noonday outspan, a waterhole amidst a group of *kopjes*, he had determined suddenly to have a look at the diamonds he and Cherub had purchased illicitly and had smuggled so cleverly from the diamond town to be sold to a Portuguese dealer. He wanted to handle them, to estimate the wealth they would bring him, the wealth which, now that Cherub was out of the way, would be all his.

Not finding the tins in which they were secreted in their usual place, he had made a frantic search of the wagon, his wrath increasing every moment.

He turned the wagon upside down, emptying cases of stores, strewing the Major's kit all over the place, looking in every conceivable place. He hauled the Dutchman out of his blankets, searching his pockets and helping himself to all the money he found there, and then—his search still fruitless—he sat despondently on the wagon seat and cursed his late partner.

"He swiped them. I might have known he couldn't play fair. But—" his eyes lighted—"I'll go back for them. As soon as we've had *skoff* we'll go back."

He raised his voice in a shout of "Thuso!" intending to give orders for the return trek. But Thuso—he had vanished at the first outbreak of Anders's wrath—made no reply.

"Hell!" Anders muttered. "Wonder where the nigger's gone?"

At the touch of a hand on his shoulder he looked up with a start to see Nessor standing behind him.

"Oh, it's you is it, Dutchy," he growled. "Better, eh? Well, here's a hell of a mess. Baines has gone and lost himself, and he's got the diamonds with him. He stole them from me. And your nigger's gone and he—"

Nessor sighed heavily. In a little while, he knew, the delirium of fever would have him again in its clutches and there was much he wanted to do.

"You are an evil man, Toad Anders," he said slowly. *"Ach sis* no; now you shall not speak. You are evil, and so, too, is Baines. I was a fool to come on this trip with you. But the money was good—specially when Baines showed me how to buy back my outfit from the Major. But that, too, was evil. I see that now. It is all evil. But now my eyes are open. I should have known. You killed a Hottentot's god, and—and so all this evil has come to us.

"Now," his hand tightened on Anders' shoulder, "now you will give back the money you took from me. Then—"

Anders turned suddenly at that and hit out with all his force. The blow landed full in the Dutchman's face and the big man, weakened by the fever, toppled backward on the floor of the wagon.

Anders laughed callously, gave another call for Thuso, then climbed back into the wagon and searched again for the diamonds.

A premonition of impending evil suddenly made him look up to see, staring through the opening at the back of the tented top, several powerfully built natives. They menaced him with their spears.

He straightened up with a start, his hand leaped to his revolver but a stinging jab in his thigh caused him to turn round. This turn brought him face to face with Jim, the Hottentot, with whom were other armed natives.

"Dutchy!" he called despairingly.

But Nessor was unconscious of anything but the fever madness and before Anders could make any move to defend himself, the natives had closed in on him.

A little later they carried him close to the camp-fire and there they pegged him out on the ground, face upward.

Squatting on the ground beside him was Jim, drawn and haggard looking, his face distorted by misery and hate for his prisoner. Grouped about them were the warriors, men of Bomva's *kraal*. Two of them held Thuso; two others were heating the blades of their assegais in the fire.

"And now, white man," Jim said in a cold, passionless voice, "we will talk together. Afterward you shall suffer many things before death relieves you. It is well that you understand my tongue a little. Only a little that dog says—" he pointed to Thuso. "And so I will talk very slowly, as to a child, in order that you may understand.

"You are a thing of evil, there is no good in you. You killed the man Baines and—"

"It is a lie," Anders whimpered.

"You killed him," Jim continued in a flat, dull monotone. "The dog, Thuso, told me many things. But that killing is no great matter save that you cheated me somewhat of my vengeance. I wanted to deal with him. And you killed a mantis—do you deny that? For that alone your punishment would be great. And yet that is as nothing to your other evil. You killed my *baas*—"

"He killed himself," Anders gasped, his face twitching with fear. "I didn't kill him. He—"

"Because of you," Jim amended, "my *baas* is dead. The rest is nothing, less than nothing. What need of words? My *baas* is dead and you live—but only for a little while."

At a sign from him the two natives who were standing over the fire handed Jim the assegais.

Anders screamed for mercy, cursed, struggled to free himself, threatened and screamed again, while Jim slowly brought the white hot blades close to the soles of his naked feet.

Then there came a shot and a voice calling, *"O-he,* Jim. Softly, Jim!"

With a glad cry of, *"Baas!"* Jim ran to greet the man who was more to him than all the gods of his superstitious creed; the man he thought was dead but, miraculously it seemed to him, lived again.

"Baas!" he cried again and his cry was echoed by the men of Bomva's *kraal* who, Anders forgotten, ran to greet the man they held in such high esteem, the man they had in other days proved to be a man amongst men.

THREE HOURS later the Major, dressed in spotless white duck, clean shaven, his hair brushed back in an immaculate pompadour, monocle glistening in his eye, climbed up onto the driver's seat and ordered the two men—Anders and Cherub—to be brought before him.

Warriors quickly obeyed him.

"Shall we free them, *Baas?*" they asked.

"Yes, but keep the gags in their mouths. I do not wish to hear their voices.

"Now, dear laddies," he said, smiling at the hate with which they regarded each other, "I regret to say that I do not feel as vindictive as I should, really. That, I suppose, is due to my relief at finding Jim unharmed. You know, honestly, I should hang you, but unfortunately there are no trees near at hand high enough for my purpose. And so I'm going to let you go free. Better than that; you will find that I have sold you two of my mules, and provisions, and your—er—lethal weapons. That is the way Jim took all the money from your pockets. I haven't stolen, you will observe, merely copied your excellent business methods.

"I fancy you will find that I have provisioned you very well—oh, very. Plenty of bully beef and flour and what not. Oh, yes; and all the tins of beef which you seemed to set so much store by. Only," he chuckled softly at the gleam which came into their eyes, "I'm afraid you'll find them very tasteless. I—er—as it were, sucked all the seasoning from them. Really! Most astonishing I found it. Talk about pearls in oysters— Oh, well! I see you get my meaning so I won't rub it in. Save—yes, I really must congratulate you on the clever way in which you hid those stones. And it was most unfortunate for you that you should have disclosed their hiding place by making such a bally fuss the time I tried to help myself to one of the tins.

"Yes, I'm keeping the stones. They represent my—er— reward for saving you, Cherub, from being lost in the wilderness, and for saving you, Anders, from the merry little tortures Jim had in store for you. Quite honest and businesslike. I think you will agree. And Nessor, I am sure will appreciate it when he is better. Of course I am going to look after him. He's a good soul at heart, I think. But rather an innocent, if you understand my meaning. And Thuso will stay with me for a while. Jim will see to him.

"And that, I think, is all. The sight of you wearies me. The warriors will escort you several miles back along the trail. Then they will tie your feet to a stout tree, and depart. By the time you have freed yourself and secured your weapons, you will find them in the packsacks, they will be well out of range of your shots and curses. And, if you're wise, you won't venture this way again. That's all. Regret I can't be on hand to see what happens when you two find yourselves face to face. Take them away warriors."

At that the warriors hustled the two men along the trail, driving the two mules, laden with packs, ahead of them.

"And all this, Jim," the Major said, the light of affection in his eyes giving the lie to the sternness of his voice, "came of your foolish thirst!"

"Golly, yes, damme no," prattled Jim, using nearly fifty per cent, of his knowledge of English. Then, in the vernacular, seriously, "But no, *Baas*. That man, Anders, he killed a praying mantis; he put his filthy hands on a Hottentot's god. That is why these things happened. But you're alive, *Baas*. What is past, is past. What else matters?"

"Nothing, Jim. And now, what, you blighted old heathen?"

"I told Bomva you would stay and hunt with him for a while. There are lions—"

"And his women have brewed good beer?"

Jim chuckled.

"Maybe a little, yes, *Baas*."

The Major climbed down from the wagon and walked over to the black horse, Satan, and thoughtfully patted his silken hide, laughing as it playfully nibbled at his fingers.

"He is butter fat, Jim," he said presently.

"Truly, *Baas*."

"Far too fat for the trail."

"I, too, thought that, *Baas*," Jim said hopefully.

"And so, Jim, we will stay and hunt for a while with Bomva's people."

Jim grinned happily.

The Major mounted, sitting gracefully in the saddle.

"I ride on ahead, Jim. You will travel slowly. The Dutchman is very sick."

"Yah, *Baas*. Truly. Thuso—" He scowled at that native who was waiting resignedly for whatever fate might have in store for him—"shall help me inspan."

The Major nodded. "There will be stories to tell after we have *skoffed* tonight, Jim. I want to hear how you got to this place. I want—"

"It was nothing, *Baas*. Nothing."

The Major laughed softly. "Tonight, Jim," he said, "you shall tell me all." Then, with a wave of his hand, he rode away.

"*Au-a!* What a man!" Jim exclaimed "There is none like him, Thuso. He is the Major and I—I am Jim, his servant."

WITCHCRAFT

"**H**ELL!" THE white man bellowed with a burst of devastating wrath. "I have paid you enough."

With a threatening gesture he raised his heavy, rhinoceros hide whip.

"But, boss," the native protested feebly, looking from the coins which glittered falsely on his open palm to the bleeding gash in his thigh, "this will not be sufficient to buy *mouti* to heal the cut in my leg."

"It is enough," the white man stormed, making the soft, musical vernacular a language of harsh gutturals. "It is all you get. Now *hamba—vootsac*—go!"

The lash of the *sjambok* curled about the native's naked back, adding force to the white man's commands.

The native cowered as the lash again wrapped about him, drawing blood, but his eyes flashed vindictively.

He backed slowly out of range of the whip, then halted and drew himself up erect and pointed a condemning finger at his antagonist.

"For this you shall pay, white man," he said slowly. "For this you shall pay. It is no little thing that you should have lied to and cheated other of my people, it is no little thing that you should have lied and cheated me. But that could be forgotten. This other—*Au-a!* Like a dog you have beaten me. That shall be remembered until the shame of it has been wiped out. I am Rivimbi, blood of Chaka flows in my veins. I am the son of Tsomebe, who is the mouthpiece of the spirits. All shadows shrink before his shadow—"

"*Tula!* Shut up!" the white man interrupted. "I spit upon you, I spit upon the shadow of your father. And so—*Hamba!*"

He advanced truculently upon the native, slicing the air with his whip, cracking it menacingly.

Rivimbi, unflinching, held his ground until the white man was almost upon him. Then his courage broke, his morale left him. He forgot that he was a worthy representative of a race of warriors. He remembered only the lesson which had been beaten, kicked and starved into him during his period of service at the diamond mines: That he was a black dog, a worthless nigger, whilst white men—all white men—were superior beings, lords of creation, to whom must be rendered unquestioning homage and obedience.

And remembering that he turned and limped slowly away, his lips firmly compressed, giving no outward sign of the pain of the blows which the white man, following him up, rained upon him.

"Take that for a parting gift," the white man panted as he launched a savage kick at the luckless Rivimbi. "Pass it on to the old dog ape who fathered you."

He laughed harshly as his victim joined himself to a number of natives who had come up unobserved and who had witnessed the white man's exhibition of brutality with incurious eyes. Then his mouth twitched nervously, a look of fear came into his eyes and his fingers gripped convulsively upon the butt of his revolver.

He tensed, listening to the loud voices of the natives. He licked his dry lips, then relaxed with a sigh of relief. They were moving slowly away from the place.

"You dogs! You swine!" He shouted vile threats and viler insults after them. They ignored him, made no answer to his insults, and presently a billow in the rolling veld hid them from view.

"Gawd!" he muttered. "For a moment I thought they was agoin' to rush me. But I'd made it hot for them if they had. They knew that."

He retraced his steps to a group of giant, termite heaps. A bony horse grazed near by. From the tops of the heaps a piece of canvas was spread, making a crude, tent-like shelter from the blaze of the African sun. On the ground beneath it was a shabby saddle, bridle, and a small folding canvas table on which stood a pair of scales.

Sitting down on his saddle the white man critically examined the stone-like object he had just purchased from the native. Blood from the wound in which it had been hidden had dried hard upon it, giving it a rusty appearance.

The white man spat on it, rubbed it clean on his gray flannel shirt, polished it with a piece of chamois leather, held it up to the light, weighed it carefully in his scales.

"It's a beauty," he said contentedly. "Means more than one good beano in Jo'burg, that does."

By profession Jake Sternberg was a diamond prospector; he had a license to prove it. But the claims he worked were human ones, mostly black. His tools were his hands, the *sjambok* and revolver with which he backed up his sanguinary threats, the toes of his ironshod boots and a pocketful of gilded farthings.

Unsophisticated natives accepted these coins as sovereigns. Others, fearing Sternberg's other tools, accepted them without open question, and did not deal with him again. Occasionally one protested, and suffered as Rivimbi had suffered.

They had no legal redress. They were sellers of diamonds they had stolen from their employers and, consequently, deserving of little sympathy. But their crimes were insignificant compared with the crimes of the men who tempted them to steal with promises of great reward, and then, as Sternberg had done, would cheat them with gilded coins. There were a few—one notable one—listed as Illicit Diamond Buyers, who played the game for the game's sake, who considered their crime a political one, a protest against the harsh laws governing the diamond mining industry promulgated by the powerful Syndicate. Such men played the game squarely, asked no one to shoulder the risks, matched their wits against the machinations of the police and the host of informers which swarmed about the diggings, and did not whine or turn Queen's evidence when things went against them.

But for the most part I.D.B.'s were an unsavory lot, their deeds sordid. They were the sweepings of the gutters of the world's big cities. Honor they had none; they were devoid of courage; they lied, stole, and bullied men weaker than themselves.

Jake Sternberg was the chief of this ilk. With sundry others of his craft he had left the detective-ridden Kimberly diggings and had come to the newly opened fields at Klipdrift. There, even if the pickings were fewer, they were able to operate with a certain measure of safety. The police were represented by one gullible overfat trooper, and the miners were too busy squabbling amongst themselves over the ownership of claims to pay heed to the wolves in the fold.

And because Sternberg was a brawny, powerful looking man with a loud, bullying voice, because he had the reputation of being a deadly shot and quick on the draw, he made himself head of the I.D.B fraternity. He alloted their beats, took a percentage of their takings and ruled them with a high hand and loud voice. Their outward submission to his rule, however, was negatived by their secret plotting to put him away, if it could be done without any risk to themselves, either by murder or legal process.

But Sternberg was *slim*. He took no one into his confidence. He lived alone in a tiny shack close to the policeman's hut. He never went out alone at night, and his business office was "somewhere" on the wide spreading veld. He always selected a place, such as his present one, near to one of the winding native paths which led from the *dorp* to the native villages beyond the hills; a place which commanded a clear view of the surrounding country, where he could treat with the natives in his own inimitable way without fear of being trapped in the meshes of the law.

To his left was a low line of mysterious looking hills. To his right, some three miles distant, was the crude new settlement of Klipdrift, a mushroom township of tin huts and canvas tents, of grandiloquently named streets which in the wet season were knee deep in mud but which now, with the dry season barely half over, were rivers of dust which whirled and eddied with every passing breeze. It was a township of men, being too new and crude yet to harbor women of any sort. It was a town of hard livers, a town whose citizens considered themselves a race apart, a law unto themselves. The brazen sun and the drifting dust induced unquenchable thirsts.

Behind Sternberg, and in front, stretched the limitless veld, seemingly dead, yet teeming with life; apparently parched, arid, yet at times a land of raging torrents.

The sun was near its setting. Violet shadows softened the hard lines of the veld.

Jake Sternberg rose to his feet. It was time for him to return to the *dorp*. The veld, when encompassed by Africa's night, was no place for him.

Quickly he packed up his meagre outfit, caught and saddled his dispirited horse, taking up the sweat caked girths with unnecessary vigor.

Mounting, he glanced leisurely about the veld to make sure no other possible clients were afoot, no lurking enemies.

A cloud of dust in the north called for a closer inspection. He levelled his field glasses at it and, in a little while, made out a tent-topped wagon drawn by twelve mules. A man on a black horse rode alongside.

Sternberg watched until he saw them swing into the dirt road which led to the settlement, watched until they passed so close to him that his glasses enabled him to pick out details; the splendid condition of the mules, the sure ability of the Hottentot driver, the graceful ease of the horseman, and the monocle which gleamed in the horseman's eye.

He laughed softly. "Some damn' hunter," he said, his vicious face contorted by a sneer. "Some precious momma's pet sent out to the Colonies to make a man of himself.

Maybe I can help in the process. I'll make his acquaintance tonight. He ought to be worth plucking."

He turned then and levelled his glasses at a little knot of natives who were advancing slowly along one of the trails.

Near a clump of bushes they halted, milled about uncertainly, then came on again until they came to a slight depression in the veld about thirty feet farther on. There they squatted down and drank from black bottles which were handed around.

Sternberg's eyes hardened, he trained his glasses on the clump of bushes and swore viciously.

"The swine!" he ejaculated and picking up his reins, spurred his horse along the trail.

As he neared the drinking natives one rose unsteadily to his feet and lurched directly into his path.

"Wait, boss," he hiccupped and grabbed the bridle reins.

"What do you want, dog?" Sternberg growled, glancing covertly toward the bushes beyond.

"I want to sell you this, boss," the native replied with a drunken chuckle, and exposed on the palm of his hand an uncut diamond of good size and color.

Sternberg's black eyes narrowed as he stared fixedly at the stone, his right hand slid stealthily into his saddle wallet, feeling for something among his day's purchases.

"Come nearer," he said, "that I may see better."

The native loosed his hold of the bridle and came to the near side, clinging to the stirrup, the diamond still exposed on his open palm.

"You dog!" Sternberg roared angrily and with a lightning move he grabbed the native's wrist, wrested the diamond from him, then leaped from the saddle onto the man, sending him headlong to the ground.

They rolled over and over, the native struggling feebly, Sternberg punching and kicking him, yelling furiously. "I'll show you! You think I'm a 'buyer,' eh? Well, this'll show you I'm not. I'm going to take you in to the policeman. Now, get up!"

He released his hold of the man and rose to his feet. "Turn round," he continued as the native, cowering, faced him once again. "Put your hands behind your back. There." He tied them securely. "Now *hamba*. To the *dorp*. Get on, now."

Half dazed the native stumbled along the path, halting expectantly as he came opposite the bushes.

Sternberg mounted and rode up to him. "Get on," he said wrathfully. "I'll learn you to—"

"Hold on, Jake!" The bushes parted and fat, good natured Trooper Sam Moore emerged.

"How in hell did you get here, Sam?" Sternberg asked and continued hurriedly. "Well, I'm glad you are here. I give this nigger in charge for trying to sell me a stone. Here it is." He handed the policeman what to an untrained eye looked like a shapeless lump of dirty glass.

The policeman pocketed it without comment.

"And," continued Sternberg excitedly, "you'd better arrest that bunch of niggers back there before they get crazy, an' kill somebody, on the rot-gut gin they're drinking."

Sam Moore laughed boisterously. "That's all right, Jake. They ain't drinking nothing stronger than water. An' you didn't ought to have used this nigger so hard. He's one of my police boys. I used him as a trap. You see," he laughed again, "Smithers told me—er, that is, acting on information received that you was a I.D.B. I made up my mind to test you. Yes, I did," he continued, waving aside Sternberg's exclamation of anger. "Why not? If you was a I.D.B. it was

my duty to know it an' run you in. But the way you treated
Tikkey here, when you had no call to suspect a trap, proves
you're running straight an' there ain't no harm done."

Sternberg stuttered with an affectation of indignation,
then laughed. "All right, Sam. Only it ain't playing the
game, to try and trap a man. It ain't fair to put temptation
in anybody's way. However, seeing as it's turned out a the
way it has, it ain't no use talking about it. By the way I seen
a dudeish looking chap riding toward the *dorp*. We ought
to get him into a little game of poker tonight. What do
you say?"

The trooper nodded. "I'm with you. I'll call for you after
skoff an' we'll go down to the Royal, Jake. He'll probably
put up there."

Sternberg nodded agreement, waved his hand in a parting salute and rode off, chuckling softly to himself. Trooper
Sam Moore was such a gullible fool!

The I.D.B. was barely out of sight when an undersized,
rat-faced man crept stealthily out of the bushes.

"Wot yer let him go for?" he asked Moore in a frightened
burst of passion. "Yer fat fool! You had him fair and square,
an' yer let him go! Oh, lor! He—"

Trooper Moore shook his head ponderously. "He didn't
do nothing against the law, Smithers. 'Smatter of fact, if
everybody did what he did, there'd be no I.D.B.'s."

Smithers spat contemptuously. "He's a I.D.B., I tell yer.
An' he'd have bought that stone only 'e must have found
out we was here in 'iding, an' was on his guard."

"You're talking like a fool, Smithers," the policeman said.
"We came out here damned careful, afoot, with a mob of
stinkin' niggers all around us. He couldn't have known we
was hiding in that bush. No, Smithers, Jake Sternberg may

be all the things you say he is, 'cept he ain't no I.D.B. At least I ain't got no proof he's one."

"You fat-gutted fool!" Smithers screamed. "Wot do you care about proof? He had the stone in his 'and. He took it from the nigger, didn't he? You saw it, an' I was a witness. Well then, there's your case. That's all the court needed to know. They'd have sentenced Jake on that evidence to ten years on the breakwater, you'd 'ave got promoted, an' us poor mining coves could have gone 'ad a bit of peace. You—"

"That's enough," Moore interposed with a fat man's dignity. "I don't get my cases that way. I don't frame a man. Put that in your pipe an' smoke it."

"No," Smithers sneered. "You don't frame a man, you fat fool, you let him pull the wool over your eyes. You 'ave a chance to nab the dirtiest I.D.B. goin', an' let 'im get away. An' what's worse, you blurt out that it was me as informed against 'im. Hell!" Smithers was almost whimpering now. "He'll make me pay for that. Unless," a crafty gleam came into his eyes, "unless I get 'im first."

Trooper Moore pulled down his tunic over his rotund stomach, straightened his helmet, twisted the waxed ends of his fair mustache fiercely upward and assumed, as well as he could, a military pose. "I've listened to you long enough, Smithers," he said pompously. "Better keep quiet, now, or I'll run you in for swearing false information against a man, makin' me walk way out here in the blasted heat, causing me to neglect my other duties. Here's the stone you gave me to try an' trap Sternberg with."

Smithers took the stone and was about to put it in his pocket, hesitated and, warned by some premonition, examined it closely.

His face fell, an angry rage mastered him, causing him to overstep the bounds of caution. "Hell!" he stormed. "This ain't the stone I gave you, you fat fool. Sternberg's rung the changes on you."

Moore eyed him coldly. " 'Course it's the same stone. He didn't have no chance to change it."

"It ain't the same, I tell yer," Smithers insisted. "The one I lent yer to trap him with was a rose diamond. This 'un's a muddy yeller an' ain't worth a damn. Mine was worth 'undreds. He rung the changes on yer or maybe," he leered provocatively, "you an' him are partners."

Fat Sam's fist shot out with incredible speed and Smithers reeled back, a hand to his aching jaw.

"I pulled that one," the policeman said complacently. "Better be careful, Smithers. Just 'cause I'm fat an' easy goin' don't mean it's safe for you to go 'round makin' accusations of that sort. Be careful, Smithers."

Smithers cowered before the threat of the trooper's ham-like fist.

"For the matter of that," Moore continued cheerfully, "it mightn't be a bad idea to watch you. Where in hell did you get a rose diamond? You ain't got no claim, an' I know you ain't got the money to buy a rose diamond in honest deal."

Smithers started and only by an effort regained an appearance of composure. "I was only foolin' about that, Sam," he said placatingly. "I got so wild at Sternberg not fallin' inter our trap that I said a lot of things I didn't ought to. Didn't know wot I was sayin', like. This is the same stone, all right. It ain't worth a copper cent. You can 'ave it if you want."

Moore eyed him dubiously. "Don't want it," he said shortly. "But you be careful what you say in future—makin' me walk out here on a fool's errand, and getting one of my police boys beaten up. Come on, let's get back to the *dorp*. I'm dry."

IT WAS quite dark by the time Jake Sternberg reached his hut, dismounted and gave his horse into the charge of the cowed, rag clothed native who acted as his spy, body-guard and house servant.

"Well?" he growled as the native, wise from past experience, waited for permission to speak before taking the horse away to the tumbledown stable shed.

"If the boss pleases—" the native began uncertainly.

"The boss doesn't please," Sternberg interrupted, thinking he was anticipating a request for a pass permitting the native to visit one of the compounds. "Tie that horse up. No need to off-saddle; I'm goin' out again after *skoff*. Hi! Why in hell haven't you lighted the candles?"

"Boss—" The native's protest ended in a squeak of fear and he dodged quickly just in time to evade the vicious blow Sternberg aimed at him. But the horse got the blow full in the ribs, and almost collapsed at the impact.

"Blast it!" Sternberg roared, and rubbed his aching wrist. "I'll teach you to stand 'round gabbling!"

But the native had showed wisdom. He had swiftly led the horse away, determined to remain hidden in the darkness until such a time as his boss' temper had somewhat subsided.

For a few moments Sternberg stood there, bellowing orders to the native to return, threatening him with bodily injury when he did come.

Then suddenly he was silent. The darkness had sapped his windy courage. He groped for the door of the hut, fumbled with the latch, lifted it and stumbled into the hut, closing the door swiftly behind him. And there he stood, motionless, breathing hard, sensing that something, some one, was sitting in the darkness waiting for him.

"Who's there?" he questioned hoarsely, and drew his revolver. When there was no response, he laughed self-consciously, returned the revolver to its holster and felt in his pocket for a match.

"I'm a fool," he muttered. "Thought somebody was here, one of Smithers' gang tryin' to get me. Wouldn't put it beyond them, at that. And Smithers, the sewer, I'll make him sorry he tried to frame me! Where in hell are them blasted matches? *Arr-r-r.*"

There was a slight scratching sound, followed by a little halo of light as the match burst into flame, and Sternberg carefully lighted the row of candles stuck on a shelf built into one side of the hut. As each candle's light further dispelled the gloom, Sternberg's spirits rose.

The last candle lighted he turned slowly, once again conscious of another's presence, and stared into the eyes of a native who sat cross-legged in a far corner of the hut.

"Greetings!" the native said calmly. He was very old, his matted hair was white, his limbs shrunken. His face was lined with deep wrinkles. Almost toothless, his articulation was indistinct. But his eyes burned as they stared unwinkingly at Sternberg until the white man was ready to swear that they floated in a mist haze of their own creating.

Sternberg shivered.

"Aye, it is cold, white man," the native croaked and drew a ragged blanket closer about his attenuated form. "It is always cold when darkness releases the spirits from the land of the dead."

Sternberg licked his dry lips. "Who in hell are you, an' what do you want?" he demanded in the vernacular.

He took a threatening step forward, then stiffened as if held by an electric current; his feet felt clamped to the floor, his arms hung limply by his side.

The native laughed. "I have many names. Some call me the Lord of Life and Death. But I am Tsombe, the father of Rivimbi. You know of that one?" It was a statement rather than a question.

"What of it?" Sternberg said tonelessly.

"Maybe much, maybe little. I come to you, white man, for justice. That is all, but that is a lot. You cheated my son—he is a fool. You beat him—he had forgotten that the blood of warriors flows in his veins. Aye, he is a fool, he has forgotten his manhood. But he is my son. And so," he grinned sardonically, "I have come to you that justice may be done. Yet know this, I would not have come to you but would have executed justice in my own way—I have many servants—had not a white man, a friend of all black ones, a man who is a man, persuaded me otherwise. Maybe you know him. He rides a black horse; a piece of glass clouds the wisdom of his eye. Maybe you know him. But no matter. Because he asked it, I have come to you that you, yourself, may be given a chance to make amends for the evil you did to my son. You shall pay me money you promised him and for the blows you gave him. Do that and I will forget the insults you put to my name. That is all, white man. I wait for your answer."

There was a long silence. Sternberg tried to voice the anger which almost choked him, but only mouthed noiselessly. His heavy jowled face was a mottled crimson, he gasped like a half asphyxiated man.

Tsombe chuckled as if at some secret thought, made a sweeping gesture of his hand. "I wait for your answer, white man," he repeated, and deliberately looked away.

Sternberg gasped, yawned widely, then—"Get out of here," he yelled. "Quick! Before I *sjambok* the hide off you."

He took a pace forward, but halted at the patter of foot-steps outside. The door opened. An inrushing breeze extin-guished all of the candles but one, and guttered unsteadily.

"Shut the door," Sternberg shouted, and his native servant retreated precipitately, slamming the door behind him.

"Your answer, white man!"

Sternberg started violently. For the moment he had forgotten the witchdoctor.

The one flickering candle failed to lighten the corner of the hut in which Tsombe sat, but Sternberg fancied he could see the gleam of the man's eyes, and that was all he needed to see. He drew his revolver, stealthily.

"It is enough, white man." The native's voice sounded very faint, as if coming from a great distance. "You know not truth."

"You dog!" Sternberg growled. "I'll blow—"

He stopped, panic stricken. The eyes in the dark seemed to move, to melt into nothingness. He was conscious of a cold current of air. Subconsciously, he heard a creaking as if of the opening and closing of a door. The eyes appeared again, larger, menacing.

"You speak with a double tongue," Tsombe's voice continued. "All your dealings are evil. Therefore justice shall be forced from you. But not now. Soon. Maybe tomorrow at sunrise, or at its setting. Maybe not until another moon has waxed and waned. But soon. This time I came to you, next time you will come to me, to my *kraal* in the hills. When I call, you will come. Is it understood, white man? Is it understood?"

Then, in the faintest of whispers, like a dream voice, "When I call, you will come. Do not forget."

Then, utter silence.

Long minutes passed. Sternberg sighed and moved uneasily. He tugged savagely at his tobacco stained, straggling beard, wincing slightly at the pain.

Once again he raised his revolver, levelling it at the far corner of the room.

"—your brains out!" he cried, finishing the threat he had commenced minutes before.

He fired four times in rapid succession, blinked hard and stared fixedly into the gloom, waving his hand before him, fanning away the acrid powder smoke which swirled about him.

Presently it cleared and he grunted with dismay. Save for himself the hut was empty.

With shaking hands he lighted the candles and pouring himself out a stiff peg of whisky, drank greedily. "Must have been dreaming," he muttered. "There wasn't anybody here, couldn't have been. Maybe I got fever coming on, or maybe it was a touch of the sun. Anyway, it's gone now."

He poured himself another drink.

"An' if they was somebody here, some dirty swine of a witchdoctor, then he got out when my nigger came in. Lucky for him he did get out, too.

"Hell! I'm a fool to get the wind up like this. Touch o' the sun, that's what it is. An' I'm hungry, maybe that has something to do with it. Where's that nigger of mine?" He raised his voice in a shout of "Sixpence!"

Almost before his shout had died away the door was violently opened and Fat Sam Moore entered, breathing hard.

"What's the *indaba*, Jake?" the trooper asked. "I heard four shots." He looked anxiously at the other. "All right, ain't you? You're pasty about the gills."

"Yes, I'm all right," Sternberg answered impatiently. "There was a snake in that corner. I shot at the damned thing, but missed. That's all."

The trooper's face fell. "That all? Thought I'd got a case at last. Thought you'd murdered somebody, or been murdered. But, hell, nothing ever happens in this *dorp*. Come on. Let's go down to the Royal an' have a drink."

"I'm not goin' down tonight, Sam."

The policeman looked incredulous. "Oh, come on, Jake. You ain't forgot that dude feller, have you?"

Sternberg's face lighted. He had forgotten. And the dude would afford him some amusement. He needed something like that to take his mind off the feeling of terror which obsessed him.

"All right, Sam," he said. "You go on down now. I'll be along later, when I've had *skoff* an' the moon's up."

The trooper nodded and waddled out of the hut, wondering why Sternberg had kept glancing over his shoulder.

"He drinks too much alone, that's the trouble with Sternberg," he mused. "I'm always tellin' him that. Looks to me as if he was in for an attack of D.T's. Well, that'ud be a bit of excitement."

TWO HOURS later Sternberg made his way down the middle of the dusty road to where light streaming through red curtained windows, indicated the locality of the Royal Hotel.

As he neared, the door opened and the form of Smithers was silhouetted for a fraction of a second in the opening, then the door closed with a slam and Smithers reeled drunkenly down the *stoep* steps.

With an angry hissing intake of breath, Sternberg pounced upon him, shook him violently, pummeled him, crashing his fists into the helpless man's face. When he released his hold, Smithers slumped in a huddled heap to the ground.

"I'll learn you to frame me," Sternberg raged. "What I've given you now ain't a patch on what's a-goin' to happen to you!" He kicked Smithers in the ribs and then passed on to the hotel, feeling immeasurably pleased with himself and the way in which he had asserted his authority over Smithers.

Entering the bar-room he found that all the habitues of the place were gathered about a tall, foppishly dressed man, who sported a monocle in his right eye and spoke in an affected drawl.

"Look at momma's pet," Sternberg chortled derisively. "Let him be, boys, an' come an' have a drink with a man."

Save that one or two of the men looked 'round impatiently, Sternberg was ignored.

This puzzled him. Generally he was treated with a sychophantic homage, men acted as if it were an honor to be allowed to buy him a drink.

He roughly forced his way to the front rank of the knot of men who were crowded 'round the dude and stood there, glaring truculently around, listening to the stranger's account of his adventures on the veld.

"So you can see for yourselves, dear lads," he was saying, "what a frightful pickle I was in. Oh, absolutely. There was dear old Jim—he's a bally Hottentot, don't you know; been with me for years an' years; he's quite a Damon to my Pythias, if you get my meaning— Well, there he was under the broken wagon which I was holding up. An' there was the bally lion, evidently in search of a meal, charging at a great rate. What was I to do? Well, I ask you? If I let the wagon go, dear old Jim would be crushed to a pulp. If I didn't let it go and grab my rifle, I was booked for a long journey, via a lion's belly, an' Jim would be done for anyway. Talk about bein' between the devil an' the well known deep sea! That was it, I give you my word. Exactly. I was in a frightful funk. I—"

"For God's sake," Sternberg exclaimed to the listeners, unable to restrain himself any longer, "are you going to stand there all night gapin' and listening to momma's pet tell lies? Him hold up the back end of a wagon? Hell, it takes a man to do that! He couldn't hold up a bantam's tail."

"Most rude of you to interrupt," the monocled man drawled. "Most rude."

"Aw, get on with your story," Sternberg sneered. "What did you do?"

The other took out his monocle and polished it absently.

"Why—er—" he stammered, "it sounds incredible, but—well I waited until the lion got quite close—then I bit it."

A titter of mirth greeted this and Sternberg flushed angrily. He felt that the laugh was against him.

"Think you're funny, don't you, dude?"

"Not at all, dear chap. Serious, very. Give you my word."

"You're a fool!"

"Granted. But then, I can't help that, can I? Born so, you know. Some are. Others achieve folly. Take yourself, for example."

Again Sternberg sensed that the laughter of the men was at him. "See here," he raged. "Don't you try to get funny with me. I'm Jake Sternberg. See?"

The dude's blue eyes hardened, steely lights came into them. The lines about his mouth tightened. Then he relaxed and his clean shaven face looked more inane, more vacuous than ever.

"I've wanted to meet you, Jake," he said smoothly, "ever since I had a talk with a—er—native named Rivimbi. He told me quite a lot about you an' the way you treated him. Old Tsombe, his father—I gave him a lift in my wagon—was frightfully annoyed at the affair. Oh, most annoyed. He was most eager to kill you in a very special way, a nasty, sticky way. But I persuaded him that that sort of thing wasn't done, really, an' told him that if he put the matter up to you, nicely, you would see the justice of his demands. He was very skeptical about it so I hope you made everything all right with him. For your sake, I hope that. He's a very clever chappy, an' I'd hate to have him for an enemy. He's a witchdoctor, you know, an' has all sorts of degrees to his name. An' he can make you see things that aren't. Absolutely! Quite the complete hypnotist, I give you my word. He told me—"

"Never mind what he told you," Sternberg interrupted. "You listen to what I tell you. You keep your nose out of my affairs, see? An' now, shut your mouth. Nobody wants to hear your gab, Percy."

"But they were listenin' until you so rudely interrupted, really. An' my name's not Percy. It's Aubrey St. John. Though," he chuckled softly, "I'm generally called 'the Major.' Don't know why, I'm not a fightin' man. Yes, I'm 'the Major.' "

He waited, expectant, evidently thinking that that title would have some affect on Sternberg. And it was a name to conjure with throughout South Africa. It was the title of a man, this soft-spoken monocled dude, who was a peer amongst I.D.B's. A man whose diamond buying exploits were the despair of the police who tried to trap him, and of the lesser breed who tried to emulate him. He was accepted by all sorts and conditions of men, white and black, as a man amongst men. Even his enemies admitted that, and his essential honesty and courage.

Jake Sternberg should have known all this, should have known that the man's foppish raiment concealed a powerful physique, that his soft, flabby appearance was only a delusion, and that his vacuous face, his silly assisms, were used as masks to conceal the swift workings of a keen brain. But something had sealed the memory cell which would have warned Sternberg to take no undue liberties with this silk-shirted dude, and in order to regain the prestige he had lost he became even more offensive.

"You pretty fool," he snarled, and to add force to the insult he swung his right to the other's jaw.

The Major moved his head slightly, and as Sternberg's big fist slid harmlessly by his ear his left hand moved with great rapidity and caught Sternberg's wrist in a grip of steel.

"You damn' pet," Sternberg bellowed again, and swung heavily with his left. His aim was spoiled by an open handed flick on the nose which caused the blood to flow, and before he was fully alive to what was happening his left wrist was imprisoned as securely as his right and both his hands were pinioned to his side. Then despite his kicks and struggles he was lifted off his feet. High up in the air the Major lifted him, then lowering him turned him over across his knee and spanked him with his open palm as if he were a child.

The loud laughter of the onlookers drowned Sternberg's curses.

"You're a very naughty man, I'm afraid," the Major drawled, and releasing his hold on Sternberg, let the fellow fall to the floor.

Sternberg's hand went to his revolver holster. It was empty.

"Tut, tut, dear heart," the Major chided him. "Don't swear. Here's your little pop-gun." He tossed the revolver he had taken from Sternberg on to the ground.

Quick as a striking snake, Sternberg grabbed it up and pulled the trigger. But instead of a report, the revolver clicked harmlessly.

"But of course," said the Major, "I took out the cartridges. You understand that, surely?"

Sternberg jumped to his feet and threw the empty revolver with all his force at the Major's smiling face.

"Hardly cricket," the other drawled, as he caught the hurtling weapon. "But I think you're out, old dear."

He tossed the revolver through an open window and turned his back on his opponent, inviting the others to drink with him.

Sternberg hesitated, weighing his chances of another run-in with the dude, thought better of it and sat down at a table and helped himself liberally from a bottle of whisky which a bartender set before him. There, presently, Trooper Moore joined him.

"He treated you like a two-year-old, Jake," Fat Sam grinned. "An' he's *slim*. You can't put one over on him. Smithers tried to pick his pockets, an' while Smithers was working on him, the Major worked on Smithers. Yeah, an' he winked at us others to let us know what was goin' on. Smithers gets a lousy bob from the Major's pocket an' the Major gets all Smithers had—matter of five quid. You ought to have seen Smithers' face when he found out he'd been done. He tried to draw his gun, an' then I butts in—I don't stand for gun-play. But I didn't need to, the Major can take care of himself. He gave Smithers two minutes to get out, and Smithers got, We've been drinking Smithers' health with Smithers' money, ever since. The Major's *slim*, Jake, an' he's a damned good sort."

"You get him over here for a game of poker," Sternberg growled, "an' you'll see how *slim* he is. He's a dude fool. Luck's been with him, so far. I wasn't feeling right tonight. That's why I let him put one over on me—an' because I wanted to get him in a good humor so's I could trim him at cards better."

The trooper nodded dubiously.

"Hi, Major," he shouted. "Jake here wants to know if you'll play a little game of poker an' let bygones be."

The Major walked slowly over to the table.

"That's very sportin' of you, Jake," he said. "An' poker, you say? 'Fraid I'm only a novice, very clumsy when I shuffle the cards, an' all that. But if you're willing to overlook little things like that, why I'm yours to command."

But two hours later Sternberg was forced to announce sullenly that he was broke and could play no more. For once he had met his master. His clever manipulation of the cards had gained him nothing.

"You've got the luck of the devil," he snarled.

"Oh, quite!" the Major laughed. "Sure you can't go on? No? Then I'll toddle along to my camp. Toodle-oo, Jake. Thanks for the instruction in the art of poker playing an' shuffling. That's the most important part of your game, isn't it? So long, you chappies."

IT WAS late in the forenoon of the following day when Sternberg, groaning with the aching pain in his head, opened his eyes and saw Trooper Moore standing by his bed.

"Hello, Fat," he said wanly. "Must have been drunker than hell last night."

The trooper looked coldly at him. "You was, Sternberg. An' now you listen to me. You drank like a fish after the Major left last night, an' you talked a lot. Remember what you said?"

"No. It don't matter, does it? A man's liable to say anything when he's drunk."

"It matters a damn lot," the trooper said heatedly. "You said a lot, some of it lies but most, as I found out by making inquiries, was true. Yeh! You said too much, Sternberg. You boasted about the way you'd been throwin' dust in my eyes, a-lettin' on you was a honest diamond digger when all the time you been I.D. buying. You must've thought you was goin' to get the men to forget the way the Major treated you by boastin' how you'd made a fool of me; specially that *slim* trick you pulled yesterday, swapping the diamond I'd used to try an' trap you fer one that was no good. Well, you boasted too loud, Sternberg. You ain't goin' to throw any more dust in anybody's eyes round here. You—"

"Oh, look here, Fat," Sternberg started to protest feebly.

"Name's Moore, Trooper Moore," the policeman snapped. "An' it's no use you sayin' anything. If I had any real evidence, I'd arrest you now. But I ain't, I admit that. An' because I'm square, I won't frame you. Not even a skunk like you. But I'm givin' you until noon to get clear of this *dorp*. If you're here after that time, or if you come back, I'll frame you so hard that you'll spend the rest of your life on the breakwater.

"Don't forget, you've got till noon. That's all!"

He stumped out of the hut, slamming the door behind him.

"Fat!" Sternberg called weakly. But there was no reply. He got out of bed, sluiced his head in a bucket of water and sat down on a rickety chair and endeavored to plan some way of righting himself with the trooper.

"It's all that blasted dude's fault," he muttered. "If it hadn't 'a' been for him I wouldn't have gone to the Royal last night. I wouldn't have got drunk an' blabbed like a fool. Blast him! An' it was him who sent that nigger Tsombe to me here, putting the wind up me with his slinking ways. But I'll get even with the monocled fool."

He looked at his watch and then, in a fit of panic, rose to his feet and started packing his moveable possessions.

"I got to go," he said. "No use tryin' to argue things out with Fat, the damn' fool. No use tryin' to bribe him, either. Well, I ain't done so bad out of this *dorp*."

He carefully stowed away the diamonds he had illicitly purchased in a pocket which had been sewn on the inside of his gray flannel shirt. Half an hour later, his possessions strapped to his saddle, he rode away from the *dorp*, outwardly ignoring the jeers of the men he passed. But each mocking greeting added fuel to the rage which was consuming him, straightened his determination to get even with the dude who, according to his warped reasoning, was responsible for all his misfortunes.

He had traveled some three miles from the *dorp*, heading for a farming settlement which he planned to reach before sundown, when he sighted a white man's camp on the veld. It was, he recognized with an exclamation of triumph, the dude's camp. The tent-topped wagon, the white bell-tent and the sleek mules which grazed near by told him that.

Drawing his revolver he rode up to the camp, determined to shoot on sight, meaning to leave nothing to chance.

As he neared the wagon, a squat powerfully built Hottentot rose and greeted him respectfully.

"Where's your *Baas?*" Sternberg asked in the vernacular.

"He has gone to the *dorp.*"

Sternberg cursed softly. "And you, what is your name?"

"My name is Jim, *baas.* I am the servant of the Major."

Sternberg cursed again. The memory of all that fear, anger and drink had hidden from him last night now all came back to him. The Major! And he had dared to match his strength and wits against that man! He shivered, remembering how greatly he had dared.

The Major! What a fool he had been not to have recognized the man that ambushed himself behind a soft exterior. The Major and Jim the Hottentot! The two men had almost assumed the importance of legendary heroes. Everyone knew of them and of their feats, laughed at their exploits and admired their strength, wisdom, and knowledge of the veld.

The two men, the white man and the black, Sternberg knew were inseparable. The friend of one was the friend of both, what hurt one hurt the other. It was this second thought which now actuated Sternberg.

"Put up your hands, Hottentot, he commanded harshly and punctuated his order with a shot.

The Hottentot obeyed with a grunt as the heavy bullet ploughed into the ground close to his naked feet.

Sternberg dismounted and, working swiftly, loosely tied Jim to the spokes of the wagon wheel. With his hunting knife he slit Jim's red shirt from top to tail, exposing his muscled back.

"And now," said Sternberg, removing his coat and running the lash of his *sjambok* through his hand, "now

I'm going to pay you for the way your *Baas* treated me last night."

The *sjambok* whistled through the air.

THE SHADOWS were lengthening.

The Major, sitting on the *stoep* of the Royal Hotel, talking to Trooper Moore, noted the position of the sinking sun, adjusted the set of his white pith helmet and arose.

"Goin' already, Major?" Fat Sam protested.

"Yes, must. Old Jim would be getting anxious."

The men who were gathered about the Major's horse, a coal black stallion, admiring its points, urged him to stay and make another night.

He laughed aside their invitations.

"Well," a miner said, "leave the horse, Major. I'll give you five hundred for him."

"He can't be bought, old dear," the Major drawled. "I need his speed when I'm—er—flying from the arms of the well known law."

There was a general laugh at that.

The Major slowly descended the *stoep* steps, mounted and sat for awhile listening to the goodnatured banter of the men. And even though the events of the previous night were still fresh in their minds, some of the men could not refrain from a contemptuous chuckle at his appearance. He looked such an effete dude as he sat polishing his monocle.

He picked up the reins, waved a farewell to the men, beaming with good nature and the joy of living.

And then Jim, the Hottentot, stumbled into view around the corner of the hotel building, his tattered shirt soaked with blood, his face haggard with pain.

"*Baas!*" he croaked, and fell face forward to the ground.

The Major jumped from his horse and ran to him, picked him up and carried him into the shade of the *stoep*. There he examined Jim's bleeding back, washed the wounds, rubbed them with ointment produced by the storekeeper, and bandaged them expertly with strips torn from a sheet.

Jim sighed deeply and opened his eyes.

"I am a fool," he muttered. "Like a woman I have acted. But all went dark before me, so that I stumbled and fell, But all is well, now, *Baas*." He tried to rise.

"Keep still, Jim." The Major gently pressed him down. "Tell me who did this."

"A strong man, *Baas*. A very strong man: At times it seemed as if his blows would cut me in two. He did it, he said, to pay you for the evil you did him last night."

"Sternberg!" the Major exclaimed, his eyes glittering wrathfully. Their color changed from blue to steely gray, the slack lines about his face tightened, his jaws projected menacingly.

He rose to his feet. "Jackson," he spoke incisively. "You will take care of Jim. Good care. You understand?"

The hotel proprietor nodded. "But where are you going?" For the Major was pushing his way through the men who crowded about him.

"After Sternberg," said the Major icily. "I'm going to flay the life out of him."

And though most of the men fully sympathized with him, they recoiled from the killing light in his eyes.

"*Baas!*" The Major turned at Jim's call. "This you should know, *Baas*. Many blows the man gave me. He was laughing as one gone mad. Then he raised his *sjambok* again, saying that he had but started. I waited, but the blow did not fall. He breathed hard, *Baas*, and the whip fell suddenly from his hand. He went white and licked his lips, as one who remembers—as one who is suddenly afraid."

"Aye," said the Major, "he remembered both Tsombe and me, perhaps. Did not Tsombe promise vengeance upon him when he used the *sjambok* the last time—and now he has whipped again."

"That may be, *Baas*," said Jim, "for he mounted his horse and rode like mad, and looked often over his shoulder at the hills where Tsombe lives."

"Then Tsombe's vengeance had best be speedy," said the Major grimly, "else mine will outride him."

And with that the Major mounted, spurred and rode swiftly away.

The miners looked at each other wonderingly.

"What's all that mean?" Trooper Moore asked. "What's he mean—the vengeance of Tsombe?"

"Don't know and don't care," someone answered. "But I'm going after the Major. There'll be something worth seeing when he gets hold of Sternberg."

The idea met with general approval and a few minutes later such men as had horses rode out on the trail taken by the Major. Fat Sam Moore, mounted on a grossly fat mule, ambled doggedly in their rear. Their numbers were augmented as they passed through the *dorp*, and they rode, whooping loudly.

Smithers joined these men as they rode past the Major's camp.

Their speed slackened now for the Major was out of sight and they were forced to follow his spoor, and none of them were expert bushmen. The trail led haphazardly over the veld, through patches of dense bush, over wide *vleis*, between groups of weirdly piled rocks.

A crisp report ahead of them caused them to spur their horses to better speed.

They finally came up to the Major. He was dismounted and bending over the prostrate body of Sternberg, and he looked up as they drew rein and dismounted.

"He's dead," he announced grimly.

"Wot d'yer mean, dead?" Smithers asked roughly, and he and the others crowded forward.

"Shot," the Major said tersely. "Through the head."

"Well," one of the miners commented. "That's better than he deserved. Let's pile some stones over him an' go back for a drink."

"That's all—fine an' large," Smithers cried. "But if Sternberg was shot, then the dude shot 'im. An' look! Sternberg's gun 'asn't been fired. It was murder!"

The miners glanced around at each other suddenly. "That's right," said one of them slowly. "And murder doesn't go, here."

"No," said another, "murder doesn't go. There's ropes for fellers that does murder."

The Major's eyes narrowed as he looked first at the man who had just spoken, then at Smithers.

"Don't be bally fools," he said. "I didn't shoot Stern—"

He was interrupted by incredulous laughter.

"Let's have a look at your gun," said one of the miners curtly.

The Major laughed. "Well—no. I don't think I care to do that, old chap. I'd feel quite naked without it. But why such interest in my—er—lethal weapons?"

"Because I want to see if it's been fired recently. We heard a shot an' here's Sternberg dead. If you didn't shoot, then we're willing to believe you didn't do it."

"Oh, I see. Clever of you, very. Well, my gun has been fired. I shot at a hyena that was hanging around."

"That's a good 'un ter tell the marines," Smithers exclaimed. "Where's this 'ere hyena?"

"Last I saw of him, dear old Rat-face, he was getting from hence as fast as his four legs would take him. I missed him, unfortunately."

"Yeh, damned unfortunate for you," one of the miners growled.

"Eh? Oh, I say, look here, you know," the Major expostulated. "I don't like all this talk. Sounds like a bally inquest. An' we're wasting time. Much as I dislike the—er—corpse, I think we should concentrate our efforts on findin' the murderer. Really."

He straightened up. By some feat of legerdemain his revolver seemed to leap from its holster to his hand. The miners halted their advance. One of them shouted. "We don't have to look for the murderer; we've found him."

"Really?" the Major drawled. He seemed intent on the polishing of his monocle. "An' who did the foul deed?"

"Aw! Come off yer perch, ducky," Smithers exclaimed. "It's plain enough for any fool ter see. All these chaps 'eard yer say yer would kill Sternberg. An' we 'ears a shot an' comes 'ere an' finds yer bending over his bloomin' corpse. Wot more does anybody want? An' wot I says," he cried, turning now to the others, "is that we ain't goin' to stand for murder. If we do, where'll us stop? I ask yer. This monocled dude'll be killin' one of us, next. So wot I'm sayin' is: Them as murders gets 'anged. An' there's a gallus," he pointed to a near by tree, "an' 'ere's a rope. An'," pointing to the Major, "there's the murderer. So, wot do yer say, boys?"

Mob psychology is an extraordinary factor. The majority of the men were hard working, justice loving miners who would no more have thought of lynching a man, ordinarily, than they'd have tried to fly. Neither would they have condemned a man on the purely circumstantial evidence before them.

But now something seemed to snap their better judgment and they surged forward menacingly.

The Major tensed. A born psychologist, realizing that this was no time for words, he made his revolver his ambassador.

Three shots ploughed into the ground, sprinkling the men in the van with red dust. Another bullet whipped Smithers' slouch hat from his head, causing him to whimper with fright. The men halted, undecided.

"Satan!" the Major called. And the black stallion plunged through the men who separated him from his master, lashing out with his heels, scattering them left and right.

The Major mounted, and before the men could rally was galloping swiftly away.

Several of the men emptied their revolvers at him, but they were poor shots and their bullets went wild. South Africa was never a gunman's country. Stragglingly they galloped in pursuit, stringing out as the fastest horses worked to the fore. But the black horse ahead was faster than the fastest, and before they were fairly in the hills the pursuit had become only a slow but untiring following of the trail.

IT WAS nearly sundown when the Major came to the *kraal* of Rivimbi, hidden in the heart of the hills. The inhabitants greeted him as an old, respected friend, and for each one he had a name, showing by his use of the picturesque idioms and obtuse proverbs of the vernacular his thorough knowledge of them and all their ways.

Giving his horse in charge of one of the warriors, he entered the hut of Tsombe, the witch doctor.

The old man was seated on a ragged blanket, staring fixedly at a small fire which burned steadily in the center of the hut.

"I did not call you, *Ndhlovu*," he said abruptly, calling the Major by one of his native names. "Yet you are here. Since noon I have been calling Black Beard, but he does not hear me. *Au-a!* I am getting old."

"He can not come," the Major said gravely. "He is dead. He remembered and was afraid and tried to flee—but an enemy killed him."

Tsombe *clicked* irritably. "That was known to me. I had forgotten." Then, harshly, "You had no love for him. Did you kill him? Dared you to come between me and my vengeance?"

The Major laughed softly. "And did the Spirits whisper *that* in your ear?"

"I know what I know," Tsombe said cryptically. "Now tell me all that you know, all that you came here to say to me. So shall I judge the truth of things."

The Major nodded. "This, then, is the way of things." And he briefly recounted all that had befallen.

"Um!" Tsombe commented. "And why do you come to me?"

"Hoping that you can point out to me and to those who follow me, thinking that I killed Black Beard, the man who cheated you of your vengeance."

"And do you not know who killed him?"

The Major laughed. "Aye, I know. Or think I know. But how can I make others believe my words? It was the rat-faced man, he whose voice urged the others to kill me."

"Could you not so have spoken to these others?"

"Without proof, my words would have been wasted. Besides, they were in no mood to listen. The blood lust had maddened them. You know how it is?"

"Aye, *Ndhlovu,* I know." The witchdoctor was silent for a little while. Then, "When, think you, will those who follow come to this place?"

"Not, I think, until the moon is high. I confused my spoor down there in the valley. But they may forsake the trail and come straight to this place."

The witchdoctor nodded.

"When they come they must find us ready. And there is much to do." He crawled to the door and shouted orders to the men who were lolling near by. Then, chuckling softly, he returned to his place by the fire.

"And now white man, friend of my people," he said, "listen. In this we must work together—"

THE MOON was high when nine men rode up to the *kraal.* Trooper Sam Moore, mounted on a horse he had commandeered, had joined the pursuing eight, much to the disgust of the miners who realized that the fat man would have weighty objections to their lynching plans.

"Have you seen a white man riding a black horse?" the policeman asked the native who stood as if on guard at the entrance to the *kraal.*

"Aye, truly, *inkosi,* we have. And great trouble did that evil one cause us! Just before sundown he came, riding on a horse which was so lame that it walked on three legs. He came to me, did the white man—I am the headman—and demanded that I give him food and another horse. But I am poor, *inkosi,* I cannot give. And he could not pay. But that was all one to him. He beat me, he beat those of my young men to come to my aid. With a *sjambok* he beat us. Like one possessed he went through the huts, taking food, insulting our women by words and blows.

Then he took my mare, fat with foal as she is, and rode away toward the north."

"Then we've got 'im, boys," Smithers I cried exultantly. "Come on. He can't 'ave got far on a mount like that."

"We can't follow spoor in this light," one of the miners objected. "Better wait 'til morning and get this nigger here to follow the spoor for us."

"That's right," said Fat Sam, who was all tuckered out and desired nothing so much as sleep. "Besides, this nigger may be lying. Where's this black horse the white man left?" he demanded, turning sharply on the native.

The man shouted an order and a boy led the horse forward.

"The nigger wa'n't lying," exclaimed one of the men. "Look at that fetlock. Must have sprained it somehow."

The others nodded sagely. But not one of them thought of running a hand down that fetlock. Even if they had, since not one of them was really veld-wise, it is doubtful if they would have detected the hair knotted tightly about the fetlock which had induced the swelling.

"There's nothing for it, boys," Fat Sam announced. "We'll stay here the night an' go on in the morning."

The others grunted their approval and commenced to off saddle.

The headman's eyes gleamed. "White men," he said tentatively, "maybe Tsombe can help you find the man you seek. Tsombe is the mouthpiece of the Spirits, he is all wise. Even now he holds a 'smelling out,' that the white man who brought this evil upon us may be punished. Will you come to the council place?"

The trooper turned to the others. "You chaps can go if you want. These 'smelling outs' are worth seein' sometimes. These witchdoctors, some of 'em, are clever devils an' make yer see things which ain't. You go. But me, I'm goin' to make me a bed of grass an' sleep."

"Me, too," Smithers echoed. "I'm 'og tired."

"There is much beer," the headman said slowly, noticing their air of indecision, "an' the maidens dance."

At that there was a break toward the council place, and Smithers was carried along with the others, protesting feebly. But Fat Sam fought his way to a pile of mats in a hut and went to sleep.

Arrived at the council place, an opening before the headman's hut enclosed by a pole stockade, the others were escorted to a place opposite the entrance and seated on skin *karosses* which had been hastily placed for them.

Girls brought them huge calabashes of beer from which they drank deeply, then idly surveyed the place, conscious of a feeling of superiority over these black deluded fools who had gathered open-mouthed to watch the tricks of a cunning witchdoctor.

A large fire blazed between the white men and the opening in the stockade, and before it an old man, hideously garbed, capered grotesquely. Fish bladders were woven into his hair, horns protruded from his temples. A cape of monkey skins was about his shoulders, whilst his face and almost naked body was smeared with white ash paint.

To their left and right were massed the people of the *kraal*, seated beyond the circle of light cast by the fire and in the shadows of the huts which stood just beyond the stockade. The white men sensed their presence rather than saw them; only white of eyes glinted here and there, and the tips of many spears. This overwhelming show of force momentarily overawed the white men who did not know that most of the spears, held upright so that the moon light was reflected by the polished blades, were in the hands of women and children.

Smithers licked his lips and drank again. The others followed his example, then, their fears dispelled, watched the caperings of the witchdoctor.

Presently they vaguely realized that the old one's leaping contortions were weirdly rhythmical, and they followed his movements with fascinated eyes.

The beating of tom-toms impinged monotonously on their ears; the measured notes of the chant the people were singing lulled their senses.

To and fro Tsombe, the witchdoctor, moved. Now leaping high into the air, slapping his thighs, beating his heels together, now running 'round in widening circles, his body bent forward, his head almost touching the ground.

Suddenly, with a piercing cry, he dropped to the ground in a huddled heap.

The beating of tom-toms ceased, the hypnotic rhythm was taken up by the soft clapping of hands, the chanting became a faint whisper.

Then Tsombe rose to his feet and stood with outstretched hands.

The clapping ceased, the chanting died away. There was a long, pregnant silence.

Then, "I have pleaded with the spirits," Tsombe's voice cried loud and very shrill, "and they have promised to aid me. Do you hear, you people?"

"We hear!" the answer rolled back like surf upon a distant shore.

"The spirits have granted me a vision of gone-by things," Tsombe continued. "Listen, and you shall see what I saw."

"We will listen. We will see!"

"Yesterday an evil white man, one whose black beard covers his face, beat my son and spat upon my Spirit."

"*Wo-we. Au-a!*" The exclamations of the people sounded as if the universe sighed.

"This morning," Tsombe's voice was now a monotonous drone, "because he was in all things evil, other white men drove Black Beard away from the place in which he dwelt. He rides away— Do you see?"

"Aye, we see him."

"He comes to the tented house of another white man, the place of *Ndhlovu* who is our friend. A Hottentot—you know that black one—is there. He greets Black Beard who beats him with a whip. And then, because the Hottentot is also our friend, I send my spirit to whisper in Black Beard's ear. He drops his *sjambok* and rides away in fear because of the vengeance I have in store for him. You see that?"

"Aye, we see that."

"Then mark well what follows. Another white man, a puny, rat-faced white man with beardless face and cunning eyes, waits hidden behind a rock. He has a fire stick to his shoulder. There is a flash, a sound of thunder, and Black Beard falls from his horse. Blood flows from a hole in his head. You see? You hear?"

"Gawd!" gasped one of the miners, stirring uneasily as a man awakening from a heavy sleep. "It was Smithers!" He looked at his comrade. That man yawned, a puzzled look on his face. Then he pointed at Smithers. "It was you!" he said.

"Don't be a damn' fool," Smithers whispered uneasily, as if to reassure himself. "This is only nigger guff. 'Ow could that old fool know what I done? Besides, I was be'ind a tree. I—I mean—" His voice trailed off into a frightened silence. He tried to turn his head to glare at the miners, but it seemed to him that his head was held in a vise, as if he could not take his eyes off the witchdoctor.

The miners exchanged significant glances and edged a little closer to Smithers. The tom-toms sounded again, the chanting swelled in volume. Again Tsombe danced.

Another pause. Again silence. An eternity passed. The tom-toms spoke again, a deep obligato to Tsombe's voice.

"Black Beard is dead," cried Tsombe. "That is no matter. He deserved death. But what shall be done to Rat-face, to him who dared to come between me and my vengeance?"

"He must die. Let the fire burn the evil out of him. Light a fire on his belly!" The cries of the people swelled above the beat of drums.

"Aye, he must die. But first to smell him out. And that I cannot do. His skin is white."

"*Wo-we!* His skin is white."

"His skin is white," Tsombe cried again. "And against such an one my power fails me. And so," Tsombe's voice pealed triumphantly, "I summon up the spirit of Black Beard to smell out the man who killed him. Close your eyes, then, if your hearts are black, lest the wonder I work be too much for you."

He stretched his hands above his head in silent invocation—the beat of the tom-toms sounded louder, louder—the beat quickened, quickened until the rhythm was lost in one continuous rolling thunder of sound which ended abruptly in a tremendous crash.

Tsombe's hand moved. The fire, which had become a glowing heap of ashes, suddenly belched out dense clouds of acrid smoke.

The witchdoctor dropped to the ground, covering his face with his hands. "Watch!" he cried, and his voice sounded faint, as if coming from a great distance.

The smoke clouds thinned, seemed to take on shape; materialized finally into a shrouded form which stepped out from the heart of the smoke cloud.

It moved with shuffling steps toward where the white men were seated. They gasped, wondering, endeavoring to disbelieve the evidence of their eyes.

It came to a halt, finally, directly in front of Smithers.

"You!" it said, and though the tones were muffled the miners recognized the voice and accent of Sternberg. "You! You shot me."

Then the shroud fell away, exposing a white, black-bearded face. Blood trickled down from a wound in its head.

Panic-stricken, Smithers cowered down, yelling, "Go away; don't yer touch me, Sternberg! I did it! I did it!"

In his struggles he upset pots of beer; the miners nearest were splashed by the liquid. The spell was broken.

Smithers jumped to his feet and made a dash for the opening in the stockade. The two miners followed him in close pursuit. All was pandemonium.

The natives surged forward. Two of them captured and held Smithers, laughing at his futile struggles, deaf alike to his attempts to intimidate and bribe them. And Smithers cared for nothing save to get away from the place he believed was haunted by the ghost of Sternberg.

But the miners by now were fully recovered from the hypnotism of the tom-toms and the weird dance. With a roar they bore down on the natives that were holding Smithers. Their cries were hoarse with grim intent. "Get a rope! Hang him! He killed Sternberg, he's the murderer! He just confessed, damn him!"

But a sudden shot and a commanding voice roared above the chaos. "Hands up!"

The natives ceased their clamor. The white men, surprised, turned in the direction of the voice and saw, standing where the glow of the fire illumined his features, the Major.

But the miners' ire was up, as much at Smithers' treachery as at the murder. Several of them growled surlily and reached for their revolvers.

"If you want to die," the Major's voice drawled coolly, "draw."

A moment's hesitation, then, as one man, they raised their hands above their heads.

"That's ever so much better," the Major continued. "Discretion is always the, oh so much better part of valor. And I am a good shot. Even if I did miss the hyena." He grinned. "Well, laddies. Have you come to your senses?"

There was a moment's silence, then from somewhere came a chuckle. More chuckles. "Sure, Major," one confessed. "We ought to have known better."

"And you know now who is the real murderer?"

"My God, yes," the other responded. "We ought to have guessed when he egged us on to lynch you. But it needed Jake's ghost to put us right. I tell you, I saw—"

He stopped short and stared blankly at the Major. That man was wiping a red stain from his forehead. Little tufts of black hair—goat's hair—still adhered to his cheeks.

"Hell!" the miner exploded. "So you was the blinkin' ghost?"

"Exactly," laughed the Major. "Quite a clever little run in play, wasn't it? Really that Tsombe is a bally wonder. You know, he almost had me thinking I really was Sternberg's ghost. I was deucedly uncomfortable, I assure you."

Just then there was a slight disturbance, and Trooper Moore pushed his way through the natives.

"What's the row?" he panted, rubbing his eyes with the back of his hand. "I bin asleep."

"Yes, I fancy you have, Sam, old dear."

The trooper turned ponderously on the Major. "Ah," he breathed, "I might have guessed you was at the bottom of it. Well, I arrest you, Major, for—"

"Don't say it, please, Sam. There's your blinkin' murderer."

The Major pointed at Smithers who was quiet now save for an occasional whimper.

The trooper looked at the miners and then at the struggling Smithers, trying frantically to break loose from his captors. Fat Sam was greatly puzzled.

"It's true, Fat," the miners assured him.

Convinced at last Fat Sam advanced triumphantly on Smithers and clumsily fastened a pair of handcuffs on his wrists.

"I want to hear all about it," he said then, turning to the Major. "However did you find out this here cove done it?"

"They'll tell you," smiled the Major, nodding toward the miners. "But they're right—you've got the murderer. And you'd better keep close watch on him till you can get him back to the *dorp* to jail."

"Will I?" cried Fat Sam. "You can bet your blinkin' boots I will! I ought ter get promoted for this. Hell, if you stayed with me, Major, I'd be C.O. before long."

THE MAJOR was in Tsombe's hut, laughing with the old wise one at the success of their ruse.

"When the drums beat," said Tsombe, "it is not hard to make men see that which you want them to see."

A native entered and touched the Major on the arm.

"Yes?" the white man questioned.

"I searched Rat Face's pockets as it was ordered," the native replied. "I found this."

He handed the Major a small, chamois leather bag.

"Good," the Major commended and nodded dismissal.

He emptied the contents of the bag onto the floor and laughed softly.

"It is true, Tsombe," he said, as the witchdoctor idly picked up and examined one of the stones—it happened to be a rose diamond. "We always receive what is due us. Consider these pieces of stones, Black Beard stole them from certain of your people who work in the mines, who stole them from their employers. Rat Face kills Black Beard and takes the stones from him. And now they come to me. Is it not just? Knowing all things, is it not most just? These are my reward for having, only for a little while, taken upon me the evil that was Sternberg."

THE TROUT IN
THE MILK

IT WAS a bizarre scene even for Africa where the unusual often achieves the commonplace. The full moon hung low in a cloudless sky, paling the splendor of the stars, illuminating the veld below with a cold brilliance which made all things appear sharply defined and allowed no compromise between light and shade, silver white or darkness unfathomable.

The tin shanties which housed the white residents of the little mining *dorp*, the mission buildings, the wattle-and-daub huts of the natives, and the low, rectangular building glorified by the name of "Hotel Splendid," all seemed to be creations of two dimensions, having length and breadth but no thickness; looked like pieces of stage scenery, like silhouettes cut from cardboard. Here and there glowed feeble blobs of light, yellow and red, with red predominating, indicating the location of curtained windows.

In the tiny mission church some one was playing a dreary hymn tune on a wheezy, asthmatic harmonium; the tune was echoed by a group of natives who squatted outside their huts, drinking until a soddened sleep enmeshed them. They had seized upon the elemental rhythm of the tune and embued it with something approaching a barbaric splendor.

Somewhere a brazen-voiced phonograph blared a senti-mental ballad of "Home and Mother," and in the barroom of the hotel sounded the excited clamor of intoxicated men, the shrill and strident voices of predatory women, the clat-ter of glasses, to which was added the feeble tinkle of an ancient, tuneless piano.

A mounted policeman returning from a hazardous patrol rode slowly down the dusty, straggling street. The bridle reins hung loose upon his horse's neck, his hands rested upon the pommel of the saddle, his head, bent forward, jerked and swayed almost lifelessly. As he passed the carousing natives their singing was instantly hushed and a clumsy effort was made to hide the bottles from which they had been drinking.

But the policeman's eyes were closed, he slept in the saddle, trusting to his horse to take him safely to the camp beyond the town.

The man who lounged outside the Hotel Splendid, half-sitting on a window sill, silhouetted against the crim-son light which shone through the red curtained window, laughed softly as the policeman rode on out of sight; laughed again when the man facing him growled inco-herent blasphemies.

"Oh, really now," he drawled. "You musn't swear, really. I won't allow it." The voice almost described the man; it was a soft, lazy, musical voice; it suggested culture, humor and foppishness; it contained more than a hint of steel.

The other's growls subsided.

"That's better, much better—" the drawl was now even more pronounced—"but as I was about to say, it's a bally good job the local arm of the well known law was asleep as he rode by. Had he been awake, dear old Fisher, he would have stopped to enquire why your hands were raised on high. Of course you might have told him that you were doing your physical exercises—and you really should do some; your, er, waist bulges alarmingly—but I don't think he would have believed you. No, I'm sure he wouldn't, specially as he would have seen that I hold a revolver in my hand, that the muzzle of said revolver is on a line with the lower button of your waistcoat and that my finger is upon the trigger and itching, literally itching, to squeeze it. And he would have wanted to know all about it, and I would have had to tell him, much to my distress, of course. One hates to be rated an informer. But when the Law questions, why, er, the truth will out."

THE OTHER grunted impatiently.

"And," continued the Major, "he might have recognized me."

"If he hadn't, I'd have told him," the other put in swiftly.

"I think not," the Major countered complacently. "My finger is very light on the trigger, and the trigger has a hair spring."

"Anyway," Fisher said blusteringly, "the truth, as you call it, wouldn't have hurt me. You've got no proof of nothing."

The Major raised his eyebrows, and a monocle dropped from his left eye into the palm of his hand. He polished it thoughtfully on the sleeve of his white, silken shirt, then replaced it. It altered the whole expression of his face; softened the square cut of his jaw, widened his cheeks, masked the keenness of his eyes, and gave him the appearance of a feather brained nincompoop.

"I suppose you're right, Fisher," he admitted. "I have no proof of nothing, as you so crudely put it. Only circumstantial evidence. Sometimes such evidence is very strong as, for instance, the trout in the milk. I am indebted to a Yankee philosopher for that neat exposition. Don't suppose, though, that you've ever heard of Thoreau? No? Never mind; one can't know everything and I am sure you'll admire the neatness of his defence of circumstantial evidence. You understand it, of course? Or must I expound? The trout in the milk proves, if you follow me, that the milk has been watered."

He laughed softly, exposing white, evenly spaced teeth.

"Yes, you're damned funny!" Fisher sneered. "You with your blather about milk an' trouts. But that don't get us anywhere. And," a whine crept into his voice, "can't I take my hands down? You know I'm not armed."

The Major nodded. "Careless of me not to have thought of it before. I ought to have remembered that you never carry weapons, that you pose as a man of peace—quite the little missionary helper, in fact. It's against your principles to carry firearms, isn't it, dear laddie? You hire bullies to do your shooting for you, don't you? Oh, well. Perhaps you can talk better, now your hands are down."

Fisher glowered malevolently and stopped rubbing his benumbed arms for a moment to reply. "I could talk better if we went into the bar and sat down to a drink."

The Major appeared to consider this, then shook his head with an affectation of regret. "No, I'm afraid I can't allow that, really. You see, I'm here quite incognito, as it were. A price is on my unworthy head. For some extraordinary reason the police of the Diamond Town have got it into their heads that I am an I.D.B. Most inane of them, really, considering that I am the most law abiding of men. Oh, quite. But there it is. Considering that the police are so anxious to send me to the breakwater that they have offered a large reward for information leading to conviction and all that, you will readily understand that I can't afford to take chances. Some one in there—" with a backward jerk of his head he indicated the hotel—"might recognize me and try to win the reward. And I wouldn't like that at all.

"So, we will finish our talk here. Then I will vanish to parts unknown and not return until the police have forgotten my, er, recent operations. And now—" he paused for a moment. Then crisply, commandingly, "Tell me all about it. What is your little game?"

"I don't know what you're talking about," Fisher said stubbornly, but a fat jowled face sweated uneasy. In his eyes was a furtive look of fear.

The Major sighed. "You're so foolish an' so bally obvious, Fisher. You're as obvious, say, as the, er, trout in the milk. You're wasting my time an' my breath, an' they're both precious. Let's be precise. I want to know why you sent three of your precious bullies to dog my footsteps back there in the desert. I want to know why you instructed them to search my kit."

"I don't know what you're talking about," Fisher insisted. "If anybody followed you, as you say, and searched your kit, it was none of my doing. You can't pin a thing like that on me." His voice rose triumphantly.

"Not quite so loud, Fisher," the Major cautioned equably, "or I shall be forced to use this in order to drown your voice." He tapped his revolver with a long forefinger. "And that would be beastly unpleasant for you. Now I will be very frank with you, expose my cards, in a manner of speaking, and thus prove to you how foolish your denials are. I repeat that three men followed me into the desert; there was no doubt about it, they were so bally obvious. And I knew them to be your men because Jim—you've probably heard of him; he's a Hottentot and my guide, philosopher and friend—recognized the horses they rode as belonging to you, followed us, keeping just within range of Jim's eyesight; he has remarkably keen eyes, has Jim. And then, desiring solitude, we decided to get rid of those three by setting a little trap for them. I became most deucedly ill, almost at the point of death, I assure you. And Jim flew a distress signal.

"Those three laddies of yours answered it, they swooped down on my camp like vultures on a dying buck. They trussed Jim up in a most workmanlike fashion and then, ignoring me—I was at the point of death, you know— commenced to search my kit. I say 'commenced' advisedly, because suddenly I was miraculously cured of my sickness and—"

"The fools!" Fisher exploded unguardedly. "They should have made sure—" He stopped, confused.

The Major chuckled softly. "They should have made sure I was harmless before they searched," he prompted. "Is that what you were about to say? Well, it would almost seem that I need say no more. You have exposed your hand, old dear, and you must not be too hard on your three bullies. Actually, I was only bluffing just now. I didn't allow them to get within rifle shot of me but as soon as I knew they were following me I doubled back on my tracks—yet left no tracks, if you understand me—and came here to interview you. They're probably still wandering about in the

Great Thirst land, cursing you for having sent them on such an errand.

"But they were following me, and at your orders. Why?"

The last word cut like a whip. The Major straightened himself, tensed, and towering head and shoulders above the obese Fisher, looked down into that man's face with eyes which insisted on the truth. He moved to the right, away from the window, so that the crimson glow shone full on the other's face.

Fisher laughed weakly and shrugged his shoulders in what was meant to be an expression of reluctant, but good-natured surrender.

A ray of yellow light for a moment suffused the crimson glow as some one inside the barroom cautiously pulled aside the window shade and peered out.

The Major, if conscious of it, gave no outward sign of his awareness; neither did he seem to remark the furtive expression of relief which passed over Fisher's face, or the silent message framed by Fisher's thick, over red lips. And yet he turned slightly, ever so slightly, toward the door on his right.

A LOOK of suspicion came into Fisher's eyes and it occurred to him that the Major was on guard, prepared for any eventuality. But the suspicion passed almost immediately when the Major assumed a lounging attitude, leaning against the wall, one hand thrust negligently into the pocket of his baggy, snow white riding breeches, the other toying with his revolver, spinning it around on his trigger finger.

At that moment the Major was a most inane looking dude and Fisher was inclined to doubt the rumors he'd heard of his prowess and keen wit.

"I'm waitin'. It's your turn to speak, old dear."

The labored drawl recalled Fisher to the present need. He remembered the clever way in which the Major had held him up and had won from him what amounted to an admission that he had set three of his men to follow the monocled dude. A brainless fop could not have done that. He must concentrate now, he realized, on keeping the Major relaxed for a little while longer. And the truth would do that, he thought, better than anything else. He risked nothing in telling the truth now.

He laughed smoothly. "It's a waste of time telling you, seeing that you know all about it anyway. But here goes!"

The singing in the barroom and the metallic tinkle of the piano stopped, then started up again with renewed vigor.

The Major smiled. His monocle distorted that smile into the half witted smirk of a stage door Johnny.

"You see," Fisher continued in a confidential rush of words, "I knew your reputation. I knew that you're reckoned to be one of the *slimest* I.D.B's in the country."

"Of all my manifold, er, accomplishments I rank that least," the Major murmured.

"Oh, I heard all about the rest, too," Fisher assured him. "Man! You're the best shot, the best horsemen, the best sport—the best everything in the country if rumor goes for anything."

"She's a lying jade. But go on."

Fisher drew a deep breath and shifted his position slightly, shuffling his feet, muffling the rattle of a lifted latch. "Well, you come up here and camp out on the veld with your nigger. You don't mix none with the rest of the boys. Them as calls on you gets the frosty mit, and you never come into the *dorp*. You never let your Hottentot out of your sight. There's only one answer to that. That's how a man acts when he's on the trail of diamonds. I know the symptoms. Then you get hold of old Klaus, an' somehow or other you make him think you're the Almighty—"

"Yes, I found that most embarrassing," the Major put in. "But the dear old boy would have it that I'd saved his life once; he had broken his leg, as I remember, and there was a lion. I shot the lion, that's all."

"Well, there you are. We've always suspected that the old nigger knew a pan in the desert which was strewn with diamonds—everybody knows there is one there somewhere. And it's a fact that Klaus has bragged of knowing where there was big treasure in the desert, and a lot of men have tried to bribe him to take them to it. But he never would, the damn' nigger! But he tells you all about it, maybe because, as you say, he figures you saved his life once. Maybe he draws you a map of the place. Anyway, off you go and I send my men to follow you. Why not? There's no call for you to be so greedy. There's enough stones there, by all accounts, to make us all rich."

The door to the Major's right was opening stealthily; on it was silhouetted the shadow of a man who held in his hand a heavy revolver.

"I can't understand," Fisher continued swiftly, glancing with apprehension at the Major, relieved to see he was still absently spinning his revolver, "why you didn't take old Klaus with you."

"Klaus is nearly seventy, I believe, and that's too old, even for a bushman, to trek the way I planned to trek," the Major replied airily, adding, "By the way, where is old Klaus now?" Again the tone that brooked no evasion.

Fisher swore under his breath. Then, "He's down at my compound. I've been taking care of him." The fat man laughed harshly. "I've been trying to get out of him what he told you. But the old devil is as stubborn as hell."

"I sincerely hope," the Major said slowly, "that you haven't, er, illtreated him?"

Fisher glanced swiftly toward the door. The shadow was materializing; the moonlight glinted on the blue steel barrel of a revolver. "No," he sneered. "I didn't illtreat him. I only *sjamboked* the nigger same as I'll *sjambok* you when—"

He finished his threat in a squeal of dismay.

The revolver in the Major's hand had suddenly ceased spinning and, as it came to rest, spat a crimson flame. Another report echoed it. A shot buried itself in the ground close to Fisher's feet and the revolver of the "shadow" clattered harmlessly to the ground, while in the open doorway of the barroom a man mouthed futile curses and looked disconsolately at the back of his right hand. The Major's bullet had creased his knuckles, leaving a bleeding groove.

The singing in the barroom suddenly ceased, the natives dived into their huts like frightened rabbits. For a fraction of time there was no sound save the moaning of the harmonium over at the mission and the whimpering of the wounded man.

"You should have reminded your killer, dear lad," the Major's voice broke the silence, "that coming events cast their shadows before them."

A shrill whistle sounded at the rear of the hotel, and the noise of men running. In the barroom there was a sudden, surging rush.

"Here's the Major, boys," Fisher yelled. "Come and get him. Come—Ough!"

He doubled up and dropped nauseated to the ground, all the wind driven from his lungs. The Major had leaped out of the window, jabbing Fisher hard in the stomach as he passed, and had lost himself in the shadows of the buildings on the opposite side of the street.

A CONFUSED mob of men rushed out of the bar and halted about Fisher and the man whose knuckles were creased, talking excitedly, some of them brandishing revolvers, shouting "Where is he?" firing haphazardly at flickering shadows. Three other men came running from the rear of the hotel, adding their voices to the clamorous din, cursing, dodging stray bullets from the excited men on the porch.

A commanding voice from the shadows ordered, "Drop your guns and hands up!" adding emphasis to the orders by a number of shots which made the dust fly up between the legs of the foremost.

They halted and obeyed as one man, peering forward, endeavoring to see beyond the shadows which draped the buildings opposite in absolute darkness.

"Face the hotel," the order came next. And again they obeyed sheeplike, as are all mobs.

"Now don't move until I've given you permission," the voice continued. "And that, I'm afraid, will not be for a long, long time. You see, as soon as I've posted my men, I'm going to search you one by one. No, don't swear. Instead, you shall sing. Yes, that will be delightful for us all.

"We will sing—" the mocking drawl now became a nasal monotone—"hymn number four hundred and seventy-five from the Diamond Diggers hymnal. I will sing the first verse as a solo, then you shall, er, carry on."

In a fine rich barytone the Major sang:

> *Over the Free State line,*
> *Whatever is yours is mine.*
> *If I've a stone*

It's all my own,
No John Fry shall make me groan.
Over the Free State Line,
I'll never have cause to pine.
The I.D.B. is happy and free,
Over the Free State line!

Loud, laughing applause greeted the Major's rendering of this well known ditty of the Diamond Fields and, ignoring the protests of Fisher who wanted them to rush the Major, they took up the refrain:

Over the Free State line,
I'll never have cause to pine.
The I.D.B. is happy and free,
Over the Free State line!

repeated it and then swung into the next verse.

For the time being they were hopelessly entrapped by the rhythm of the song. They stamped their feet and thumped each other on the back to accentuate the beat.

And so they did not hear a horseman gallop down the dusty street and not until they had come to the end of the song's many verses did they remember just why they had been singing.

They nudged each other sheepishly. One or two looked covertly over their shoulders. The man whose knuckles had been creased, sheltering himself behind a big Cornishman, stooped cautiously and retrieved his revolver.

"He's gone, you fools!" Fisher cried, being the first to realize that the Major had departed.

"Glad of it," answered one of the men. "I've got nothing against him. Neither have the rest of us."

"There's a big reward out for him," Fisher spluttered.

"An' what the hell's that to us?" another cried indignantly. "We didn't come in to this for the blood money—my God, no—but for a bit of fun. An' we've had it. I bet that song's never been sung as well as we sung it." He laughed good-humoredly.

"This Major may be an I.D.B., as you say, Fisher," said another, "but I've heard enough about him to know he plays the game on the square. It's only dirty hounds like you who've got it in for him. I.D. Buying!" He spat contemptuously. "What's that to us? We've all done a bit of it in our time, and with less reason, I'll gamble, than the Major. And there's none of us here so damned bad off that we've got to earn blood money from the Syndicate. They've got their police, let them do their own dirty work. An' you do yours, Fisher. Me? I'm for a drink."

HE REENTERED the bar followed by most of the others who, as he had said, had been actuated solely by a thoughtless desire for a little excitement.

But the four men who remained outside with Fisher were of an entirely different caliber. They existed on the failings, physical, mental and moral, of others. The hardest work they ever did was the avoidance of work. They were cardsharpers and pickpockets; they cheated natives with spurious coinage; they were prepared to commit murder, provided they ran no risk, for a handful of loose change; and they were always ready to follow the leadership of any man who promised them, as Fisher had, easily acquired wealth.

They listened somewhat sullenly now to his curses.

"Hell! Shut up, Fisher," one of them, a tall, cross-eyed individual named "Cupid" Dawes, exclaimed at length. "What in hell could we have done? He had us covered in the beginning, an' how was we to know he didn't have any other men hidden in the shadows over there like he said? For the matter of that, you didn't do so much to brag about yourself, letting him hold you up the way he did."

"That's right, Cupid," agreed the man who had been the victim of the Major's marksmanship. "Look at what Fisher let me in for." Removing a dirty, blood stained handker-chief, he exhibited his knuckles. "It's only by luck the Major didn't kill me."

"But what I wants to know is," a burly, black visaged man chimed in, "what was the Major doin' here in the *dorp*? If, as Fisher says, he has a price on his head, what does he want to come here for? Specially as he left in such a hell of a hurry a month ago. Are you playing square with us, Fisher? If not—"

"Of course I am," Fisher said savagely. "He came here because Steinman, Kite and Smith are as big fools as you lot are. The way they followed him made him suspicious, he knew they were hand in glove with me, and so he rides into the *dorp* to find out what it's all about. As if the dirty blighter didn't know!"

"In that case," suggested Cupid, "what in hell's the good of us blattin' here? We ough to be doin' something. But what?"

"Get on the Major's trail, follow him, don't let him out of your sight! But don't let him suspect you're following him. You go, Cupid, and you, Blackie," Fisher turned to the black-bearded man. "He don't know you two. An' you've both got the reputation of knowing the desert. But for God's sake don't give the game away like them other three fools did."

"Sounds nice," Cupid Dawes said sarcastically. "We trail the bounder through the desert, risking our blooming lives—and that's no joke; even bushmen get lost there once in a while and die of thirst. Well, there we are, risking our lives. And what are you doing? Nothing. And you expect to grab seventy-five per cent, of the takings for doing it, while us others share a beggarly twenty-five per cent!"

"You forget," Fisher cut in hastily, "that it was me who got on to what the Major was after. You forget that it was my money that outfitted them other chaps, an' it's my money that'll outfit you and Blackie. You couldn't do anything without my backing. And as for risk, hell, you don't take no risk. All you got to do is follow the Major, and he's too *slim* a cove to get himself lost. Risk? Bah! If it wasn't for my business here which I can't leave, I wouldn't have to take you coves into the scheme at all. I'd follow the Major myself."

THE OTHERS greeted this with derisive laughter.

"Anyway," Cupid continued, "how do we know the Major's on the trail of the diamond pan? For the matter of that, how do we know there's diamonds in the bloomin' desert?"

"Everybody knows about the diamond pan," Blackie said earnestly. "We don't have to bother about that, Cupid. It's there, all right. Wasn't it me who found young Tom Hardcastle just beyond the town here? He'd discovered the pan, no doubt about that. The poor devil hadn't much on when I found him; the desert had beaten him, and he'd tore off most of his clothes, the way men do when they get lost. He only had a ragged shirt on when I came up with him, but he gripped a good sized diamond in each hand, and he babbled a lot about a salt pan covered with stones before he died. I tried to get him to tell me where it was, told him I wouldn't give him any water until he told—but he was too far gone."

Fisher nodded. "Oh, the pan's there," he said. "No doubt about that. There's plenty of proof of that."

"Well, it'll take a lot of diamonds to pay me for facing the blinking desert," Cupid growled. "Hot? If hell's any hotter, I'm going in for religion. All right, I'll admit the pan's there, but I ain't convinced yet that the Major knows where it is. And if he don't, what's the good of following him?"

"He knows," Fisher said confidently. "He admitted that old Klaus was under an obligation to him—it seems he saved the nigger's life once—and everybody knows Klaus knows where the diamond pan is, and he's told the Major. Besides, if the Major wasn't after the diamonds, why should he go to the trouble of throwing them others off the trail and coming back here to warn me off sending others after him? Hell," a note of contempt came into Fisher's voice, "if only Watson here had shown a little sense, he'd have held the Major up and we could have forced the blasted dude to give us the lay of the land. Instead of which Watson creeps around like a villain in a stage play and gets a bullet across his knuckles for his pains."

"And that's your damn' fault," Watson countered hotly. "You tipped me the wink that he was off guard."

"That's neither here nor there," Blackie said decisively. "We had a chance to get him, an' missed it. But what the hell's the good of cryin' over spilt milk? Come on, Cupid, let's go and get some drinks. Mornin'll be time aplenty to start after the Major, an' it'll be dry work from then on for a bit. You go an' get our outfits ready, Fisher, and see you don't skimp us on provisions, blast you. The best and plenty of it."

Fisher nodded agreement. "The best I've got, of course, Blackie," he said, and scowled as the others trooped into the bar.

He stared pensively before him, wondering if his partners would play square with him once they had located the diamond pan, considering vaguely means whereby, once the desert's store of diamonds had been located, he could take to himself the total profits of the undertaking.

"I'll be honest with them," he mused. "I'll pay them for their time and labor and, maybe, a little over. Say, two pounds a day. That'd be more than fair. After all, they put no money into the business. They don't risk nothing."

Then suddenly he was conscious of a confused clamor and a reddish glare in the sky at the lower end of the town. He located it, presently, as being near to his house and native compound.

"Fire!" he shouted hoarsely and ran down the street, wallowing clumsily, gasping "Fire!" at every other step.

TROOPER RICH of the mounted police sighed as he pushed back his chair from the *skoff* table, and listened to the lengthy complaint of Fatty Fisher.

"It seems to me," he grumbled at length, "as if something always happens when I'm away on patrol, an' that you, Fisher, are always the complaining person, or the person complained against. If somebody 'ud only hide a bullet in your fat guts, life 'ud be lots easier here."

Fisher smirked. "Maybe. Maybe not. At any rate, I'm alive, Rich, and it's your duty to act on all complaints made to you. You needn't get it into your head that you can squirm out of this business just because you've just came off a long patrol. You'll go, or I'll report you to headquarters."

"I'll go," Rich said evenly, "if I think I ought to go. I happen to be in the government's employ, Fisher, not in yours. Now, what makes you think the Major set fire to your compound?"

Fisher spread his fat, pudgy hands in an expressive gesture. "Who else would have done it? Who else has a grudge against me?"

"Most of the decent folk in the *dorp,* I imagine," the trooper replied dryly. "And whoever did it deserves a vote of thanks. That compound of yours was a stinking pig sty."

Fisher rose ponderously to his feet. "Of course," he began with an assumption of dignity, "if you're setting yourself up to act as judge and jury, I better waste no time in reporting you to headquarters."

"Sit down and don't talk like a fool," the trooper said testily. "I'm only expressing my opinion. Now, about the Major: I say it's not like him to burn places down unless—unless, mind you—you gave him a damned good reason."

"You talk as if you knew him," Fisher sneered.

"I do. And whatever his opinions on the I.D.B. act, and they happen to be against the law, he's too big a man for a toad like you to appreciate, Fatty. Steady, now, don't choke. The truth about yourself once in a while is good for you, and it's no use gagging over it. Now then: you say the Major held you up last night?"

"Yes, and I've got plenty of witnesses to that, even if you didn't see him when you rode by. But maybe you did see him but pretended not to, you being a friend of his?"

"I didn't see him. I was probably asleep," the trooper replied evenly. "I'd been in the saddle eight hours that day. But never mind that. The Major held you up, you say, and took from you a map which old Klaus had made for you, showing the location of a salt pan strewn with diamonds.

Then, when there's signs of a rescue, the Major holds the rest of the men up, shoots Watson in the hand and—"

"He shot to kill," Fisher interposed. "It was a lucky thing for Watson that I managed to joggle the Major's hand just as he fired, and made him miss,"

"He didn't miss," Rich said with a laugh. "He hit Watson where he meant to hit him. When the Major shoots to kill, he kills. You can take my word for that. It's lucky for chaps like you and Watson that the Major ain't the killing sort. He'd rather make a fool out of his worst enemy than kill him, and he generally manages to do it. So watch out, Fisher."

"I can take care of myself," the fat man snorted.

THE TROOPER laughed. "I wouldn't gamble on it. But all right, he holds you up, then gets away and takes old Klaus from your compound—saved me the trouble of doing that, Fisher. One of my police boys tells me the old chap's back was all bloody from the thrashing you gave him the other day. I was going to pay you an official call about that."

"You ought to know better than believe a nigger's tale against a white man, Rich," Fisher exclaimed heatedly. "You ought to know I wouldn't thrash a nigger."

"I know you well enough not to put any stock in your psalm singing over at the mission on Sundays. That don't mean a thing. I believe my police boys, but if old Klaus has gone off with the Major, it's no good my taking that matter up with you. Maybe the Major saw how you'd ill-treated the old bushman, and that's why he took him off. Yes," he nodded, "that's just about what the Major would do."

"And I tell you," Fisher raged, "that he took old Klaus because the nigger knows where the diamond pan is."

"I don't see why he'd hamper himself with Klaus if he has the map as you say."

"It's plain enough. He took Klaus so the old chap couldn't tell me again where the pan is; he's making sure that no one else can find the pan. That's what."

"Sounds feasible," the trooper agreed, "Well, what do you expect me to do?"

"Go after the Major and get my property back, and bring old Klaus back, too. My God, I don't see why I should have to instruct you in your duty. If you know your job, you'll arrest the Major. Apart from the fact that he held us up, shot Watson, abducted a native in my employ and set fire to my compound, he's a noted I.D.B. If you read your circulars you'd know that there's a warrant out for his arrest; he's suspected of being at the bottom of that big clean-up down at the 'Fields' last month. The way he acted last night is enough for you to arrest him, and once he's under arrest, it ought not to be so damned hard to pin this other business on him."

The trooper looked contemptuously at Fisher. "You mean I could 'frame' him?"

"Well, I would," Fisher said. "But maybe you're too tender hearted for that. Anyway, you might find it wasn't necessary to frame him; he might have the diamonds with him."

"That's not likely. Use sense, Fisher. He's too brainy to go wandering around the country with stolen diamonds in his possession—or, at least, they're not exactly stolen, I take it, but some he's bought illicitly."

"You never know," Fisher said sententiously. "The chance is worth taking, I say. Should you get him with the goods, you're as sure of a commission as I'm sure my name's Fisher."

The trooper's eyes glistened. The thought of a commission tempted him. He was ambitious. "I've a good mind to have a shot at it," he said thoughtfully. "But it's ten to one that the Major'll be able to clear himself of the charge and the laugh'll be on me. I bet no magistrate'ud convict him, either, on these charges of yours, Fisher."

"Why be squeamish?" the fat man urged. "Why not frame him?"

The trooper shook his head decisively.

It was, possibly, this attitude of so many of the police toward the Major's diamond dealing operations which had kept from him the fact which had overtaken so many of the lesser lights of the illicit diamond buying fraternity, the fate of a long sentence to hard labor at the Cape Town breakwater. Not, it should be understood, that the police aided and abetted the Major in his operations—far from it—but that they understood and sympathized with the motives which actuated him. They realized that his illicit dealings formed his protest against the unjust clauses of the I.D.B. act, and they admired his courage in making a lone stand against the powerful forces of the Syndicate. Admiring the Major's many manly attributes, his horsemanship and knowledge of the veld, his shooting and his understanding of natives, and knowing too that he would never take an unfair advantage of them, that he never broke a promise and was always to be found on the side of the weak, the police had come to regard the Major as royal game. They hunted him, anxious to claim the honors which would accrue to whoever would be fortunate enough to arrest him "in the act" as it were, but they hunted him fairly. Others they might trap, but not the Major. A few, it is true, had tried but their failures were always applauded. The Major had become, almost, a legendary hero. Certain hard and fast rules were set down governing the chase of him, and they were rules formed by sportsmen. And as no true sportsman will shoot a "sitter," or shoot a cow antelope, or dynamite a river for the wary trout, so the policemen of South Africa, at least the majority of them, kept to certain rules in following up the Major.

"Look here," said Trooper Rich, "you say you've got plenty of witnesses that the Major held you up and all the rest of it?"

Fisher nodded.

"And you'll come with me to the Magistrate and swear out a warrant against him?"

Fisher nodded again.

Rich sighed. "Then, in that case, I'm willing to go after him. But not otherwise. Ten to one he'll be able to prove that he had nothing to do with that affair down at the diamond fields. But I'm not going to arrest him on that charge. If there's anything in it, why, I'll have him safe. If there's nothing to it, and he can clear himself of these complaints of yours, I can let him go and no harm'll have been done. At any rate, the chaps won't be able to include me in the list of men who've tried to get the Major and failed!

"Come on: We'll ride over to the magistrate's. But, while I think of it, Cupid Dawes and Blackie rode by here this morning. They're your men, ain't they? Well, they said they were going after the Major. What about that?"

Fisher affected a start of indignant surprise. "The scoundrels!" he swore. "Then they're either in with the Major, or they're planning to follow him so that they can find out where the diamond pan is, and then help themselves. They're all trying to do me out of rights, blast them."

The trooper shrugged his shoulders.

"You've got to arrest them, too," Fisher insisted.

"Don't be a fool, Fatty. That diamond pan, if there is a diamond pan, belongs to whoever finds it and files on it first. You can't go sticking 'Trespassers will be prosecuted' signs all over the blinking desert."

"Maybe not," Fisher whined. "But it was me that got the information from old Klaus. And I had to pay through the nose for that information, too; he's a cunning old devil. And so I say it isn't right that these other men should cheat me out of what's mine. I tell you you've got to arrest Cupid and Dawes as well as the Major."

THE TROOPER laughed. "On what grounds? Because they're following the Major? Don't be a fool. That's no grounds for arresting them. I can't pull them in, much as I'd like to. But if I had proof of what I suspect of them two," he looked keenly at Fisher, "I'd be justified in shooting them on sight, let alone arresting them."

Fisher clutched eagerly at his arm. "I can give you that proof, Rich," he said eagerly. "You'd like to know who stuck up the mail coach, wouldn't you? And who killed 'Mother-lode' Charlie?"

"I know already. What I want is *proof!*"

"I can give you that proof! Yes, and proof of other things, besides. Proof that'll hang Cupid and Blackie higher than Haman."

"Then let's have it," the trooper replied tersely.

Fisher winked. "Not so fast, Rich. First you and me have got to come to an understanding."

"I'm listening, but promising nothing."

"You'll have to promise, or get your own proof. You've got to manage this business the way I say, or I'm dumb. Look here: I don't care a damn about the mail robbery, or the murder of Charlie. I'm not a policeman, and it don't concern me whether the robbers and murderers are caught or not. All I'm interested in is this diamond pan; I want what's mine; I want to make sure that the Major and them other two fellows don't get away with any of the stones. So here's the situation. The Major's got the map and he's got Klaus, and he's heading across the desert for the pan. *My* pan. Blackie and Cupid are following the Major, planning, I bet, to wait until the Major locates the pan before they show their hand. Then they'll probably try to force him to take them in as partners. Failing that, they'll probably kill him and take all there is for themselves. I'm thinking they won't waste much time trying the partnership line, either. All right, what you've got to do is follow them and not show your hand until they've shown theirs. Then, when they're all together you can arrest them, kill 'em for all I care. Maybe that'ud be better than trying to bring them out of the desert. And then, when you come back here, you've got to give me a map showing the location of the pan, a sample of the stones you found there, and take an oath not to say a word about it to any one, and to forget all about it yourself. Are you on?"

Rich considered this for a moment, then realized that the only way he could hope to capture the three men and bring them back safely out of the desert was to wait until they had gained their objective. And then, he knew—always supposing he could effect their arrest—he could count on one of his prisoners, the Major, to help him bring in the other two.

"All right," he said briskly. "I'll go and see about my outfit. Then we'll ride over to the magistrate's and you shall tell me what you know about Blackie and Cupid. If it's law-court proof, I'll promise to do things the way you say. It's the best way at that."

As the trooper left the hut, Fisher chuckled complacently and inwardly congratulated himself on his astuteness.

In one move, without any personal risk, he had put into operation a plan which would square his account with the Major; which would win for him the location of the diamond pan; and which would remove from his path two men who would have undoubtedly proved a stumbling block when it came to apportioning the proceeds of this desert treasure trove.

Fisher considered that he had been very clever, very clever indeed.

THE HEAT of the Great Thirst Land had sapped the strength of Cupid Dawes, and he sprawled under the shade of a small *wit boom* tree, indifferent apparently to time, place or this undertaking which was to bring him great wealth. East and west, north and south, stretched the desert, immense, mysterious, implacable. A desert of shifting, treacherous sand, it seemed to hold all the heat of countless centuries of Africa's sun; it dazzled the eyes. To the naked flesh its touch was comparable to white hot needle points; it dried up the blood and seemed to choke the very pores.

In places the sand had drifted, forming hills and valleys which limited the vision. Enormous dunes, like ocean billows broke up the surface of the arid waste and made of it, for the unwary, a fatal maze.

Occasionally Cupid Dawes looked toward a nearby dune, a truncated cone-shaped hill of sand which towered above all the others in its immediate vicinity. On top of it, silhouetted against the electric blue of the sky, was the man Blackie, a pair of field glasses glued to his eyes.

"The damn' liar!" Dawes cursed. "He bragged he knew the desert better than me, an' look at the hell of a mess he's got us into! I'll make him pay for it, sometime, some'ow."

His fingers closed convulsively on the butt of his revolver.

Then he cursed again at his own impotence, at the knowledge that his physical strength was a child's by the side of Blackie's.

"Course I could shoot him," he muttered. "Shoot him when he wasn't looking. But that would be damned foolish. I can't get out of this hell alone. God, me tongue feels like a bit of blotting paper."

He licked his cracked lips, then put a small pebble in his mouth and sucked it in order to promote a flow of saliva.

At a shout from Blackie, whose voice sounded very near, and a beckoning wave of his hand, Cupid half rose then dropped back again, muttering, "I ain't going up there—not likely. If he's discovered anything he can come down here and tell me. Ten to one there ain't nothing an' he only wants me to get up there, out of breath an' off me guard, so's he can kill me easy. No, I ain't going. Let him come here."

Blackie shouted again, waited a moment, then came slithering down the dune. Reaching the bottom he made his way toward Cupid, walking slowly, impeded by the soft sand which clogged his footsteps.

His eyes were sunk deep into their sockets; like his partner, he seemed to have reached the end of his tether. Yet, despite it all, there was a triumphant gleam in his eyes.

"Cupid," he called softly as he neared. Receiving no reply, he half drew his revolver and walked now with great caution.

"I wouldn't if I was you," Cupid said suddenly, sitting up and covering Blackie with his revolver.

"I thought you was asleep, Cupid," the other exclaimed, exposing his secret hope.

"Well, I ain't. I had you covered all the time, blast you, sneaking up on me that way, planning to do while I was asleep what you ain't got the guts to try an' do when I'm awake an' on the lookout."

Blackie shrugged his shoulders. "You're all wrong, Cupid," he said with an affectation of good humor. "I was coming up on you quiet-like, because I thought you was asleep, and I didn't want to wake you. I knew you needed sleep bad. You don't think I'd shoot a pal, surely?"

"I don't think, I know," Cupid replied vindictively. "But I'm no fool. I'll see you don't get the chance to do me in like you did your last partner."

Blackie scowled, started to make a protest but Cupid, ignoring him, continued, "What was you yelling about up there?"

Instantly Blackie's face became animated. "My God!" he exclaimed. "The desert does get into a man's brains, no doubt about it. Here we are rowing like a couple of wash-erwomen, and I'd almost forgotten about what I'd seen from the top of the dune there. Listen: We've both been off color these last few days. We've been thinking things about each other which ain't true. That's what the desert does to a man. But we can buck up now. Another week at the outside an' we'll be out of this hell."

Cupid rose to a sitting position. "What do yer mean?"

"Why," Blackie's words came with a rush, the excitement of his news entirely possessing him, "I've located the Major again. He's camped back there near a big salt pan, got his tent up an' everything. An' listen, Cupid: When the mirage lifted a bit I could see him and his nigger, large as life, pottering about the pan, picking up things which they kept putting in their pockets.

"That can only mean one thing, Cupid. He's located the diamond pan, and by this time tomorrow, it'll be all ourn. We'll creep up on him in the night—it'll be easy, he won't be expecting anything—an' that's all there is in it."

"You're sure you saw him, Blackie?" Cupid's voice trembled with excitement. "You sure it wasn't the mirage that made him seem so near?"

"By God, Cupid," Blackie answered, spitting contemptuously, "I'm no green-horn to be fooled by a mirage. Course it made him look nearer than he really is, but I've allowed for that. Trust me. Tomorrow we'll be picking up diamonds, an' the next day we'll head for the settlement. But we won't go near Fisher, blast him. If he wants diamonds, let him come in the desert and find 'em same as we done, eh?"

Cupid's eyes sparkled. For the moment he forgot his great physical weariness and his feeling of resentment toward his partner. Blackie was a good pal; they'd share fifty-fifty with what they made, and to hell with Fisher! They'd both be rich men, richer than Joel or Barnato. Richer than all them coves at Kimberley. They'd—

THEN HIS face clouded as recollection of their present predicament came to him. "Yes, it all sounds nice. But how far is the Major's camp from here?"

"A day's trek at the outside. That ain't nothing, Cupid."

"The hell it ain't," the other screamed. "An' how do you think we're going to get there? On our feet? With me weaker than a cat. An' it's all your blasted fault. I told you it was as good as committing suicide coming into the desert on horseback with pack mules. We ought to have had a oxcart, same as the Major. But you knew best! An' now our animals is dead, an' there ain't enough water in this stinking water hole you was so proud of finding to fill our water bags. An' if there was, the bags wouldn't hold it. They're rotten, same as Fisher, blast his dirty soul. An' if they would hold it, we couldn't drink the stinking stuff.

"Well, why don't you say something instead of gaping there like a fool? Tell me how we're going to last another day out, trekking on foot, without water—considering we ain't had more than a mouthful for two days. Tell me that!"

"Sure, I'll tell you," Blackie replied, "though by rights I ought to let you stay here and stew. Blaming it all on me, as if it ain't your fault as much as mine. When I was up there I spotted a pan I know. There's a old mine shaft near it, an' at the bottom of the shaft there's always water; it's never been known to fail, a old bushman told me. An' it's right in the line we have to take to the Major's camp, an' it's only a couple of hours or so away. So come on. We don't need to take any grub or nothing but what we stand up in. We'll get all we want of things like that after we've settled with the Major. He always travels soft.

"Me? I ain't even taking my rifle or my cartridge belt. Only my revolver. An' if you're wise, you'll do the same as me. Now come on."

He stretched out a hand to help Cupid rise to his feet and when that man took it, closed with him and, after a short, silent struggle, disarmed him.

"Just for safety's sake," he said, thrusting Cupid's revolver into his own belt and grinning at the little man's vicious curses. "I don't like the way the desert gets you, Cupid. It might send you mad, and then you'd get to thinking I was your worst enemy, and shoot me. So, I ain't taking chances.

Now, come on—or stay here. It's all one to me. For the matter of that I don't know why I don't shoot you and have done with it."

"I'll tell you why," Cupid said sullenly as he rose. "It's because you ain't got the guts to face the desert alone. That's why. Go on, lead the way."

IT WAS long past noon when the two men, both limping painfully on bleeding feet, came to the pan which was their first objective.

From a short distance it had looked like an immense lake, and the illusion was heightened by the "waterspouts" which swept across it. The smooth surface of the pan mirrored the surrounding dunes and the few white feathery clouds which like whisps of gossamer floated across the sky. So much like a lake did it seem that Cupid, his brain thirst tortured, thought he could hear the *lap lap* of little wavelets as they broke upon the shore. He increased his pace, and coming to the edge of the pan, actually dropped down on all fours, intending to gorge himself with water. And then the illusion passed. He knew that the "lake" was only a salt-encrusted pan, that the "waterspouts" were really *zand duivels*, sand whorls.

He dragged himself erect and hurried after Blackie who was half way across the pan.

BOTH MEN were bewildered by the uncanny mirage. Sometimes a dune on the opposite bank would appear but a few feet away and Blackie would turn to encourage Cupid to stick it out. "A few more yards," he'd croak, "and you shall have all the water your belly'll hold." Then, when he turned again, the dune would have vanished or would appear many a weary mile distant. At times, though the pan was scarcely a mile in diameter, the surrounding dunes were invisible, and it seemed to the men that they, were walking on the surface of an immense, tideless sea.

To Cupid a hundred yards or more behind Blackie, it seemed at times as if he were following twenty or thirty men strung out in a line at regular intervals. Then they would merge into one gigantic figure which seemed to be up to the waist in water.

It was a maddening mirage, to appear to be in the midst of water and yet be ploughing through dry sand.

But after a time they reached the backs to the pan the mirage ceased to torment them. Ahead were the dunes again, shifting sand and physical hardship, easier to bear than the other.

Blackie led the way along a narrow *straat* between two dunes, where the grass was waist high. At the lower end of the *straat,* where the grass ceased as suddenly as it had begun, was a shaft about fifteen feet deep and barely wide enough to permit a man to descend it. A tree trunk had been left in it by some forgotten prospector. It had, apparently served as a ladder.

All about the shaft was the spoor of animals; gemsbok and duiker, ostriches and leopards, steenbok, and a huge lion. They had apparently been attracted by the water which gleamed refreshingly at the bottom of the shaft.

With an access of strength Cupid prepared to climb down the shaft. Then he dropped to the ground, apparently prostrated. But there was a malicious gleam of triumph in his pig-like, squinting eyes, and he lolled half way over the top of the shaft, depriving from his partner a sight of what awaited below.

"I'm all in, Blackie," he whined. "You'll have to go down and bring me some water up in your helmet or something. And hurry up, blast yer. I'm perishing of thirst."

Blackie laughed and without any hesitation, not waiting for his sun blinded eyes to become accustomed to the gloom of the shaft, climbed down the tree ladder.

Cupid watched him eagerly, saw him come to a halt at the bottom, heard the musical splash of water, saw him bend over to drink—saw a bloated puff-adder strike viciously and glide lazily away.

He heard Blackie's startled oath of fear, heard a revolver shot—it sounded like a peal of thunder in that confined place. He saw a mortally wounded reptile thrashing about violently in the water, and then he watched Blackie's panic-stricken climb to the top of the shaft.

"What was you shooting at?" he asked as Blackie reached the top. "Ghosts?" And he grinned malevolently.

"A puff-adder bit me in the cheek!" Blackie gasped. "I'm a gonner! I—"

His face was contorted with pain; the poison was acting swiftly, finding no resistance.

"Do something, blast you!" he cried, and advanced threateningly on Cupid. Then he collapsed suddenly, horribly nauseated.

A quarter of an hour later he was very still. And Cupid, after firing several shots down the shaft into the body of the adder, for he wasn't taking any chances, climbed down the tree and drank his fill; rested, and drank again. He filled his helmet and returned to the top of the shaft.

Climbing then to the top of a nearby dune he took his bearings, laughing almost hysterically when he spotted the camp of the Major. It was so much nearer than he had dared hope.

He looked at the sun; another three hours of daylight remained. If he hurried he could, he thought, reach the Major's camp before darkness came; could get within sight of his camp fire at least.

He returned at a run to the shaft and descended to the water once again, drank and soaked his clothes in the precious fluid.

Again coming to the top he took his revolver from Blackie's belt, kicked the inert carcass of his dead partner, and set off at a jog-trot in the direction of the Major's camp.

"It'll be all mine now," his thoughts ran. "I don't have to share with anybody. An' my conscience is clear, no bad dreams for me. I didn't kill Blackie, it was that blasted puff-adder. Poor old Blackie!"

He laughed merrily—but the laugh ended in a whimper of fear. He was alone, the shadows were lengthening, and one dune looked so much like another. It was so easy to get lost. He might pass within a hundred yards of the Major's camp and not see it because he would be on the opposite side of a flanking dune.

Then he shouted aloud with delight as a long *staat,* the valley between two long furrows, opened before him. It led in the right direction, no doubt about that, and trekking there would be easier, the sand would be firmer.

THE MAJOR'S camp was pitched in a desert oasis, bordering the bed of a long dried-up river where water could only be obtained by digging.

It was carpeted with long stretches of grass which supplied fodder for the trek-oxen, and fringed with *cameel doorn* trees. Gaily colored hornbills and blue jays and scarlet finches made the air seem alive with flying jewels. Game of all sorts abounded and so tame, not realizing the menace of man's presence, that even the most timid of the bucks trooped inquisitively up to the camp and dug for water with their sharp hooves quite close to the man made holes. Lions killed nearby, and leopards made the night echo to their hunting cries.

Just beyond the oasis was a series of salt pans. Most of them appeared at one time to have held vast quantities of water, for their margins were covered with pebbles of jasper and banded iron-stone. The surface of many of them was covered with spongy, powdery alkali, the surface of others was hard, sun-baked, reddish mud. Some were covered with greenish colored pot clay under which was black mud, still others were of blue clay—and diamonds are found in blue clay.

Each day since their arrival at the oasis the Major and Jim had explored the pans, searching for diamonds, but so far without success. Green garnets, tourmalines, peridotes, beryls and a few emeralds had been their only reward.

"There are no diamonds here, *Baas*," Jim said as, after a back breaking day, scorched by the sun and half blinded by its reflected glare from the pan they had been prospecting, they made their way slowly back to the oasis.

"Maybe you're right, Jim," the Major said absently in the vernacular.

"And so the *Baas* will give up the search?" the Hottentot asked hopefully.

"I did not say so, Jim. There are many more pans hidden there in the dunes. We have not seen them all yet."

The Hottentot made a gesture of disgust. "It is folly to walk in the sun when there is shade at hand," he said.

"Maybe. But those who sit always in the shade see nothing, find nothing."

They were silent for a little while, each intent on his own footsteps as they forced their way through a thick patch of *haak dorn* bush. That obstacle left behind, the Major said, "Soon, Jim, I think, we will have callers. But who will come first: the men on horseback who ride to our east, or the policeman on the camel who keeps always to the west?"

"Who knows? Who cares, *Baas?* We will be ready. But if they do not come, *Baas,* how long do we stay here?"

"Until old Klaus dies."

"Au-a! That will not be long. He is dying like a plant uprooted and left in the sun. The sap of life has gone from him."

Again silence—a silence which lasted until they came to their camp.

Before going to his white bell tent, the Major halted beside Klaus, the bushman, who was lying on a pile of cut grass.

"Greetings!" the old man croaked, and his lips parted in a toothless grin. "And again you found nothing?"

"Nothing, Klaus."

The bushman chuckled. "Tomorrow I will lead you to the place."

The Major shook his head. "When you can throw a spear fifty paces, then you shall lead me, Klaus."

"Wo-we! Maybe that will never be. I am very old. At least let me tell you where it is."

The Major shook his head and passed on to his tent, sighing a little at the thought that the old hunter's hours were numbered for all his indomitable spirit. The treatment the old bushman had received at the hands of Fisher had cut fully five years off his life.

When Jim had rounded up the trek-oxen and penned them in the thorn stockade, he took a canvas bucket full of water in to his *baas,* and then squatted down on his haunches beside Klaus.

"How goes it, old one?" he asked.

"Well, Hottentot. Very well. With the setting of the sun I shall be made young again and go a-hunting as I did in the days of my youth."

"*Wo-we!*" Jim exclaimed softly. "Is it as near as that?"

"Truly. And this is a good place to die."

They were both silent for a little while. From the tent came the sound of splashing water and the Major's voice singing one of the Freebooter songs.

"Your *baas,*" said the headman, "is a man."

"Without doubt," Jim agreed, his eyes lighting as he thought of all the years he and his *baas* had been together playing whatever game Life set before them, and playing it well. "I could tell you—"

"There is no need. Of my own knowledge I say he is a man. And you, too, Hottentot, are a man."

"He is my *baas,* I am his servant," Jim replied simply.

"Yah. You are both men," Klaus continued. "Now tell me: If it was not because I know where diamonds are, why did your *baas* take me from that place of evil and bring me here?"

"It is always my *baas'* way to use his strength and wisdom for the welfare of the weak. He knew you had been unjustly treated, and so he took you from the compound of that evil white man. He, himself, dressed your wounds. *Au-a,* a great part of him is as soft and tender as a woman. And he brought you to this place because it was here you said you wanted to live out the little of life that was left in you."

"You say he brought me here, came here himself, because an old man babbled foolishly? Not because of the diamonds?"

Jim nodded.

"Is there any doubt? Not once has he asked you where the pan is."

"No. Yet each day he goes seeking."

"Would you have him sit in the shade and watch a foolish old bushman die?"

Klaus shook his head, greatly puzzled.

"If he would listen to me I would tell him where the diamonds are. Why will he not listen?"

"Because fallen fruit is often rotten. It is his custom to stalk his own game, to pick his own fruit. The hunt means more to him than the kill."

The bushman nodded, faintly comprehending. "Yah, he is a man," he muttered. "I express a desire, the desire of a foolish old man. And lo, your *baas* brings about that desire's fulfillment. Is the sun near the setting, Hottentot?"

"Very near, old one."

"*Wo-we!* That is good. I am very tired. But listen, Hottentot. I will tell you things and you shall tell them to your *bass*.

"A half day's trek from here, heading north, is a dune shaped not unlike a crouching lion; it is the highest of all the dunes about. At the foot of it is a water hole. A tree is in it and down that tree you can climb to the water. I put that tree there; from this place I carried it. By that water hole you shall camp, and the next day you shall go to a salt pan which is just beyond, and search the ground about its northern edge. And there your *baas* will find the diamonds." He chuckled softly as if understanding the jests of fate.

"That," he continued, "is a white man's treasure. But I know a still greater treasure. *Wo-we!* The desert has no secrets from us bush folk.

"Listen again." His voice was now barely above a whisper, and Jim had to bend low in order to hear him.

FINALLY THE whisper died away and the old hunter was silent, breathing hard.

The Major came from his tent, dressed immaculately in a suit of white duck. A monocle gleamed in his eye, his jet black hair was brushed back in a pompadour.

He came over and knelt beside the bushman, looking inquiringly at Jim.

"It is the end, *Baas*," the Hottentot whispered.

At that Klaus opened his eyes and smiled into the face of the Major. "Thank you, *Baas*," he said clearly. "You are a man. This is a good place and a good time to die."

He closed his eyes and— "The sun has set, *Baas*," Jim said softly.

About this time Trooper Rich, ten miles to the west, shot his camel which had broken its leg, and set off on foot for the Major's camp.

At this time, too, Cupid Dawes, emerging from the *straat* he had followed, discovered that it had not led straight as he had supposed, but had curved to the east so much that he had entirely lost his bearings.

Panic stricken, he retraced his steps at a run, intending to make for the water hole and start again from there in the morning.

THE NEXT day, long before sunrise, Jim and the Major were hard at work packing up their gear, ready to trek back to civilization.

By the time the sun had risen above the horizon they were on their way, Jim and his *baas* walking at the head of the oxen, heading—because of the Major's indifference and Jim's insistence—due north.

"We will be at a water hole by sundown, *Baas*," Jim said. "Old Klaus told me one was there. So we travel light now and fill our barrels there." Then he continued, warming to his theme, "Since those two who followed us have not come to us, we will go to them."

He said nothing about the diamond pan. That was to be a surprise to his *baas*.

They had almost reached the limit of the oasis when a magnificent, black-maned lion leaped out of the long grass directly in front of them. It crouched, its tail waving gracefully.

The Major and Jim froze in their tracks; the oxen came to a plunging halt and bellowed fearfully. The Major's rifle came up to his shoulder as the lion suddenly came forward, head down, tail erect, in a devastating rush.

Then the Major's trigger finger contracted, and a heavy bullet tore into the lion's lungs. But he still came on whilst the Major dropped in an inert heap to the ground.

Jim, wild with fury, giving no thought to the hidden enemy whose shot had creased the Major's temple, leaped in front of his prostrate *baas* and lashed at the lion with his driving whip.

But his blows, although they opened the flesh to the bone, did not check the lion. He rose in a magnificent spring and Jim threw himself on the top of his *baas*, shielding him with his body as well as he could. When the lion was at the peak of his spring another shot sounded, and another, and the tawny beast dropped lifelessly on top of Jim.

Jim struggled free and frantically dragged the dead lion from his *baas*. In this he was aided by Trooper Rich who rushed out of the tall grass, white faced, stammering explanations.

They carried the Major to the wagon, made him comfortable on a pile of blankets, bathed his wound with water and gave him whisky to drink. And presently the Major opened his eyes, the blood came back to his face and he smiled, first at Jim, then at Rich.

"I'm all right," he said. "Beastly headache, that's all. Suppose I have you to thank for that, Rich, old dear?"

"By God, Major," the trooper stammered, "I swear I didn't mean to shoot you that way. I was siding in the grass there, waiting to see if Cupid and Blackie were with you before I showed myself, and I saw you suddenly stop and level your rifle. I couldn't see the lion and I thought you had spotted me and had got the drop on me. Then you fired and I took a pot at you. God! I'm as sorry as hell. But I didn't see the lion and—"

The Major laughed. "Then that's that," he said. "No harm done. I quite understand. Oh, quite. Sort of thing any one might have done. Most natural mistake. But what are you doing here? And where's your well known ship of the, er, desert?"

"I'm here to arrest you for arson, abduction and God knows what else. My camel, it broke its leg and I had to shoot it."

"Ah, Too bad. Jim! *Trek jou!*"

The oxen lumbered forward, Jim at their head.

"And now," continued the Major, "do you mind explaining a few things, Rich? If you were out to arrest me, why did you hang about so long?"

Rich hesitated a moment, then outlined the plan conceived by Fisher's fertile brain.

"I see," murmured the Major. "It would seem that Fatty Fisher is responsible for many things. I must have a heart-to-heart talk with him. He'll be grieved, I know, to hear that my labors here have been in vain. Old Klaus is dead and his secret died with him."

"And he didn't tell you where the diamond pan is?" Rich asked incredulously.

"No. He was an obstinate bounder. But, by the way, what were those 'God knows what' charges you wanted me for?"

"The diamond business at Kimberley, chiefly, Major."

"Ah! I was afraid of that. You'll have to take my word for it that I am perfectly innocent. Quite!"

"There's a warrant out for you, and you came up here to evade arrest," the trooper countered.

"True. Most neatly put, laddie. But the good flee when the wicked pursue, and—"

"Well, you're my prisoner," Rich broke in, "and I warn you that anything you say may be used as evidence against you."

"Letter perfect! Marvelous!" the Major exclaimed.

"If you'd like to give me your parole, Major—"

"Of course," the Major agreed swiftly. "Otherwise you would have to handcuff me, and that would be most objectionable. Now let's talk of pleasanter things."

IT WAS nearly noon when Cupid Dawes came to the shaft down which he had so callously allowed his partner to go and meet a horrible death. He was in a terrible plight; his eyes were badly inflamed, the sight of one almost gone; the soles of his shoes were worn through, his feet were bleeding badly, and he was crazed by thirst and fear.

Now that he was in sight of the water hole a measure of sanity returned to him. Feverishly he increased his pace, almost tripped over the rib bones of Blackie, upon whom the desert scavengers had long since done their work, and so to the shaft head. And there he stopped aghast, petrified by the awful stench which arose from the hole.

Forcing himself to look down he saw the bloated body of the puff-adder, already decomposed, floating on the top of the water which was, of course, undrinkable.

And then, quite suddenly, he went entirely mad. He fled from the spot, blaspheming, cursing Blackie—wasn't it Blackie who had killed the adder? Wasn't it Blackie, therefore, who had purposely contaminated the only drinking water in the desert—the only water in the world?

He ran as if pursued by evil devils, tearing his clothes from his body—lost, mad.

He saw ahead of him presently, a crystal clear lake.

Shouting with joy he dashed toward it, collapsed at its very edge and died violently, his outstretched hands clawing at the salt crusted surface of the pan.

THREE HOURS later the others came to the shaft, and their well-trained eyes enabled them swiftly to reconstruct some part of the tragedies which had been played there.

"We'll have to go back for water, Jim," the Major said slowly, "and it will be heavy going. But first we will try to find Cupid, poor devil."

Jim shook his head. "No, *Baas*. We will not go back yet. First we will try another place for water. It is near here, Klaus said. And we must have water before we look for the white man. *Wo-we!* He has the desert madness. Maybe he is dead; maybe he has gone far. Come, *Baas*. And you," he turned to the policeman, "will stay here with the oxen."

Half an hour later he and the Major were skirting the northern rim of the salt pan, and there they put to flight a number of vultures, exposing the little that was left of Cupid Dawes.

"Poor devil," the Major muttered, not knowing how richly Cupid merited the fate the desert had meted out to him.

"Look, *Baas*," said Jim, and exposed on his open palm several oddly shaped stones, looking like lumps of discolored glass, which he had picked up close to Cupid's outstretched hands.

"*Bai* Jove," the Major murmured, taking the stones from Jim, looking at them and then at the stones which were all about him. "Diamonds by the bushel. A regular Tom Tiddler's ground. But," he licked his dry lips and let the stones fall to the ground, "I'd rather have a drink of clear water than all the diamonds here, Jim."

"Maybe I can give you that too, *Baas*. But first I will take some of these." He filled the pockets of his ragged trousers with the stones, selecting with the eye of an expert the better colored ones.

Then he led the way back from the pan, 'round the end of the low dune, and there they came upon a chaos of rocks in the center of which, protected from the heat of the sun by an overhanging ledge, was a large, spring fed pool.

"This is the bushman's treasure, *Baas*," the Hottentot said with a happy grin.

The Major tasted it, gurgled appreciatively, drank again and—"Therein a bushman's wisdom is greater than a white man's, Jim, and his treasure more desirable. Now you go for the policeman and the oxen. But do not take him near the pan. That is our secret.

A FULL two months later the Major and Jim brought Rich back to the police camp and handed him over to the care of Jones, the other trooper at the camp.

"He's had fever and he's still weak," the Major said. "But he's a plucky devil. He arrested me back there in the desert and brought me in, fever or no fever."

"And what charge am I to hold you on?" Jones asked with a grin after they had put Rich to bed.

"Arson, abduction and what not."

"I suppose by 'what not' you mean that affair at Kimberley?"

The Major sighed. "Exactly."

"Well, that warrant against you has been withdrawn."

The Major chuckled. "I thought it would be. Jim will be glad to hear it and so, I think, will Rich. He found it very hard to do his duty. The dear man thought he ought to let me go because I—oh, well! As if I could desert a sick man in the desert."

"Some could, Major," Jones said tersely.

"Well, you tell old Rich about that. Now, ta-ta. I must be toddling along."

"Not so fast, Major. I must still hold you on that arson and abduction charge. Who's the complainant?"

"Fisher"

"That bounder?"

"Exactly.

"But I suppose if I can get him to withdraw the charge it will be quite all right?"

Jones nodded.

"Good. Then I must ask you to accept my parole until sundown, while I have a little chat with Fisher. He'll be most surprised to see me and hear what I have to tell him. Sure it'll be all right?"

Jones nodded.

"That's bally nice of you, Jones. And, I say, I wish you'd share the contents of this little parcel with Rich. They will make you both rich— Ha, ha! no joke intended. They're, as it were, little mementoes. I picked them up here and there in the desert. By-bye! I'll drop in for tea if Fisher won't be merciful. But he will. Yes, I feel quite sure of that. You see, he's been responsible for so many things that I think he could be rewarded. So I'm going to show him a place in the desert where he can pick up diamonds by the hundreds. Absolutely."

A MONTH later the Major came again to the diamond pan. With him, blindfolded, came Fatty Fisher.

"There," the Major said pleasantly as he removed the bandage from the fat man's eyes, "you see I've kept my promise. I showed you yesterday where Blackie died. And this is where Cupid died. And here—much more interesting to you—you will see diamonds. Diamonds! That's the word, eh, laddie? Well, diamonds it is. Look around you. You're walking on them. Here," he gave Fisher a large cloth tobacco bag, "I'll stay here with you long enough for you to fill that. Take your time. Pick the good ones, but don't try to slip any in your pockets when you think I'm not looking. I shall be looking all the time, I assure you."

Like a man possessed, Fisher went down on his hands and knees, chuckling with delight, creeping backward and forward, exclaiming in wonder at the richness of the deposit.

Finally, his bag filled, he rose to his feet.

"I don't see why, Major," he began, "you can't let me take more, why you don't take a sackful, or a cartload full, for the matter of that. We could fairly shovel them up!"

"You are greedy, and you exaggerate," the Major said coldly. "Even the number you have in that bag would flood the market unless carefully traded."

"I'll take care of that end, Major," Fisher said eagerly. "I—"

"As a matter of fact, Fisher," the Major said, "you're taking too much for granted. Far too much. Actually, you know, I'm not going to let you take away any diamonds at all. That wasn't part of my bargain, you know. I simply said that I would bring you to this place. I've done it—and now I'm going to take you away."

His revolver leaped from its holster into his hand, the muzzle of it was aimed at Fisher's paunch.

"Empty that bag on the ground. Quick."

Fisher cursed, raved and threatened, but obeyed.

"Now turn around. Pick out some landmarks, if you can. Then you can come back and find this place yourself someday—if you can."

Fisher looked wildly around, hoping to find some distinctive landmark, and failed.

A moment later, blindfolded, he was being half led, half pushed back along the trail leading to the oasis.

FOOL'S FOLLY

GRAY CLOUDS scurried across the face of the moon, dimming its white splendor. One by one the stars were blotted out; a piercing wind swept its way unchecked across the open veld. The temperature dropped. By comparison with the heat of the noonday sun, a heat which had sent all white men to the fancied coolness of the bars and the drinks purveyed there, the cold was intense, freezing, chilling heat-thinned blood.

South Africa is like that: Charming by reason of her whimsical vagaries; damned because of her hell inspired changes.

The horseman, riding back from Diamondtown to his camp on the veld beyond the commonage, turned up the collar of his heavy coat and blew on his numbed fingers.

"Judging by the blaze," he muttered, staring ahead at a yellow pin-prick of light which shone through the swift gathering gloom, "Jim's got a good fire goin' an'it'll be bally welcome. Jove! If I were at home, I'd prophesy skating in the morning, or at least a good, old-fashioned snowstorm. Instead of which—" he sighed—"it'll probably rain all the night through,' making the veld a bally quagmire. But by noon it'll be steaming hot an' dust devils'll be dancing everywhere. What a country! An' what a fool I am to stay in it. Specially when I don't have to. I could go home an'—

He shrugged his shoulders and rode on for awhile in moody silence, the bridle reins hanging loosely about his horse's neck, flapping his arms to promote warmth.

Suddenly he broke into song, hummed a Yule-tide carol:

"I saw three ships come sailing in—"

As if choked by Africa's unsympathetic alien atmosphere the song ended as abruptly as it had begun.

"But, my word!" exclaimed the horseman, giving voice to the thoughts which had prompted the song, "I've made up my mind. Rather. I'm going home for Christmas. If I start in the morning I can get the *Ghoorka* at Cape Town. She'll get me home just in time. But what on earth will I do with Jim? Take him with me, or—"

Again he was silent, making and rejecting plans, letting his mind feast on the good things he would do when he got home—after an exile of twenty years.

The clouds had merged into one black, lowering canopy which had extinguished the moon and stars and, once the wind dropped, would spill its contents on to the sun parched earth.

The horseman's keen eyes were not blinded by the darkness. Topping a slight rise he could see his bell-tent and, beyond that, the light canvas-topped trek wagon to which were tethered his sixteen mules.

To the left of the tent was a native, his Hottentot servant, squatting before a fire, a blanket thrown over his shoulder, intent on stirring the contents of a big "kettle"; intent on that, oblivious to all else save, perhaps, the words of the song he was singing.

The white man reined in his horse and listened, but he was still too far away, and the wind was in the wrong quarter, to get anything but meaningless words. Meaningless because isolated, not because they were spoken in the harsh, clicking guttural of the Hottentot.

HE RODE on again slowly, choosing his way with care, concentrating on getting as close as he could to his camp before being challenged by the Hottentot.

It was a game which had never failed to delight these two—white master and black servant—in all the years they had been together. It was a matching of bushcraft against bush-craft.

"Of course," the horseman mused, "Jim, the bally old heathen, knows I'm on my way. He must have heard me singing, he must have heard the jingle of Satan's bit." He patted his horse's arched neck. "But if I can get a little nearer before he hails me I shall score one to myself. Only," he concluded ruefully, "the deuce of it is, he'll probably wait until I ride up to him and then—and, my word, how sarcastic the old lad can be:—he will tell me all my movements since I left the *dorp:* here I lighted a cigarette; there I turned to avoid a gully; here I drew rein to listen to him sing— But speaking of gullies—"

He turned his horse into a deep hollow, one of the wave-like billows which broke up the level expanse of veld, and rode along it. For a little while it led him to the east of his camp, then, curving sharply, headed to a point beyond the campfire opposite the place where he would have appeared had he kept to his original line.

And having reached that place he halted for a moment, before riding up out of the depression, to listen to the Hottentot's chant. He could distinguish every word now, and it puzzled him.

It was a hunting song the Hottentot was singing and the white man knew it well; he had sung it many times, glorying in the words of the savage saga and the elemental, barbaric rhythm.

Yet his attitude now of intense concentration was of one hearing the song for the first time. He was endeavoring to find the clue to the puzzle it presented him; wondering what had destroyed the regularity of the rhythm.

Suddenly he understood: The Hottentot was interpolating isolated words, sometimes whole sentences, into the age-old, tradition-sanctified chant.

The white man, listening breathlessly, separated those words and sentences, put them together, shuffled and rearranged them, finally obtaining this:

> Go back. Oh, man who comes riding a black horse. Oh, man who waits in a donga to my north. In the white hut evil waits. A woman waits with death in her hands.

"I suppose by *'White hut'* Jim means the tent," the horseman mused. "And the old boy's clever, deucedly clever, to get over a warning like that. But then I've come to expect that of Jim. One might catch a weasel asleep, but never Jim! So he thinks I ought to go back, eh? And simply because a woman waits to—er—interview me. Granted the well known weaker sex is much too strong for me, I do not feel inclined to show my heels tonight. No. Tonight I must pack and whatnot. Also, I'm curious. This must be looked into."

HE FUMBLED in his tunic pocket and, producing a monocle, fixed it in his eye. Even in the darkness one would have been aware that that monocle had a magical effect on him. From the moment he wore it he seemed to emanate "silly assisms," seemed to surround himself with the personality of a vacuous, inane fop.

Then, whistling gaily, he rode forward, up out of the hollow, and into the circle of light cast by the fire.

The Hottentot looked up swiftly, an expression of reproach, warning and despair on his ugly, good natured face. Then he turned his attention again to the stuff he was stirring in the kettle and continued his song.

The white man dismounted.

"Take care of Satan, Jim," he ordered and, his hands thrust deep into the pockets of his white drill riding breeches, sauntered lazily toward his tent.

As he neared it a woman suddenly appeared in the opening, and, levelling a revolver at him, commanded sharply, "Hands up, Major!"

With a wondering, vacuous expression on his round, smooth-shaven face, he removed his hands from his pockets and raised them above his head, removing his helmet with his right and bowing profoundly, as he did so.

"And now what, dear lady?" He asked in a pleasing drawl.

She looked slightly nonplussed for a moment but answered stoutly enough, "We are going to have a little talk together, you and I. And then—"

"And then?" He prompted, noting her hesitation.

"That all depends," was her cryptic answer.

The Major laughed gaily.

"That all depends," he echoed. "Bally lot of meaning in those three words. On them you can hang all the law and the prophets—what?"

"You would try to make fun of a woman," she remarked sourly.

"Oh, I say," the Major exclaimed, "that's not fair, really. Such a thing was far from my thought, 'pon my word, yes. I was only tryin' as it were, to make conversation. This is a deucedly awkward position, you know. Oh, very. You see I don't know you—or your—er—errand. And my arms are aching, you know. And, yes, I'm in a very awkward position."

"You are," the woman agreed grimly. "Well, you're going to listen to me and agree to a proposition I'm going to make. If you don't, you'll be in a much more awkward position I assure you. Ever seen a man drop with a bullet in his brain?"

The major fidgeted.

"Oh, I say!" he murmured. "What a ghastly sense of humor you've got."

"It isn't humor—" the woman sniffed—"I'm just letting you see I'm here on serious business and not to be put off by any of your smart-aleck tricks."

HE LOOKED covertly over his shoulder, wondering what the Hottentot was doing; surprised that he had not, before this, made some move which would have helped the Major turn the tables on the woman who was holding him up.

But Jim had not moved from his place by the fire and, apparently, had not the slightest interest in his *Baas'* welfare.

The woman laughed coldly.

"You needn't look for any help from Jim," she said. "I can speak the lingo—well enough, at least, to convince him that at any false move from you or him I shoot. And I don't miss what I aim at. Yes, your nigger's convinced I mean business. That's why he didn't warn you I was here. He knew he'd get a bullet in his yellow hide if he did."

"But he did, dear lady," the Major murmured. "And very cleverly too. Oh, never mind," he continued with a shrug of his broad shoulders, answering her look of scornful disbelief. "The only thing that counts is that I disregarded the warning and you have me—er—where you want me. Yes, very much so, by Jove!"

She eyed him narrowly, but, because his back was toward the fire-light, failed to read the expression on his face.

He continued easily, advancing toward her, she backing slowly into the tent, "Because my bally arms are tired I'm going to take them down and if you must shoot—why, I suppose you must. Only, reflect, dear lady. Murder's a beastly occupation for a woman."

He lowered his hands as he spoke, took a cigarette from his case and lighted it calmly.

Then he held the flickering match between his cupped hands so that it illumined his face; held it until the flame reached his fingers, searing them. Then he dropped it, but with no show of nervous shock invariably exhibited by smokers so caught. As an exhibition of nerve control it was masterly, taking into consideration the fact that, at the same time, a revolver was pointing at his vitals—and that revolver in the hands of an overwrought woman. Her forefinger was alternately straightening and crooking about the trigger.

"And now," the Major continued softly, "I think we'll have a little light on the subject."

He reached for a lamp which hung from the tent pole, and a moment later the tent was illumined by its soft, yellow light.

Besides a camp bed with snowy linen, the tent contained a table, two deck chairs and a number of black, uniform-sized cases. On the floor was spread a number of well tanned skins—that of a magnificent black maned lion being the most conspicuous.

"Jim killed that laddie, alone, with a spear," the Major remarked casually, much in the manner of a host making conversation with his guests. "It was quite an affair! I had a—er—worm's eye view of it all. You see, I was under the lion at the time. But—" he drew a chair forward—"won't you sit down? Unpardonable of me to keep you standing so long. Please sit down."

There was a world of courtesy in his voice, and of sincere sympathy.

It startled the woman, A look of doubt crept into her faded gray eyes; sorrow softened the hard lines of her face into what they really were, the wrinkles of age.

She tried desperately to pull herself together, and failed; she looked helplessly at the Major then back at the revolver she held in her hand.

SUDDENLY THE revolver dropped with a dull thud to the ground and she collapsed into the chair the Major had pulled out for her, covered her face with her hands and wept noiselessly, rocking ceaselessly to and fro.

The Major looked down at her uneasily; his hands, firm, white, capable, fluttered helplessly before him. He made a motion as if he would pat her reassuringly on the back, thought better of it and, instead, toyed nervously with his monocle.

Then he stooped quickly, picked up the revolver, placed it on the table close to her, sat down in the other chair, waiting for the woman's outburst of grief to wear itself out.

And while he waited he eyed her keenly, endeavoring to find a clue to her presence at his camp and her violent antagonism toward him.

Her face had seemed vaguely familiar, but his unusually keen memory failed him for once and he could not place her.

She was, he judged, a woman of fifty-five or thereabouts and had once been, undoubtedly, beautiful in a hard metallic way. Her hair, what little of it showed beneath the wide-brimmed hat she wore, was a nondescript, rusty brown, lifeless, dull, indicating that for many years it had been a peroxide blond.

Her ungloved hands were large, and the stumpy red fingers were covered with tawdry rings.

Presently she raised her head and looked across the tent at the Major, furtively dabbing at her eyes with a much belaced handkerchief, straightening her hat, patting a stray wisp of hair into place.

"And now what, dear lady?" the Major asked softly.

She started at his voice, confusion for a moment took possession of her and the fingers of her right hand played a nervous tattoo on the top of the table which stood by her side. And so they came in contact with the revolver, closing convulsively upon its butt. Its cold metallic touch acted like a cold douche upon her, shocking her into a state of self control. Once again her eyes glittered with a hard light.

"Better begin at the beginning, don't you think?" The Major murmured.

"There's no beginning," the woman said harshly, "where the likes of me's concerned. My name's Jane Brunton—

Joburg Jane. You've heard of me, no doubt. There ain't many men in South Africa who haven't."

She paused defiantly, waiting for some comment from him; steeling herself against an expected coarse insult.

"Yes, Mrs. Brunton," the Major replied gravely. "I've heard of you. And, if all I hear's true, I'm probably one of the few men in South Africa you haven't helped with a grubstake. There are a lot of men who owe their present success to the start you gave them."

Jane Brunton laughed harshly.

"It's always easy for my sort to be generous. It's the only virtue we possess."

THE MAJOR was silent. He knew Jane Brunton's reputation; knew of all the evil credited to her when she was a leader of South Africa's feminine underworld. But all that belonged to the past, to the days when she had been an autocratic beauty. Of the woman she now was he knew nothing, save that she was undoubtedly in great trouble. And nothing in his expression or the tone of his voice when he again spoke indicated that he thought of her other than he thought of any woman: an unexplainable mystery and therefore to be feared; a woman and therefore to be held in great respect. It was this fear, this respect which explained his awkwardness in the presence of women, reduced him to a state of inanity which matched his monocle-masked face.

"We're goin' to have a most bally frightful storm," he remarked helplessly, "an' it's getting cold. Would you like some coffee? Jim makes—"

He half rose from his chair intending to go to the Hottentot to give directions.

He collapsed, gaping foolishly, at Jane Brunton's terse command. Once again the revolver, held in an unwavering hand, was levelled at him.

"Don't want any coffee," she said tonelessly. "Now just you listen to me. What are you going to do about my boy?"

The Major stared at her wonderingly and passed his hand over his smooth, jet black hair in a puzzled gesture.

"Your boy!" he murmured. "But I don't understand. I didn't know you had a son. And, in any case, what have I to do with him?"

"A damned sight too much," she snapped angrily, but there was despair, too, in her voice. "Listen: I sent him away to school when he was only a brat of eight. I sent him to England and kept him there so's he wouldn't never know what sort of a woman his mother was. Get that: *was*. For nearly fourteen years I didn't lay eyes on him. For the last eight I been making myself respectable, making myself the sort of woman he ought to have for a mother. And I done it. Damn it—I done it!"

She repeated the assertion passionately, challenging him to contradict her.

"I'm sure you have," the Major murmured with a gentle courtesy.

"A year ago," she continued in a softer vein, "he came back to me on the farm I'd bought, fifty miles north of Diamondtown. Red Drift it's called: You've heard of it?"

The Major bowed.

"It's one of the best stocked farms in the country I'm told."

"It is. I got three thousand *morgen* of land an' most of it's prime grazing ground; an' I got a couple of hundred acres under cultivation an' one of the best homesteads in the district. An' I did a lot of it myself. Wouldn't have a white man near the place lest people 'ud talk. Worked beside my niggers, I did." Her eyes glowed with the pride of achievement. Then they faded; misery clouded them.

"But Frank," she continued, "didn't care for farm life. He was young, needed company, an' maybe I was wrong to try to pin him down so soon. After all, you're only young once, an' it's best to make the most of it. But, I wonder!"

She paused, considering the wisdom of that age-old, easy philosophy.

"Frank is your son, I suppose?" the Major commented.

"YOU KNOW damn' well he is," she retorted savagely and continued, ignoring his protests; "of course you know, an' you know all the rest, an', in a way, I'm wasting time goin' through it all now. But it helps me think out what to do.

"Well, Frank got restless—missed the company of youngsters his own age; no wonder, with only me to talk to. My God! An' the way he used to talk to me of parties he'd been to in London. He hinted at things that he said 'ud make me blush if I was to hear the whole story. Make *me* blush. God! If only I could. But that was the way I wanted him to think of me: a mousey, quiet, little woman who didn't dream how bad men could be. I used to laugh and cry myself to sleep over his tales. He was so damned innocent, an' young, for all his talk!

"But, as I say, he got fed up with the farm very soon an' got into the habit of riding into the *dorp* every Friday an' coming back Monday. It was no use my saying anything, I felt sure of that. He was a man in years, anyway. An' I couldn't warn him, as I ought to have warned him. That was the hell of it! How could I, a quiet little homebody, warn him, a man of the world, against all the things he was likely

to run up against, an' did run up against, in Diamondtown?"
She laughed mirthlessly. "Maybe, I'd have held him better
if I'd made myself out to be more of a woman of the world.
I've paid and I'm paying for that mistake."

She was silent, for a little while. The revolver was lying
now unheeded in her lap, her hands were clasped loosely
about her knees and she stared dull-eyed before her.

The tent bellied as a shrieking gust of wind swept by,
threatening to break it from its moorings. There followed
a dead oppressive calm.

Outside, Jim, the Hottentot, was passing swiftly amongst
the animals, soothing them, looking to their lashings, for
they sensed the impending storm.

The woman continued abruptly, ignoring the period of
silence which had interrupted her narrative.

"Yes, Frank wanted life an' he went to Diamondtown
for it."

"And he found it—the old, bad kind?" the Major
hazarded. "Women, wine, an' that sort of thing?"

"You know he didn't," the woman replied shortly.
"Frank's clean, I'll gamble on that. No. He found a hero.
Only, because he's young, he didn't have the sense to see
his hero's got feet of clay. So he dresses like a Bond Street
dandy, an' talks as if he got a plum in his mouth, a hot one
at that, an' wears a monocle, an' brushes his hair back in a
pompadour an' acts like a silly, stage door Johnny. Do you
recognize yourself, Major?"

The Major moved uneasily.

"But that, alone, wouldn't be so bad," the woman continued relentlessly. "Everybody knows—everybody who really
knows you, that is—that your silly ass ways are only a pose;
knows that for all your soft, womanish ways you're all steel
underneath. They say you're the best shot, the best horse-

man, the best trekker in South Africa. An' Frank, poor lamb, he's taken you as a model. An' you're a good model up to a point. I'll admit that. From what I hear you don't booze or run after women. But inside you're rotten."

"Oh, I say!" the Major protested feebly.

"YOU ARE," the woman continued. "You play your own game in your own way; you got the reputation of being the best of good fellows; but you play a rotten game an', because you are what you are, my boy didn't see how rotten it is. He thinks you a Robin Hood—an' is bent on playin' it with you."

"And my game is?"

She snorted indignantly.

"You're an I.D.B.—a man can't go any lower than that: Not in this country. Because an I.D.B.'s got to lie, an' cheat his best friends. God! He ain't got no friends, He don't trust nobody nor nobody trusts him. He tempts niggers to steal stones from their masters an' buys them, like as not, with a bottle of rot gut booze or a farthing gilded to look like a quid. Hell! Don't I know what the game's like? Me as saw so much of it in the years gone by. An' folks think because you're clean outside you're clean inside an' ain't tarred with the same brush as all the others of your kind. An' my boy Frank he's taken you for his hero!"

She laughed bitterly.

The Major was about to make some comment, thought better of it and, frowning thoughtfully, waited for her to continue.

"Yes," she said, "you're his hero an' you're going to make him your assistant—he's full of it—make him the rotter you are. Are you though?"

She sat suddenly erect, the revolver grasped firmly in her hand once again. "Not if I know it. An' this little affair you an' him are pulling off—day after tomorrow, ain't it?—ain't goin' to happen. Planning to rush a 'parcel' of stones, Frank tells me. God! To hear him tell it it's clean adventure.

" 'It ain't really stealing, Mom,' he says. We're only taking stones from people who have no right to them. At least we've got as much right to them as they have. An' we'll most like give all we make to a mission or something.'

"That's the way he talks! It ain't stealing, eh? But he'll get ten years hard labor if he's caught. An' maybe you'll fix it so's he is caught with a few stones, leaving you free to get away with the rest. That's just the sort of thing your sort does. I know. There ain't a straight thought in your body.

"But you're scotched, Mister Major. You're not goin' to ruin my boy."

"I don't suppose you'd believe me," the Major said wearily, "if I told you I'd never done any of the things you accuse me of. Of course I have the reputation of being an I.D.B.—"

"The cunningest one in the country!" the woman snapped.

The Major bowed.

"It's hardly an honor," he murmured, continuing, "I've never bought *stolen* stones from natives. And though, technically, I may once or twice have—er—overstepped the legal line, most of my operations have, as it were, been forced upon me and my dealings constituted acts of self defence. I have, you must believe me, dear lady, merely pilfered the pilferers, returning, where possible the stones to their legal owners, retaining only a small percentage for my labors; retaining merely sufficient to outfit for a trek way up country—to hunt an' so forth—where Jim an' me are far happier than in the *dorps*."

"EVEN IF that was true," the woman said slowly, "that don't clear you. Because of you an' your reputation I'm in danger of losing my boy. An' it ain't true! You're a dirty hound. But I'm going to scotch you. You're goin' to promise to send my boy back to me or—"

She indicated her revolver with a threatening gesture.

The Major laughed softly, sadly, at her illogical words.

"Would you," he drawled, "accept the promise of a dirty hound? A promise extracted under the threat of death?" Before she could reply he continued swiftly. "An' as a matter of fact—you'll have to believe this—I don't know your boy Frank. Wouldn't know him from Adam of Eden."

She sneered wrathfully.

"I expected something like that. Here—look what I received just when I thought I was making headway with my boy, getting him to see sense. What's your answer to that?"

From a pocket hidden deep down in the folds of her voluminous skirt she produced a note which she handed to him.

Unfolding it, he read:

Dear Joburg Jane:

Me and your boy, Frank, are great pals and I don't like to hear that you're trying to persuade him to have nothing to do with me because I'm a danger to his morals. That don't sound nice, coming from an old friend who knows all about your morals.

So this is a sort of warning-like: If anything should happen— and I ain't going to bother trying to find out what—to make young Frank double-cross me on this little scheme we're in, or if he should suddenly show more pleasure in my room than my company, why then he's going to know what sort of a woman his mother was, and still is for all I know.

If you feel like calling in to talk over old times you'll find me at Tikkey Ike's place most nights.

Yours,

The Major.

The Major read this through twice, carefully noting the ornate flourishing handwriting, then folding the paper handed it back to the woman.

"Well!" she demanded, her wrath mounting as she detected, as she thought, a sneering smile on the Major's face. "What you got to say to that?"

"There doesn't seem much I can say, only—"

"There's no only to it," she interrupted hotly. "It proves you're a liar, saying you don't know my boy. It proves you a dirty dog threatening to throw a woman's past before her son if she don't agree to stand by an' see him ruined. If—"

"Why did you come here to see me—" his drawl, calm, assured, overpowered and silenced her tirade—"when the note said I'd be found at Tikkey Ike's?"

"I went there." Her voice was toneless now again; all spirit seemed to have left her; she looked old, tired, spiritless, beaten. "And they told me you were out here."

"And you've been here—how long?"

"It was noon when I came."

He whistled.

"You've had no food—nothing?"

"Nothing. But what the hell's that to you? I was watching to see your nigger played no tricks, and thinking about my kid."

"Jim!"

"Yah, *Baas?*" the Hottentot called, answering the Major's shout.

"Make *skoff.* Hot stew, coffee, quick. Get—"

"BLAST YOU!" the woman screamed. "Are you trying to play a trick on me? Tell your nigger to stay where he is by the fire. An' don't you call him again until me an' you have settled this business."

The Major rose quickly from his chair, deep concern on his face. He realized that the woman was reaching the end of her strength, mental and physical. Worry over her son, distress at the fear that her past might be raked out into the light—and that, too, she dreaded for her son's sake—lack of nourishment, all had taken their toll of her.

"First we will eat," he said calmingly, his eyes fixed upon her.

"Sit down," she screamed again. "You won't? Then take that!"

But the Major, reading in her eyes the order her brain was sending to her stiffened fingers, reading it a fraction of a second before the fingers could carry out the brain's command, flung himself to the ground. Even so the bullet from her revolver tore its way through the shoulder of his coat, grazing his skin and drawing blood.

Before she could fire again he had reached up and snatched the revolver from her just as a deafening clap of thunder, following a brilliant lightning flash, made the earth vibrate.

Outside, Jim's voice sounded eerie as he called soothingly to the animals, then demanded anxiously, "Is the *Baas* all right?"

"All right. Make haste with the *skoff,* Jim, before the rain comes."

"The food is ready, *Baas*. In a minute I will bring it—and the rain is here."

As he spoke a cold, wet gust of wind swept into the tent; the canvas throbbed to the heavy beat of the rain, the air was filled with the sound of falling water, water cascading from the skies, churning the hard red earth into an oozy quagmire.

The Hottentot sidled into the tent enveloped from head to foot in a tarpaulin sheet from which descended rivulets of water.

He looked enquiringly at his *Baas*, then at the woman. She was sitting back in the chair now, covering her face with her hands, moaning despairingly. Her attempt had failed. But—she vaguely resented this—the woman she had *been* would not have failed. *That* woman had been harder.

"Is the *Baas* all right, truly?" Jim asked again. "I heard a shot—" He glared angrily at the woman.

"It was the thunder you heard, Jim."

The Hottentot's eyes turned to him, noted the tear in the Major's coat and the dull stain around it.

"And doubtless," he commented dryly, "it was the thunder which tore your coat, *Baas*, and drew blood from your shoulder."

"You talk too much," the Major said curtly. "The food—where is it?"

From under the tarpaulin Jim produced a food laden tray which he put down on the table and then, at a sign from the Major, withdrew.

A LITTLE while later the Major joined him, running swiftly through the downpour to where he sat under the canvas shelter of the wagon.

He swiftly discarded his soaked garments, stood out for a moment in the rain, glorying in the invigorating lash on his naked body, his muscular body which had looked slightly obese in the garments he affected, then climbing back into the wagon he briskly towelled himself and dressed again in patched, formless khaki slacks and a tattered gray shirt. On his head he put a battered felt hat, his uncombed hair stuck out, looking trampishly unkempt, and a pair of veld *schoens* covered his sockless feet.

Jim watched the preparations uneasily.

"The *Baas* plays a game?" he asked suddenly.

"Yah, Jim," the Major replied absently.

"And at the woman's bidding?"

"Truly, Jim. Aiming a gun at me she said I must do thus and so. And, to preserve my life, I obey."

"What folly, *Baas!*" Jim exclaimed. "The gun is no longer threatening your life, then why obey? For the matter of that, had you listened to my warning—"

"I didn't, Jim. And I'm glad I didn't. So now I go to do what I have to do for my name's sake." He wrapped himself in the tarpaulin Jim had been wearing and climbed down to the ground, slipping in the ooze.

"The *Baas* goes like that—and on foot?" Jim asked incredulously. "He will get wet—"

"And also dirty, Jim. But it is part of the game. See that the woman is made in all ways comfortable, Jim. She is my guest, my honored guest. You will stay here to protect her. It is understood?"

"Yah! But, *Baas,* is there no part for me in this game you play?"

"None, Jim. Filth has been thrown on my name. I go to wash it off."

"But the *Baas* will take care?"

"Great care, Jim." Then, with a mirthful chuckle, the Major said, imitating Jim's voice, and almost exhausting Jim's knowledge of English, "If I don't see you. S'long. Hullo! Damme, yes, no."

Then he trudged off through the darkness, heading for the township.

An occasional lightning flash which turned the leaden rain to ribbons of gleaming silver, made him visible to Jim's keen eyes. Then came a flash and Jim saw nothing but a waste of water.

"*Wo-we!* What a man," Jim breathed softly. "But he is also a liar! For his name's sake, he would have me believe, he dresses in rags and goes on a night like this to the *dorp* of evil men. But I, I who have known him these many years, I know better. A woman's tears—*wo-we!* I have seen it before—blinds his eyes to caution. Into the darkness he goes, and in the darkness how can he see the snares which may be set for him.

"*Wo-we!* I, Jim, the Hottentot, I am his servant, therefore it is my part to follow and see he comes to no harm. Yah! That is my duty. I am his servant."

His mind made up on that point Jim jumped down from the wagon and was on the point of following in the direction taken by the Major when the woman's voice, raised in a shout of, "*O-he,* Jim!" brought him to a confused halt, brought to him a remembrance of the Major's orders.

"*Au-a!*" he muttered. "But he is my *Baas*, and my *Baas* gave an order. So— Coming Missy!" he shouted and slithered his way through the mud toward the tent.

THE BODEGA BAR at all times fully lived up to the evil reputation of its proprietor, "Tikkey" Isaacs.

It was a place where the scum of humanity which flocked to the Diamondtown could pander to their perverted vices, unmolested, provided they paid tribute to the fat, greasy, sycophantic Tikkey.

A hard visaged woman, dressed in tawdry finery, pounded waltzes and barn dances on a tuneless piano and to its labored rhythm others, their partners men of color if not of substance, danced with an affectation of gaiety.

Whites and full-blooded negroes, and all shades between, coolies and Malays, were welcomed by Tikkey; the possession of money broke down all color bars and the oily Tikkey waxed fat, financially as well as physically, on the shortcomings of his fellow creatures.

Around the walls tables were placed and about each table sat men and women, drinking heavily, not daring to object to the vile doctored stuff served to them or the exorbitant price they had to pay.

And Tikkey Isaacs, the evil genius of the place, constantly circulated about the room, his pasty face appearing ghoulish through the haze of smoke; his ears strained to hear any scrap of conversation which might be of value to him, frowning heavily whenever his eyes alighted on a group who talked in whispers and whose glasses were empty.

In a far corner of the room sat two men quite alien to the rest of the motley crowd. They were clean; their garments were immaculate and somewhat foppish; specially was that true of the younger man; and they both wore monocles.

But whereas the younger man seemed to find the atmosphere of the place distasteful, the other evidently revelled in it, exchanging coarse jests with the dancers as they pirouetted by.

"This is the life, eh, Frank?" the older man said suddenly in a harsh voice. "This is better than helping the old woman run a farm, ain't it?" Then he continued, after a furtive look at his companion, in a labored drawl which seemed more in keeping with his clothes and monocle, "My word! It's simply rippin', what?"

"Oh, rather, Major," the other replied. "Quite." And he laughed self-consciously. "Just the same, old chap, I'll be beastly glad to get away from the *dorp*. I can hardly wait for the time when we—"

"Ssh, you fool! Not so loud. Don't want to let everybody know." The man who called himself "the Major" looked around uneasily. "Don't mention diamonds here."

"I wasn't going to, dear lad. What a sell for you. I was—er—merely goin' to refer to our hunting trip. But really, dear old lad, I'm beastly fed up with this place. Bad gin, fearful noise, smoke and what not. It isn't necessary, surely, for us to wait here? It isn't the sort of place I'd expect to amuse you, and—"

"It doesn't amuse me, Frank. But it's a safe place to come and transact business. Don't you see? You know my reputation? Well, remember that."

"Ah, I see. You're just pretending to enjoy all this so you can get on the trail of some stolen stones. Is that it?"

"My word! What a brain! Now, look here: you see that woman over there? No, not that one. The half-caste with a red flower in her hair. That one. Now you go and dance with her. Do the pretty with her. She's one of the gang I'm after and, if you handle her cleverly, you may get some useful information out of her. Go on. I'm trusting to you."

HE WATCHED the youth reluctantly make his way through the crowd to the woman he had indicated; watched, with a contemptuous, sneering smile, Frank's elaborate bow and the gallant way in which he offered his arm to the more than willing girl.

Once the two had started to dance, he took out his monocle, emptied his glass with a sigh of relief, and, shouting an order for another, slumped back in his chair, his feet resting on the table top.

Tikkey himself brought the drink and eased himself gruntingly into the chair Frank Brunton had just vacated.

"Vell! How goes it, me poy?" he asked, rubbing his hands together.

"I'm getting damned sick of it, Tikkey," the other growled, holding his drink up to the light. "What's this, more rot-gut?"

"It's some of my special whisky. Real Irish that is, mister. But you ain't yet answered my question: How goes it?"

"And I'm telling you I'm damned sick of it. I ain't had a real drunk since we started this damned game, and I've been living like a bally monk. The bally— Oh, hell! That's what I mean. I've been talking like a—dude so long I've forgotten how to talk any other—way. An' look at me get up! It's God's truth, Tikkey: I been propping me eye open so long with that blinkin'—*bleedin'*—piece of glass that I can't shut it at nights. I—"

"I ain't asking 'ow you feels, mister," Tikkey interposed sourly. "You ain't got no grounds fer complaint. I've fed yer vell and dressed yer—an' oy! How I've dressed yer! But all that's no never mind. Fer the third time I ask yer: How goes it?"

The other flinched slightly and was unable to meet Tikkey's basilisk stare.

He pointed to Frank Brunton who was talking earnestly to his dancing partner.

"That answers you, don't it?" he asked. "The kid don't like the women you keep here, Tikkey. But he's dancing with her because I told him to. I told him he might be able to get some information from her that 'ud help me. She'll keep him busy 'til I call him off. He'll do anything I tell him, for the present. But just the same he's getting restless; beginning to have doubts I'm the sort of man he thinks I am."

"Vell! Vat of it?" Tikkey rubbed his hands gleefully together. "You ain't, are yer? My vord! You an' the Major are as different as chalk an' cheese; you ain't any more alike, less than, a diamant an' a piece of filth. An' you ain't the diamant. You vouldn't be any good to me if you vas. I like you just as you are. Hell, yes. So the dear poy's getting restless, is he? Vell, vell! An' maybe you are too?"

"That's right, Tikkey. An' I'm wondering what my rake-off'll be. It ought to be a big 'un, considering all the risk I take."

"Risk!" Tikkey almost squealed his contempt. "Vot risk do you take? Not a penny of money do you risk. But me: I risk much. Free food an' drinks, an' clothes, an' lodgings I give you. Vhy! But for me, you'd be sleeping out on the veld. An' it's raining like 'ell. So much I give you, an' maybe I get nothing back."

"You'll get plenty back," the other grumbled. "I've done everything; it's my plan; I get the kid where we want him; I take the risk. An' you, you dirty little money-grinder, take all the profits."

"I'LL BE generous, my poy," Tikkey promised grandly, but the expression on his face, shaded from the other's observation, belied his words: Tikkey, a physical coward, never openly resented insults, but he generally made the insulter pay.

"I'll believe it when I see it," the other commented incredulously, adding. "Just the same, things wouldn't be so nice if the Major happened to show up. He don't like people borrowing his name."

"He ain't likely to come here, so vhy vorry? Besides, if he should come poking his nose vhere it ain't vanted, he'll get a knife in his gizzard afore he can get up to any of his monkey-shines. I've arranged with one of the girls to see to that. It's funny—" he chuckled evilly—"get the right kind of hold over a girl an' she'll do anything you tell her.

"So, you got no cause to vorry about the Major. All you got to do is keep your eye on Frankie. That's all. An' then, by day after tomorrow, we'll know where we're standing, eh? We'll be on our way to being rich. That's a good farm old Joburg Jane's got, but there's better stuff under the soil than she knows of, I'm gambling. An' if there ain't, we're sure to get enough out of her to clear expenses."

"An' over, blast you."

"Sure! Why so fierce? An' over, of course." Tikkey rose awkwardly to his feet. "I got to go an' talk with Jake now. Don't keep that monocle out of your eye too long or you'll be forgetting vot sort of a man you're supposed to be. Ta-ta, Mister Major."

He grinned derisively and insinuating his way through the dancers joined a thickset, red bearded Dutchman who was standing at the bar clamoring for a drink.

The man who, in order to win the admiration and confidence of young Brunton, was impersonating a renowned character of the diamond fields, glared resentfully after Tikkey.

"Wonder," his thoughts ran, "if it'ud be safe to double-cross the dirty fat swine? Suppose I went to Joburg Jane an' told her the tale, an' told that damn' young fool, Frank, all about it too. God! What a fool he is, acting up the way he does. At that, he comes by this dude pose easier than what I do. Comes natural to him, almost. Well, suppose I gave the game away, Joburg Jane ought to be damned grateful; reckon she'd treat me well. Probably I could get a couple of hundred quid from her and she'd be on hand to bleed any time I wanted more capital—which 'ud be often."

He licked his thin lips with wolfish greed and, for a while, let his fancies revel in an anticipation of the good times he could have on money obtained by blackmail.

Conscious, suddenly, that Tikkey's eyes were focussed on him, menacing him, seeming to read his inmost thoughts, he started uneasily. Instantly his dreams of luxurious ease vanished and, instead, his mind was filled with memory of the fate of others who had thought to double-cross Tikkey.

He shivered slightly, fixed his monocle in his eye and with an outward appearance of calm assurance watched the dancers.

The music ceased with a discordant crash and the dancers returned to their tables, talking and laughing noisily as if by noise they wished to prove that they were thoroughly enjoying themselves.

YOUNG BRUNTON, having ordered refreshment for his partner, bowed elaborately, ignoring her invitation to sit and drink with her, and rejoined his former companion.

There was a puzzled look of indecision in his eyes as he sat down at the table. Presently he laughed.

"What is it, old chap?" The other queried in an affectation of good humor.

"I was laughing at what that girl said—the girl I danced with."

The other looked at him sharply.

"Oh! And what did she say?"

"Why—er—that she was due to have a busy night if a certain party you reminded her of showed up, but she guessed she could stop any harm being done, at that I asked her how, and she said, 'Why, easy enough; I got orders to knife the Major before he can do anything.' And when I asked her what she meant and that if she planned to knife you she'd make a mistake in confiding in me, she looked at me oddly, then suddenly colored up, as if she were embarrassed, and said I wasn't to take any notice of what she said, that she was only spoofing. Oh, and before that, she said my mother came here this morning! My word! That's too funny! The idea of my mother coming to a place like this! She was looking for the Major and this girl sent her away to look for you on the veld. That puzzled me for a time, but I see it now. She was making a game of me. My word, yes!" He laughed heartily. "But where are you going?" he asked as the other rose to his feet.

"Just to have a few words with Tikkey; I'll be back in a moment."

He was back again, as he promised, in a very little while and they sat, in silence, sipping their drinks and staring with an assumption of boredom about the room.

Two men, two of Tikkey's bullies, went up to the girl who had been Brunton's partner and for a time the three conversed together, the girl shouting shrill refusals to the low-toned orders of the men. But presently she rose and walking between the two men—each had a firm, brutal grip of her wrist—made their way to the door of a room leading off the big one. There Tikkey joined them and the four passed on into the inner room.

As the door closed behind them the pianist commenced another noisy, jangling tune and the dancers took the floor again, singing raucously to augment the tinny tune of the piano; while those who preferred to sit and look on, stamped their feet and banged their glasses on the tables in order to accentuate the beat.

The din was overpowering, but the man who sat with Brunton seemed unconscious of it. To his ears, because he knew what to listen for, came the thud of a lash on naked flesh and the moans of a woman, muffled by a heavy, closed door. He smiled cruelly, knowing that Tikkey was rewarding, in his own peculiar way, the girl who had talked too much and far from wisely.

EVENTUALLY THE door opened again and Tikkey came into the room, escorting the girl with an air of paternal solicitude. On her cheeks were heavy tear marks. He took her back to her table, saw her seated, brought her a drink and then, after a few whispered instructions to which she listened apathetically, went back to the door leading to the inner room and motioned Brunton's companion to join him.

"Mister," he said as that man lounged lazily up to him, "ain't you got no brains at all. What are you hanging about here for? Get under cover, quick; an' take that Brunton kid with you."

"But what for?" The other protested.

"Because, you fool, seeing as that fool girl Belle sent Joburg Jane out to the Major's camp—an' Jane all ready to raise hell—I wouldn't be a bit surprised if the Major don't pay us a visit."

"What if he does? You say you got it fixed for Belle to take care of him. But maybe she ain't to be trusted now, and—"

"*Ach!* Just like a fool you talk! She'll obey orders now, the fool! She's had her lesson. And even if she did fall down, there's plenty of others ready to do a bit of knife sticking in return for a bottle of whisky. But that ain't it. Suppose the Major turns up an' the kid sees him! Vell! The kid knows right avay vich of you two's the Major; it ain't going to take him more than two-three minutes to tell the real Major from the false. Vell! An' that means he ain't a-goin' to play with you any more, ain't it? Who the hell's that?" He broke off suddenly.

As Tikkey spoke the street door opened and a rain soaked man stood swaying on the threshold blinking owlishly at the lights.

"Only a drunk *kopjie* walloper," the pseudo-Major said contemptuously. "Better kick him out Tikkey. He don't look as if he had the price of a drink on him."

As if answering the statement he could not have possibly overheard, the newcomer slammed the door behind him and swaggered up to the bar.

"All the drinks on me," he invited hoarsely. "What'll you have?"

Men and women crowded about him, shouting their thirsty desires. But the barmaids made no move to serve the thirsty ones; instead they looked contemptuously at the newcomer: Tikkey had trained them well. They wanted to see the color of the generous stranger's money before they poured out the drinks.

And presently, now that all the bar's habitues were looking at him significantly, the bedrabbled one realized what was expected of him.

"Hell!" He bellowed loudly. "Think I ain't goot for it, eh? That's a good 'un. Me—I'm I.B.D. Owen—maybe you've heard of me, maybe you haven't. And if you haven't, look at me well 'cause you're going to know me a lot afore I'm done with this *dorp*. Hey! Do you think that'll pay for a round of drinks?"

From a small canvas bag he extracted a stone about the size of a marble and flicked it into the hands of one of the barmaids.

"Do you think that'll pay for a round of drinks, hey?" He asked again, winking at those around her, stowing the canvas bag carefully into the breast pocket of his tattered coat. "And there's a plenty more where that came from. I buy diamonds cheap. Yeh! I buy diamonds. See? That's my nickname: I.B.D. And if you switch the letters round some to I.D.B. you won't offend me none."

TIKKEY CAME up to the bar and under cover of the loud laughter which greeted Owen's labored wit, examined the stone and whispered instructions to the bar-maid.

When the drinks were served he took his stand next to Owen and grinned ingratiatingly at him.

"That'll pay for two more rounds yet," he shouted. "I'm fair, I am. I give good value always. No stinting about Tikkey."

"No," growled the man who called himself Owen. "You're—generous. That stone's worth two or three hundred quid, easy. So, as you say, it'll pay for two more rounds, all right. However—"

He shrugged his shoulders and, taking a bottle of whisky from the counter, retired with it to a table on the opposite side of the room. Sitting there, he drank with noisy ostentation and glared insultingly at Brunton and that man's evil genius.

They ignored him, and this seemed to anger him for presently he rose and lurched over to their table.

"And who the hell are you pretty darlings?" He hiccupped. "What are you sitting here for like stuffed dummies. Why ain't you drinking my health? You—!" He struck the self styled Major across the cheek with the palm of his hand and laughed harshly as the man cringed.

Young Brunton looked in amazement at his companion, wondering that his ideal should submit so tamely to such an insulting blow.

He rose to his feet.

"If you're wise, my good fellow," he said firmly. "You'll get down on your knees and apologize. The gentleman you have insulted is the Major. Maybe you've heard of him."

"Gor lumme!" Owen exclaimed. "You don't say? The Major—an' me playing with death, I was!" He held out his hand. "Shake Major an' let's be friends. Us I.D.B.'s ought to stick together. You do things your way an' I do things my way. But the end's the same, ain't it? We get the stones. I'll gamble we do."

He held out his hand, a grimy, mud-encrusted hand.

Hesitatingly the other responded to the gesture.

"Yep." Continued I.B.D. Owen, retaining his grip on the other's hand. "I've always wanted to meet you, Major. I've heard a lot about you. Ain't you the man what got some niggers to swallow some stones, so's you could smuggle 'em out of the compound, and then cut the niggers open to get the stones out? Sure you are. Smart trick that—an' dead niggers tell no tales. An'—ain't you the man—"

He related with great gusto, incident after brutal incident; stories of the I.D.B. fraternity, stories of callous cruelty, of honorless men, of white-livered cowards. And the leading role of all these stories he attributed to the man whose hand he held in a firm relentless pressure.

The narrative was finally halted by a scream of pain and helpless rage.

"Let go of my hand, you great oaf!" the "Major" wailed. "You're breaking my fingers; you're—"

"Blimey!" I.B.D. Owen exclaimed reproachfully as he released his hold and, with wondering eyes, watched the other massage his numbed hand. "Blimey! I was only just pressing a little."

"Pressing, you damn' fool! You—"

Then, catching Tikkey's warning eye the speaker rose hastily.

"Come along, Brunton old chap," he drawled slowly. "We'll toddle along an' leave this chappie to stew in his juice. He's filthy!"

He led the way out of the place followed closely by the youngster, on whose face was a look of relief that his hero was at last acting up to true form. At the same time Brunton was puzzled; his loyalty had been shaken by the things he had just heard and seen. There were a number of things he meant to ask the Major, and, if that man failed to answer them to his satisfaction, he intended to go no further with the scheme they were planning.

I.B.D. OWEN, laughing noisily, returned to his table and there was joined by Tikkey. "What's the idea?" he growled. "That fool ain't the Major. An' you know it as well as I do."

Tikkey looked keenly at him.

"Then you know the Major—not?"

"Course I know the bloody hound! He's crossed my path too many times. But he's too *slim* for me to lay hands on. Up to now, that is. Up to now!"

"You don't seem to be friendly toward the Major, Mister."

"I ain't, and neither, I take it, are you. So, come on now, tell me the lay of the game. What's that fool playing the Major for? And who's the kid he's got in tow?"

Tikkey rubbed his hands briskly together.

"Let's have a drink," he said. "Talking's dry work."

He poured out two drinks. A big one for his companion; barely a swallow for himself.

"Maybe, mister," he resumed presently, "maybe you've got some diamonds to sell."

I.B.D. Owen's hand instinctively clutched at his breast pocket.

"Maybe. Maybe not," he growled.

"You better let me keep 'em for you," Tikkey said persuasively. "It ain't safe to carry 'em about like you do. Suppose a detective should take it in his head to search you? Why, you'd be booked for a long stay at the breakwater. Better give 'em to me. I'll take care of 'em for you. Have another drink!"

They emptied their glasses once again.

"Look here," said I.B.D. Owen after a moment's heavy thought, "the stones I got in here—" he produced his canvas bag and tossed it on the table—"ain't worth a damn. They're mostly borts. I just carry them around so's I can pay my way. Take 'em if you want 'em. They're no never mind to me."

He grinned as he watched Tikkey empty the contents of the bag on to the table. He laughed softly as Tikkey, after one swift, appraising glance, picked them up and returned them to the bag which he pocketed.

"It's as you say, Mister," Tikkey sniggered. "They ain't worth much. Them as ain't splints are off-colored an' no size."

His tone was casual, yet inwardly he was elated for amongst the "stones" was one of value.

"Never mind them." Owen's voice matched the casualness of Tikkey's. "I reckon you can feed and booze me for a time in return. Later we'll talk about bigger stones. I've got a big parcel safely cached out on the veld. But you ain't answered my question about this fool who's aping the Major. What's the game? Let me in on it. Maybe I can help you."

Tikkey looked at him dubiously, thumbing his thick, protruding, lower lip.

"You're a fool if you don't take me in with you," the other continued. "But you don't have to tell me anything. I can guess a lot. Come to think of it, that youngster favors Joburg Jane. He's the dead spittin' image of her; damn me if he ain't. You remember Jane, don't you? Ah, yes! I sees you do. And Jane's goin' straight now and she's well off. Might be possible to do a little blackmailing there, eh?"

"It's you vot's guessing," Tikkey replied ponderously. "I ain't saying a 'yes' or 'no.'"

"It's 'yes' all right," the other said confidently. "But that dolled up fool—Blake's his real name, ain't it? He's the man who split on 'Red' Rankin an' got him put away. Squealed on his pal, he did, and cleared off with all the takings. And he'll do the same with you, Tikkey. I don't want anything out of this play you're making, but I'd like to get even with the chap who split on my pal Red Rankin."

Tikkey thoughtfully pulled his bottom lip.

"BLAKE'S GETTING too big for his boots, Mister, an' his mouth's too noisy. He'll be getting me into trouble if I ain't careful. Maybe you can help me, maybe not. We'll see. The Reef gang are running a parcel of diamonds day after tomorrow. Blake an' the kid's goin' to hold 'em up. Robbing the robbers, see. That's all. Vell! Supposin' you take a hand an' see as Blake don't run off with the parcel. 'Course, I shall have men watchin' him too. I'll be on hand meself. But supposing you should find a vay of putting a bullet through his brain, vhy, I'd considered you'd elected yourself a member of the club I'm running."

He laughed harshly.

The other frowned.

"I'll take you up on that," he said slowly, "only I got to have something more to go on. Where's this hold-up goin' to take place?"

"That, Mister," Tikkey grunted as he rose to his feet, "is something for you to find out. It'll be good exercise for your wits, not? S'long!"

He waved his pudgy hands and made his way across the room to where a group of men and women argued noisily.

The other sat for a while, toying with his drink, then rose, lurched his way to the door and passed out into the night.

The rain had ceased; the sky glowed with the light of a million stars; the air was clean, invigorating.

The man inhaled deeply, luxuriously. Then he straightened himself and, walking fast, made a bee-line for his camp on the veld; the camp of the Major.

"I must have a talk with Mrs. Brunton," he muttered as he walked. "Must calm her fears. By Jove, yes! And tomorrow I'll have Jim scout about with his ears open. It's remarkable what the old lad can pick up in the way of inside information. Yes, indeed. An', come to think of it, I'll do a bit of scouting myself. 'Pon my soul, yes."

FROM THE south of the town crawled a wagon, loaded with *kaffir* trade truck, drawn by sixteen oxen. An undersized, pockmarked native, the "leader," walked ahead of the span. He was naked, save for a scanty loin-cloth. In his left hand he held the leading reins, in his right, over his shoulders, a bunch of knobkerries. He suggested, above all things, a hunter; his roving eyes were on the lookout for game to kill.

On the driver's seat sat an uncouth Dutchman who occasionally flourished his enormous whip and shouted harsh, guttural expletives at the slow plodding oxen. But for the most part he sat dourly silent, scanning the veld ahead of him.

The morning dew was still on the grass, a white mist shrouded the far distant hills, the sun was not yet above the horizon, but rising fast. Everything was very calm, peaceful, the veld seemed deserted, void of all life.

Occasionally small game and birds were flushed by the native. He always gave chase to them, throwing his knob-kerries at them, crowing with delight whenever his aim proved true. Then, recovering his sticks, he would return soberly to the place at the head of the oxen. Strangely he never retrieved the game he knocked down. Apparently he killed for the sheer love of killing.

THE SUN rose, dispelling the mist. For a little while the grasses steamed then snapped dryly as the wagon passed on.

An hour passed, two.

The Diamondtown was no longer in sight, hidden by the billows of the seemingly flat veld.

Ahead, to the right, to the left, was only a yellow-red expanse of dreariness; a dreariness accentuated by the dump and ruined hovels of some long since deserted mine which presently, as the wagon tipped a slight rise, appeared close at hand.

"*Pas op!*" Almost coinciding with the Dutchman's "Take care" warning, the native apparently flushed a small buck, for with excited shouts he threw his knobkerries into a clump of grass.

The last one had barely left his hand when two men, Blake and young Brunton, both elaborately dressed, rose from their hiding place backing up their command to halt with the threat of leveled revolvers.

The native, with the fatalistic resignation of his race, squatted silently on his haunches whilst the Dutchman stared at the two in resentful silence.

"Come on now, Van Hess," Blake said irritably. "You know what we're after, Hand over."

The Dutchman spat.

"Almighty!" he said. "If you know what you want, come and get it. You are so *slim:* Maybe it is my trade goods you want."

Blake laughed.

"Yes. They're trade goods, all right. But not the kind you sell to niggers, but the kind you buy from them. But to hell with all this chatter. I know you, and you know me. I know you're running a parcel of diamonds out of the country, and I want them. Do you give 'em to me, or do I have to look for 'em?"

The Dutchman shrugged his shoulders. "I am in no hurry," he said. "It is no use telling you I have no *gonivas* (stolen stones); you would not believe me. *So-a!* Outspan, Hans."

The native jumped to his feet.

"Tie up that nigger, Brunton." Blake ordered. "And you Van Hess, you sit still."

"Almighty! There is no need for you to get mad, man. I was only going to outspan. I am in no hurry and can as well wait here while you look for what you want as anywhere else."

Blake scowled angrily.

"Tie the nigger to the wheel, Brunton," he said harshly, "and don't be so—squeamish. Pull the ropes till they cut into the rascal's flesh."

Brunton, white faced, shaking with nervousness and distaste of his task, made a feeble protest, which Blake silenced with a curse.

"Now you, Van Hess," Blake continued, "get down. And mind I'm watching you. Stand with your face to the hind wheel, your hands stretched out. That's it. Now lash him up, too, Brunton."

"Are we going to search the wagon now, Major?" Brunton asked breathlessly.

"No, you fool!" Blake answered roughly. "It'd take the best part of a day to go through that lot of stuff. Besides, the 'parcel' we're after may not be in the wagon at all. The nigger may have swallowed some, or Van Hess. Or maybe they've hid 'em in the oxen somehow. There's ways of hiding stones you'd never dream of. No. We don't waste time searching."

"Then we give this lot up?" Brunton said hopefully.

"Like hell we do! We're going to make Van Hess, or the nigger, tell us where they've hidden 'em. On second thoughts I don't reckon it's any good questioning the nigger; he ain't likely to know anything. So we'll confine our attentions to Van Hess—unless you want to give the nigger a few for love."

AS BRUNTON stared at him in puzzled wonder he laughed and, picking up Van Hess' driving whip, lashed the Dutchman across the shoulders, cutting through his thick flannel shirt, drawing blood.

Van Hess yelled at the pain of the lash, Brunton looked as if he were going to be sick.

A second and a third blow followed the first.

"You can't do this sort of thing, Major," Brunton protested disgustedly. "It isn't done. It's—"

"Shut up! Van Hess! You damned Dutchman! Where've you hidden the stones?"

He made the whip whistle about the Dutchman's head.

"Almighty!" Van Hess was almost sobbing. "Some day you shall answer to me for this."

"Where's the parcel?" Again the lash cut into Van Hess' back.

"It—you *verdoemte gonoph*—is in the water keg."

Blake grinned.

"Get it!" he said, turning to Brunton.

Quickly Brunton obeyed and a few minutes later, having knocked in the top of a water keg he had found in the wagon, he handed to Blake a chamois leather bag bulging with "stones."

Blake emptied them onto the palm of his hand, examined them swiftly, then returned them to the bag—all but one, the largest, which he cleverly palmed—and tossed the bag to Brunton.

"You keep it, kid," he said. "And now let's get our horses."

"But you're not going to leave these two tied up like this, surely?"

"Why not? Someone's sure to be along soon and set 'em free. Now, come on."

He led the way at a run toward the deserted mine.

TEN MINUTES later they rounded the dump where two horses were tethered. "You go and get the packs while I saddle up," Blake ordered.

Obediently Brunton went over to one of the tumbled down shacks and opening the door entered.

The door forcefully closed behind him and, blinking with astonishment, he found himself confronted by two men in uniform while Tikkey Isaacs, leering triumphantly, hovered in the background.

Before he could make any move to escape or to shout a warning Brunton was bound, gagged, and searched.

With a squeal of delight Tikkey pounced on the bag of stones.

"This is mine, officers," he cried. "This is what them other thieves stole from me; an' the Major an' this youngster stole it from the thieves, an' now it comes back to me. Vell, vell. That's as it should be."

Brunton glared at Tikkey, but could say nothing. In a way, he was not at all distressed by the predicament in which he found himself. This, he thought, was the sort of problem which would show the Major up in his real colors. With much inward contentment, he waited for his idol to appear and neatly turn the tables on his captors. That was just the sort of thing which the Major was famed for.

He had not long to wait.

Footsteps sounded outside and Blake's voice shouting, "Hurry up, Brunton. Have you gone to sleep in there?"

Then the door opened and Blake entered.

"What's the meaning of this?" He gasped.

"Simply," replied one of the uniformed men, "simply that this *yonker* is an I.D.B. We've caught him with the goods."

Blake nodded.

" 'Course I'm not surprised," he said. "I warned you about him, didn't I, Tikkey? The silly young fool! Well, well! He'll get a long stretch at the breakwater unless his mother comes across with a little palm oil; eh, officers? But here—what's the idea?" This last exclamation was one of indignation as the two men commenced to search him thoroughly.

"It's alright, Mister." Tikkey said soothingly. "You've been with this youngster and he might have slipped a stone in your pocket."

"Gee—he has!" One of the uniformed men handed Tikkey the stone Blake had held out from the bag. "The cunning devil!"

Blake swore and looked nervously at Tikkey.

"Oh, that's all right, my boy." Tikkey said soothingly. "You're innocent. I know that. You ain't no I.D.B. But it's a good job I had you searched, ain't it?" He laughed loudly. "Now you," he continued, addressing the two uniformed men, "you take young Brunton into the back room an' put the fear of God into him whilst me an' the Major here have a little business talk."

As he spoke he emptied the stones from the bag onto a black velvet cloth he took from his pocket and, spreading it out carefully on the ground sat down with a grunt of satisfaction.

"Yah!" he exclaimed. "Now we can talk, Mister. And, first of all, let me say I don't like the vay you tried to hold a stone out on me."

"An' let me tell you, Tikkey, I don't like the way you're talking."

The two men glared at each other and Blake's hand rested near the butt of his revolver.

SHORTLY AFTER the departure of Blake and Brunton from the wagon the Major, smiling, debonair, rode up on his black stallion.

With exclamations of concern he dismounted and cut loose the two men—the Dutchman and Hans.

"I am sorry I am late," he said to Van Hess. "I knew those chappies were after you and I meant to forestall them. But-er—I was unavoidably detained. I suppose they got what they were after?"

"*Ja!*" Van Hess replied stolidly as he climbed into the wagon. "But it is all no matter. Today, for them; tomorrow for me. Let us trek, Hans."

"Yah, *Baas!*" the native replied. "But first I get my knob-kerries."

"Move quickly then, you black rascal," And, turning to the Major, Van Hess continued: "I'm too soft with my niggers. I let them do as they like. So much time I waste because Hans there—" he pointed to the native who was searching in the long grass for his knobkerries—"is always playing the hunter—throwing his sticks at anything that lives. The *schelm! Pas op* Hans!"

"Ready, *Baas.* Only one more stick—the big one to find. Ah! Here it is. Now we can trek, *Baas.*"

With his bundle of knobkerries over his shoulder he placed himself at the head of the span of oxen.

The Dutchman's big whip cracked, and the interrupted trek was resumed.

The Major stood motionless and watched the wagon until it passed out of sight, hidden by a dip in the veld.

Then he whistled softly and Jim, the Hottentot appeared, grinning widely, as suddenly as if materialized from thin air.

"It was very easy, *Baas*. And all was just as you said."

The Major nodded absently.

"What now, *Baas?*" Jim continued.

"Go back to my camp, Jim, and tell the white woman I will be with her soon—bringing her son with me."

"Yah, *Baas*. And the stones?"

"Keep them until I ask for them. Now—"

"Be careful, *Baas*," Jim warned, and started off across the veld at a steady, space destroying jog-trot.

The Major waited until Jim was a good mile distant then he mounted and rode slowly up to the mine.

There he dismounted and crept noiselessly up to the shack from which sounded the voices of men raised in heated altercation.

"This is better luck than I had any right to expect," the Major muttered. "If I wait, they'll probably do my work for me."

He listened intently.

"I tell you, Tikkey," Blake was saying hoarsely, "that I've played straight with you. Them are the stones I got from Van Hess. If they're false 'uns, then let me get after Van Hess an' I'll make him pay for putting a trick like that over on me."

"Is it likely," Tikkey's voice sneeringly answered, "is it likely I'm goin' to let you go until you've told me where you've hidden the real parcel? Is it likely now, you double-crossing—!"

"And I tell you I'm playing straight, Tikkey! Use sense. That stone I held out now—you say that's false, too. Well, don't that show you? Look here—" a note of suspicion now showed in his voice—"how do I know you ain't trying to double-cross me. I don't believe it. I ain't examined 'em closely—didn't have a chance before an' you've kept your paws on 'em since. They looked good enough to me."

"Sure! They look alright. But see here."

AND THE MAJOR, peering through a crack in the door saw Tikkey smash a stone into powder with a blow of the butt of his revolver.

"And you can do that to all of them," Tikkey remarked. "Now then: hand over the real 'uns an' let's talk business."

"An' I tell you you've got the parcel I got from Van Hess. An' you've switched 'em you double-crossing Jew. You—!"

"Pete! Snyder!" Tikkey's call was one of fear.

A shot sounded, the fall of a heavy body, another shot— then two in quick succession.

Revolver in hand, the Major burst into the shack, almost pitching headlong over the prostrate, lifeless body of Blake.

Recovering himself, he saw two men in uniform, smoking revolvers in their hands, bending over Tikkey.

They straightened themselves at the Major's terse command.

"Well, well, my dear lads," he continued. "So you kept your uniforms when you were discharged from the force, eh? And now what?"

They looked sheepishly at each other. Merely Tikkey's watchdogs, they at least had the good sense not to endeavor to match their wits against the Major's.

"Blake shot Tikkey, and Tikkey shot Blake—they killed each other," one muttered.

"Very convenient, very," the Major murmured. "And so the world is rid of two most horrid villains. Well—that is only just. And now, if you're wise, you two gentlemen will make yourselves very scarce. Yes, I should leave the district entirely if I were you. You might find it hard to convince the real police, who are on their way here, that you did not murder these two men. You see, the fact that you are wearing a uniform you're not entitled to— What I mean is, the police chappies are very touchy about things like that."

"We're going, Major," one of the men said. "Come on, Snyder." And they hurriedly left the place, mounted their horses which were hidden in another shack and spurred swiftly over the veld.

The Major stooped over Tikkey, saw that he still gripped his revolver. Aiming it through the open doorway he pressed the trigger twice.

"That'll do to explain why Blake's got three bullets in him. And if I leave the stones where they are, that'll make the police think they fought over the division of the spoils. And they did. Most horridly. Of course what happened, I suppose, was this. Tikkey called for his two bullies, and Blake gets in his first shot which fells. Tikkey. Then Tikkey, in a sort of dying muscular contraction fires a shot which, by chance wounds Blake and Tikkey's two men finish him off.

"Well, all that's not worth thinking of. Just the same I'm glad it happened that way. I rather funked the idea of killing them myself. And I would have had to in order to free Mrs. Brunton of the fear of blackmail.

"Oh, well! Never would killing have been more justified. And now for young Brunton. The silly young ass!"

THE SUN was nearing its setting. Young Brunton and Jim, the Hottentot, were saddling the horses on which the Bruntons were presently going to ride back to their homestead.

The Major and Mrs. Brunton were standing by the tent.

"I can never thank you enough, Major," she was saying. "And Frank will thank you some day."

"You think," the Major drawled, "that he's cured of wanting to be a famous I.D.B.?"

She nodded confidently.

"He was ready to back out, I think, when Blake flogged Van Hess. By the time Tikkey framed that arrest on him he was sick of it all. But it was the way you talked to him afterward—"

"After all," the Major demurred, "I did nothing."

She laughed softly.

"I know better. But there, I can't talk of that now. Look! They're ready. Good-by, Major, and—God bless you!" He bowed.

A few minutes later they had mounted and had ridden off.

He sat down moodily in a deck chair, cursing himself, calling himself a quixotic fool.

Tomorrow the boat sailed from Cape Town and he would not be on it. He would have to spend yet another Christmas on the veld alone!

He cursed again.

Jim, good old Jim, was preparing the evening meal.

Perhaps it was just as well he was not going home. Jim could not have stood the cold, damp English houses.

And yet—Christmas! Carol singers, holly, youngsters laughing, plum pudding!

"Oh, Major!"

He looked up with a start. Mrs. Brunton had returned.

He rose and waited for her to continue.

"I'd forgotten," she said breathlessly, "I'm giving a big party at Christmas. All the young people for miles round will be there. We'll have all the old dances on. You'll come, won't you?"

"You'll have plum pudding?" he asked anxiously, "with brandy sauce?"

"Of course—yes," she laughed. "And snapdragon and everything."

He took a deep breath.

"Then I'll come. Thanks most awfully." She waved her hand, and rode off again. The Major returned to his chair, singing softly.

Presently he called, *"O'he'*, Jim!"

The Hottentot came running to him.

"You wanted the stones, *Baas?*"

"Yes, Jim."

"They are in the wagon, *Baas.* I will get them."

"No—never mind, Jim. They are good stones, Jim?"

"Yah, *Baas.* Twenty of them, all of good color and size. It was clever of the *Baas* to know they were hidden in the hollowed head of one of the knobkerries. *Wo-we!* And the right one was not hard to find. The stones rattled in it. I found it whilst the man Blake and that other tied up the Dutchman and his 'boy.' The top screwed off, *Baas.* I took out the 'stones' and put in pebbles in their place. *Wo-we!* There will be much trouble for the Dutchman by an' by."

They both laughed at the thought.

THEN SAID the Major, in a slow affected drawl, speaking his thoughts aloud, addressing them to Jim although that man understood but a scattered word in a hundred:

"It's quite a bally problem, really it is. Undoubtedly the stones are stolen ones. Van Hess' crowd bought them from natives who stole them from their *Baas'* claims; and I—

er—pinched them from Van Hess—just as Blake, had he had any brains, would have pinched them. And it doesn't really alter the fact that no one can possibly know the legal owners of these stones. Actually, I doubt if the legal owners know they've lost any stones from their claims. If I keep them, I'm a bally thief. And there you are."

He shrugged his shoulders.

"There seems only one thing to do and that—hand them over to the police and claim a reward. Yes. I think I might safely do that—my word yes. And quite ethical, too. But I'll bargain for the reward first an' insist on it being a healthy one. My word, yes. An' with the proceeds we'll take a trip to Jo'burg an' do a little Christmas shopping. And what do you say to that, Jim, you grinning heathen?"

"Me!" exclaimed Jim with a start. "If I don't see you, s'long! Golly damme yes."

"An' that's that," said the Major with a chuckle.

A SOUTHERN
CROSS

"**JIM**," **SAID** the Major, his dejected tones ill fitting his dudish attire and appearance, "I'm broke. Not a bally copper to my name or a friend to turn to. Broke and fed up. That describes me to a T. Of course, it'd be possible, maybe, to swell the depleted exchequer, as it were, by breaking the well known law an' buyin'—to sell—a few diamonds *sub rosa,* as it were. But I'm sick of playing the giddy goat with the law. So that leaves me in my original state of bankruptcy. Eh, Jim?" The Hottentot looked doubtfully at his *Baas.* He hadn't understood a word his *Baas* had said, but he gathered from that man's tone that he was worried. Consequently, Jim, too, was worried.

"Golly damme, yes, no. Hell!" he exclaimed. Jim's knowledge of English was neither refined nor extensive.

The Major sighed and looked vacantly over the veld.

A mile or so distant, to the south, sprawled the tin-roofed buildings of a typical South African mining town. It seemed unreal, an ugly phantasy of a town, as it trembled in the heat haze. The thud of the stamps at the mine sounded very loud and near; the metallic *tot-tot-tot-tot* impinged on the eardrums with a maddening force.

Save for the Major's animals and the crude township—and that added to the general air of desolation—there was no sign of life in any direction. Only the bare, treeless veld, a waste of land over which sand-devils constantly hovered. It was encircled by an unbroken line of distance-blued hills, giving it the appearance of a gigantic basin—a dust smothered basin from which there was no escape.

The Major sighed again and scowled at the tent-topped wagon which had been his home for so many years. That wagon, or ones similar to it, had been practically his only lodging in all the years he and Jim had roved up and down the face of Africa. That wagon, the goods it contained, the sixteen mules and the coal-black horse which grazed nearby, represented the sum total of the Major's wealth.

"A poor showing," he reflected bitterly. "I'm only a degree removed from a Sundowner, God help me!"

He started slightly at the sound of his voice. He had not realized that he had uttered his thoughts aloud.

The Hottentot who was squatting on his haunches by the side of the Major's chair, read in his *Baas'* tone the despair and self-disgust expressed by the words. He gently patted the white man's booted foot.

"We have lived, we two, *Baas!*" he said softly in the vernacular. "We have lived—and lived well. There should be no regrets. We have met death face to face many times and have not known fear. At least, we have not whined to the Spirits to save us. We have paid our way and fought our way. *Au-a!* When old age comes to us and we talk of our deeds, the young men will exclaim, 'Truly they are men amongst men!'"

THE MAJOR fixed a monocle in his eye and, in so doing, masked his bitterness of expression, appeared a care-free, brainless fop.

"It is more likely, Jim," he said—and his accent in the native language was as pure as the Hottentot's, "that they'll say, 'All old men are boasters and liars.' "

"Even if old age turns my bones to water," Jim vowed grimly, "I should rise up to deal with such ill-mannered ones. But why is the *Baas* sad?"

"Because—because—I don't know, Jim. Maybe it is a desire for the things I have not."

"And what have you not, *Baas?*"

"Everything, Jim."

"*Tchat!* What folly," the Hottentot scolded. "You have strength. Even I, who am no weakling am as a child in your hands. You have friends. Where can you go and not find men, white and black, whose faces do not light with joy when they see you? The veld and its people is an open book to you. *Au-a!* You can do all things, and do them well. I say you have everything."

"I am a wanderer on the face of the earth, Jim. I have no habitation."

"*Wo-we!*" Jim was evidently greatly disgusted. "If it is a hut you desire, if you desire to be one of a herd and fill your lungs with air poisoned by a multitude—then there is no answer."

"I am a beggar, Jim. I—"

"If your heart is set on a store of yellow dirt—and gold *is* dirt, *Baas*—I can as you know, show you plenty. If you desire diamonds—they are only worthless stones—there is that place we know of in the desert."

"What pleasure, Jim, in wealth so acquired? No; words are useless, It now comes to me that I have wasted my life."

Jim considered thoughtfully.

"I am now thinking," he said slowly, "of the things you have done that others might know happiness. With words they thanked you, *Baas,* little realizing that the deed itself was your reward. And now it comes to me that it would be well considered if we returned to first one of these, then another—and another—until the game sickens you. *Au-a!* We will go to them as beggars, needing help. We will inflict ourselves on them and, *Baas,* we will mark the depths of their gratitude."

The Major opened his eyes wide and, as he looked up at Jim in astonishment, his monocle dropped from his eye, shattering to pieces at his feet.

"By Jove," he exclaimed as he fished absently in the breast pocket of his tunic for another monocle. "By Jove—" he screwed the new one into place—"you're a bloomin' A number one at Lloyds psychologist, Jim, old lad. 'Pon my soul, you are. You've diagnosed my complaint and prescribed a cure: I'm just a bally infant needing jam on my bread, wanting to be appreciated. My word, yes, And I'm a bloomin' egotistical ass suffering from a sense of inferiority; I'm cryin' to be assured I'm not a bally failure. So, old lad, devoted companion of my wanderings, and so forth, we'll do the blinkin' Arabian Night's stuff. We'll do the Caliph business, you know—only of course you don't know—and go up an' down the earth to find out what men really think of us. So let's away, Jim. Who's the first on our callin' list?"

Jim looked bewildered, for, of course, he understood not one word of the Major's excited acceptance of his plan. But he knew that the prospect of something definite to do which appealed to the Major's love of play-acting—and therein was demonstrated the Eternal Boy which is part of all true men—had put to flight his *Baas'* mournful, introspective mood. And, realizing this, though ever so vaguely, Jim's bewilderment was a happy one.

"Golly, damn my eyes, yes, no," he exclaimed with a chuckle.

THE MAJOR had jumped to his feet and was inhaling deeply, expanding his barrel-like chest and flexing his muscles. His eyes sparkled and the strong lines of his clean-shaven face completely gave the lie to his pose of inanity.

The veld about him seemed, of a sudden, to live. The distant hills were no longer a forbidding, unclimbable hedge, no longer hemmed him in. They beckoned to him, inviting him to surmount them.

"The *Baas* says?" Jim queried. And he, too, rose. His was a squat, but abnormally powerful figure: in a sense, a misshapen figure clad in cast-off garments of the Major which were too big for him, save that the sleeves were far too short and the seams of the coat were strained almost to the point of bursting. A ludicrous figure, topped off by a wound-scarred, broad-nosed, thick-lipped face. An ugly face; but in the dark eyes shone a light of great devotion which, somehow, lighted up his whole countenance.

The Major looked at him affectionately. They had starved together and feasted together, and the understanding which existed between them discounted color—yet never broke down the bars. The Major was always the *Baas,* the white man, who could do no wrong. In all things he was a man. And Jim, the Hottentot, never presumed, yet never cringed. His skin was black; he maybe belonged to an inferior order, but he, too, was a man.

The Major turned to him.

"I was just saying, Jim, that your words dripped wisdom. Where do we go first?"

Jim scratched his woolly thatch.

"We could go," he said slowly, "to that *dorp*." With a jerk of his broad thumb he indicated the mining town.

"What do you know, you old heathen?" the Major protested uneasily.

"Only that yesterday the *Baas* had much money, and today, after a visit to the *dorp*, he has nothing. Therefore— But that may be forgotten. The *Baas* may have lost his money and did not give it to some one whose need seemed greater than his own. But no matter. We will not go there. It is the act of a child to give today and desire to take back on the morrow. So I say, in order that we may see how long the memories of men are, we will go to the country of Magato."

The Major was silent for a moment, recalling memories of that wily old chief whose fabled calabash-full of diamonds had attracted adventurers—the Major amongst them—to his country.

"We have hunted and been hunted in Magato's country, Jim," the Major said presently. "But I do not recall anything that gives us a claim on Magato's gratitude."

"*Wo-we!*" The Hottentot laughed derisively. "That may be. Yet I think of Magato's only son who, but for you, would have been killed by evil white men at the place of the mines."

"Oh, that!" the Major interposed contemptuously.

"And I think," Jim continued steadily, ignoring the interruption, "of the time when Magato almost lost his country through the cunning of the Portuguese. *Au-a!* He would have lost it, and his people would be now groaning because of labor forced upon them and taxes to be paid, had not my *Baas'* wisdom shown Magato a way out. And then I think— But *tchat!* I have said enough."

"Truly you have, Jim. So let us trek and put my folly to the test."

HALF AN hour later the sixteen mules were harnessed to the wagon and Jim, seated beside his *Baas* on the driver's seat, was amusing himself with testing the suppleness of his long-stocked driving whip.

The mules were dancing excitedly, and the horse, tethered to the tail board of the wagon, reared playfully. It seemed as if the animals sensed the long miles before them and were anxious to be off.

The Major took a firmer grip of the reins and braced his feet against the footboard. But he still hesitated. The mood of elation had passed; doubts again troubled him.

"Already, *Baas?*" Jim prompted anxiously.

"Yes, Jim." The answer came tonelessly.

Jim rose to his feet, gripping his whip in two hands.

"Ah, there! *Treck jou!*" he cried and the whip *cracked* over the heads of the two leaders, recoiled and flicked the sterns of the wheelers.

The mules moved off at a trot; the trot became a canter and, in a short space, the mules were galloping at breakneck speed over the veld, heading north, and requiring all the Major's craft to keep them to the line.

The veld was dotted with boulders and stumps of trees; it was crisscrossed by water-worn gullies. The wagon swayed precariously to and fro, tilting like a ship in a heavy sea.

Gradually the Major's face brightened and when, by a superhuman effort, he swung the pace-maddened mules cleverly around a gaping hole—and abandoned mine shaft—he laughed gaily at Jim's well feigned cry of fear.

THAT EVENING they outspanned at the foot of the hills, in a green valley knee-high with lush grass. A rippling stream gurgled its way down the center of the valley, winding, doubling back on itself, leaping over boulders. It had its birth in some hidden spring high up in the hills and, cascading down, laced the black rocks with the gossamer thread of its spray.

Darkness swiftly followed the fading of sunset's crimson afterglow from the western sky. Then, presently, sprinkling the black velvet canopy of night with phosphorescent dust, the stars appeared.

The wind soughed softly, rustling the grass and the air was laden with sleep inducing scents distilled from sun's cleanliness.

The Major, his bed a sweet smelling pile of cut grass, stared dreamily up at the sky. Subconsciously, he was searching for that constellation which symbolizes the yearning, the call to the veld, which Africa's white children know if once they stray from her.

"In a sense," he murmured contentedly, apostrophizing four kindly stars, "you're bally frauds. You're not over-brilliant, an' a chappy needs to stretch his imagination a lot to see that you form a Cross. Just the same, the sky would seem very empty and meaningless without you."

A few minutes later he was fast asleep.

BACK IN the private bar of the little mining settlement's only hotel, two men were discussing, idly enough, the fact of the Major's departure.

"It's a fact," the tubby, flaxen haired little man was saying. "My nigger saw them go. He says the Major drove off as if the devil or the police were after him."

"It must have been the devil," the other commented. "He wouldn't run from the police."

"Or the devil either, for the matter of that," added the angular barmaid. "It's a pity he's gone. We'll miss him."

"Who's gone? Who the devil you talking about?"

The barmaid turned with a start to face a black-mustached man who had just entered. He was well built and, in a way, handsome. His lips were parted as if he was constantly laughing at some secret joke. But his eyes did not smile; they were cold, hard, unsympathetic.

"Who's gone and where?" he asked again.

"We were speaking of a gentleman, Mister Fane," the barmaid said icily. "In other words—the Major."

Fane cursed viciously.

"You sure? When did he go—and where?"

"Early this morning," the flaxen haired man replied. "He headed north. Why, Fane?"

"Because—Oh, hell! Never mind why. You go an' get some kit together, Tubby. We'll need a light wagon, an' store an' plenty of provisions. We start at sun-up tomorrow morning on the Major's trail."

"But why? What's the rush, Fane?" the flaxen haired man asked as he rose to his feet.

Fane sneered.

"Use your brains, Tubby. What's the Major's reputation? What did he come up to this deserted, poverty stricken hole for? Not his health. Not he. He's been hanging around here for most a month, waiting for something, if you ask me; or trying to throw somebody off his trail. An' what does his leaving so sudden mean to you? Eh? Not a damn thing, I suppose! But it's my guess that he got the message he was waiting for last night, or this morning, an' off he goes in a damned hurry. And, because I know the Major's little ways, I'm gambling he's on the trail of something big: a gold-field, maybe; or diamonds, or ivory—something with big money in it, you can bet your life on that. *That's* why I'm following him in the morning!"

TWENTY DAYS had elapsed since the Major and Jim had started out on their journey to the land of Chief Magato.

Twenty days: And during that twenty days much had happened to them, delaying them, making a painful experience of what they had fondly hoped would be an easy, pleasant jaunt.

For four days they had driven through an unseasonable, devastating succession of rain storms; they had been caught by flood waters whilst fording a wide river and almost drowned; they had been obliged to dig the wagon out of mud holes.

Then, when one element had worked its evil on them, its opposite threatened to complete the wreckage.

They had been caught at night in a veld fire. To escape they had been obliged to inspan hastily and drive through a converging ring of fire. Both men had been badly singed and for a time they were riding in a chariot of fire as the canvas top of the wagon burst into flames.

The vicious exploding of cartridges made their work of salvage a dangerous one.

Four of the mules the Major had been obliged to shoot. The coats of the others—and that of the black stallion— singed by the fire, looked moth-eaten.

And so, by reason of all these misfortunes and others— such as Jim getting a bad attack of malaria, and such as three consecutive, sleepless nights when lions roared around their outspan, threatening to stampede the animals—when they finally did enter Magato's country their outfit was well suited to the part they meant to play.

Ragged, fire-scorched holes gaped in the wagon's canvas hood; the paint had been burnt off the woodwork, and the side boards splintered by bursting bullets. Several of the mules, their feet tender from the red ash covered ground over which they had so recently traveled, limped badly. Both the Major and Jim looked haggard, grimy and unkempt.

And now—

It may have been that, relaxing their caution now that they were so near their objective, both men closed their eyes and found a respite from their exhaustion in sleep. It was, certainly, only a momentary lapse, but it was sufficient to crown their misfortunes.

Startled by a herd of zebras which trotted up curiously to inspect them, the mules bolted and before the Major and Jim, arousing themselves with a start, could gain control over the stampeding animals, the wagon crashed into a big tree, effectively halting the runaways.

The force of the shock sent the two men back over the driver's seat onto the floor of the wagon; the mules were jerked back on their haunches and they milled about, squealing, biting, kicking.

The wagon tilted precariously, then toppled over on its side, smashing a wheel, staving in the woodwork, littering the ground with its contents.

Ruefully the Major and Jim crept out from the wreckage and eyed each other anxiously.

THEN THE MAJOR grinned and Jim shouted abuse at the mules. Shaken, but unharmed, they went to the animals, soothed them and restored them to some degree of order.

Not until that was done did either man allude to the smash. Then Jim said, "I am a fool, *Baas*. I slept. The fault is mine."

"No; mine, Jim. I, too, slept," the Major replied, feeling absently in the breast pocket of his tunic, cursing softly when he cut his fingers on bits of broken glass which represented all that was left of his monocle.

"Bally nuisance!" he murmured. "And that was my last one. Might be deuced awkward. A monocle is, in a sense, my calling card," Aloud he added, "I was dreaming as I slept, Jim. I would rather have continued the dream than awake to this."

"Me, too, *Baas*," Jim said sadly. "I was dreaming I was in my *kraal* with my own people. A beer drink was being held in my honor. And then—*Au-a!* It must have been one of my wives who hit me on the head—or all of them—and I woke up."

The Major laughed.

"And now, what, Jim?"

"It would be best, *Baas*, for you to ride the horse to the *kraal* of Magato and have men sent to carry in the provisions. I will keep guard here until they come."

The Major shook his head.

"No, Jim. We play this game together. I am no longer the *Baas* who commands, but the man who begs. So—we will make packs of such stuff as we can and load them on the mules. The rest we will leave here with the wagon."

Jim nodded, the idea pleasing him. Actually, he had no desire to be left alone. He had a lively memory of the tempers of Magato's warriors. They were too apt to resent the presence of a stranger—certainly of a Hottentot stranger—in their country. And, by way of showing resentment, they would be quite capable of spearing first and questioning afterward.

And so, the Major assisting, he industriously set about improvising packs and making neat, compact bales of the stuff they could load on the mules.

And so engrossed were both men with their task that their bush sense was blunted and nothing warned them of the approach of a party of armed warriors who crept silently through the bush, flitting from tree to tree, taking advantage of all possible cover. Reaching a point when to advance forward brought them out on the less covered ground just around the wagon, they halted, then filed off to the left and right, encircling the place.

This surrounding movement had been almost completed when one of the warriors, his eyes on the two strangers, his mind full of thoughts of the loot which would fall to his share, relaxed his caution and a dried twig snapped under his foot.

It was a trivial sound, but it carried its note of warning.

Jim looked apprehensively at his *Baas* and both men straightened themselves—the Hottentot stretching himself with a loud yawn, the Major, leaning back slightly, his hands to the small of his back, as if easing an ache caused by prolonged stooping.

THEY LOOKED about them, casually. But the cracking of the twig which had warned them had also warned the warriors and not one was visible. Trees, boulders, tufts of grass even, sheltered them from view.

"But they are there, Jim," the Major said softly. "Something tells me that we are surrounded by warriors—and there is nothing we can do but wait."

"I do not like waiting, *Baas*. I grow cold and, also, very hot."

The Major laughed softly.

"What would you have me do, Jim?"

"Call out to them, *Baas*. Tell them who you are. That will be sufficient."

"Maybe, Jim. But I dare not put my name to the test. No. So we will wait until they come to us."

Jim nodded.

"No harm in that, *Baas,* unless—unless they send a messenger ahead of them."

The Major looked puzzled.

"A messenger, Jim?" he queried.

But Jim only grunted and bent to his task again.

The Major lighted a cigarette, puffed unconcernedly and then continued his interrupted task.

They worked slowly now, with less than half a mind to the occupation of their hands. But only a slight tightening of the facial muscles gave evidence of the strain under which they were laboring. They listened intently for any alien sound.

And now, to their danger sharpened ears, it seemed as if all the bush about them rustled stealthily: They fancied they could hear the quickened breathing of creeping men.

Without warning, surprising them to startled exclamations, an assegai whizzed through the air, passing between their heads, and hung quivering in the trunk of a tree.

Somewhere in the bush a man grunted a laugh.

"That is their first messenger, *Baas*," Jim said grimly. "What answer shall we give them?"

The wild yell he then gave was one of reproachful surprise, for the Major had jumped to his feet and was running aimlessly to and fro, calling for mercy, ringing his hands in abject fear.

Understanding suddenly came to Jim and, grinning, he threw himself full length on the ground, hiding his head ostrichlike, under a bale. His *Baas* was playing a game—and a safe one. It was unlikely that the hidden warriors would send any more messengers; there is no glory in the killing of a white-livered fool. They would show themselves now, would come forward to parley with the *Baas*, threatening death. But Jim was sure that his *Baas* would know how to deal with them; the Major's name alone would strike fear into their hearts. Was not the *Baas* a friend of Magato, the chief? And, apart from that, the Major had successfully dealt with hostile natives many times ere this.

And so Jim helped on the Major's game by yelling in fear.

HE WAS silenced presently by loud, mocking guffaws of laughter and, looking up apprehensively, saw a number of warriors converging on his *Baas*. Spears, thrown by men hidden in the bush on the opposite side, behind Jim, feathered the ground close to where the Hottentot was kneeling. He realized that they were thrown to intimidate, not to kill, but the knowledge gave him little comfort. If one, by accident pierced him, the hurt would be no less because it was not intentional!

And so he called to the Major, "Make haste and put an end to their folly, *Baas*. These messengers have death dealing tongues."

As he spoke two warriors leaped upon the Major, pinioning his arms to his sides, and Jim gaped in astonishment as his *Baas,* protesting mildly, suffered himself to be bound hand and foot.

With a cry of rage Jim jumped to his feet, in his hand one of the assegais.

"Dogs!" he shouted hoarsely. "Let the white man go. He is the Mah-jor, Magato's friend. He is the White *Induna! Au-a!* Let him go, I say!"

They answered him with mocking laughs and one pricked the Major in the calf of the leg with the point of his spear.

Beside himself with wrath at the sight of his *Baas* being so abused, Jim did not hear the Major's quiet, "Steady, Jim! You will spoil the game." He only heard mocking laughter, and went berserk.

Casting his spear, which grazed the thigh of the man who had pricked the Major, he rushed forward, as if alone and barehanded he would annihilate the warriors.

And then another messenger came to him. Its form was that of a heavy knobkerry thrown by one of the warriors. It struck Jim on the forehead, between the eyes, checking his mad rush. Blood spurted from his wide nostrils and he dropped stunned to the ground.

The Major tensed, an anxious look came into his eyes. Then, softly, "That was a well-aimed throw, yet there was little merit in it. The man was unarmed. Are the warriors of Magato afraid of an unarmed man?"

They crowded about him threateningly. All, save their captain, were very young. To the captain, recognizing in him an old acquaintance of other days, he said, "And, Tomi, is it at Magato's orders your brave warriors attack strangers?"

The old graybeard stared, wondering how the stranger knew his name.

He gave orders to his warriors, instructed them to finish the task of packing which the Major and Jim had commenced, before answering the Major's question.

"No harm has come to you, white man," he then said. "No harm would have come to the Hottentot had he not suddenly gone mad. We obey orders. We take you to the *kraal* of the chief as, in these days, we take all strangers."

"And after that?"

"*Tchat!* Who shall say? The 'Ears' will hear and the 'Mouth' give judgment."

The Major nodded.

"I am content to wait for that judgment. But let the Hottentot's wound be tended to. It is a little thing I ask."

But, as he spoke, he saw Jim sit up and look around him as one dazed. He made as if he would rise to his feet, intending to continue the mad rush the knobkerry had halted. But warriors anticipated him and, despite his struggles, bound him securely.

The Major smiled: Jim's hurt could not be a very serious one.

AN HOUR later the warriors, with their prisoners, were taking the winding trail which led to the *kraal* of Magato, two days' trek distant.

The Major, roped to four warriors—two walked ahead and two behind—was permitted to ride; Jim was astride one of the mules. He was dull-eyed and muttered continuously.

All the warriors were laden with stuff looted from the wagon; the mules, too, were heavily packed; nothing was left behind.

By the Major's horse marched Tomi.

The Major tried to draw him into conversation, but met with little success. His questions were answered in such a way that discouraged further questioning. Only once did Tomi show any interest in his prisoner's identity, and that was after they had been trekking several hours.

"Are you indeed," he asked casually, "as your black dog said, the man we knew as the White *Induna?*"

The Major smiled.

"And what think you?"

Tomi looked up at him appraisingly.

"In some ways you look like that one," he muttered. "A trick of the voice, a look in the eyes. And he was a friend of Magato." Then, positively, "No, you are not that one. In all things which matter you are different. *Wo-we!* You are dirty; at the sight of my warriors you cried out in fear. A maiden would have made a better fight than you who made no fight at all. And that other one whom you in part resemble, he would have spoken to us, a laugh in his eyes, and we would have called him 'Chief!'—even though we still obeyed orders and bound him. No, you are not that one."

The Major stared thoughtfully ahead.

"Fire will dry up the sap of the strongest tree, Tomi, if the fire is hot enough. And it may well be that some evil, working on a man, will dry up a man's spirit."

Tomi gave this due consideration before he rejected the implied suggestion.

"No," he said again. "You are not that one." He added, smiling reminiscently, "It was always a wonder that that one could take out his eye and hold it in the palm of his hand."

The Major groaned in mock despair.

"I knew," he muttered in English, regretting the broken monocle, "I knew I'd want my calling card."

They were passing now over very rough ground and the Major was forced to concentrate his faculties, bound as he was, on keeping his seat as Satan slithered down a steep, rock-strewn trail. Thorn armored bushes tore his clothes and he was in constant danger of being swept from the saddle by low hanging boughs of trees under which they passed.

Jim was singing wildly now, interposing his songs with gales of laughter. The warriors regarded him uneasily, thinking him mad and it was with evident relief that they sighted the cooking fires' smoke which indicated their nearness to the *kraal* which was to be the night's resting place.

It is not good to be in the bush, at night, with a madman!

IN THE darkest hour that night the Major, awakening suddenly from sleep, was conscious of another's presence in the hut into which his captors had thrust him.

He could hear labored breathing; could visualize some one crawling to him on hand and knees.

The Major tensed. Bound though he was, he had no intention of passively submitting to a stab in the dark.

A light touch fell on his shoulder; a voice whispered in his ear.

"Awake, white man. Awake—softly."

He relaxed. It was the old man Tomi's voice.

"I am awake," he said. "And now what?"

"If I cut your bonds and lead you from this place, where will you go?"

"To Magato—to tell him how his warriors treat his friend."

"Au-a! That is folly. Listen; doubts have ridden me all this night. I could not sleep. So—I have come to set you free, impelled thereto by memories of the man you might be."

"Wo-we!" The Major murmured, conscious no longer of the night's chill.

"But you must *not* go to Magato."

"Wherefore not?"

"Why question, foolish one?"

"To gain knowledge."

"Then know—" Tomi's irritation made him somewhat relax his caution and he raised his voice—"know that Magato has changed. He hates those who were his friends. *Wo-we!* I say it is death, in these days, to be a friend of Magato."

"Nevertheless, I go to him."

"Fool! I will cut your bonds. The Hottentot, too, I will release. So—you will go?"

"Aye," the Major replied easily. "To Magato."

"Fool!" shouted Tomi. "Fool! Is death so greatly to be desired, then? You—" He stopped, aghast.

Apparently the whole village was awake. Men called to each other and demanded their women to bring torches; children wailed, frightened by the uproar; dogs yapped and the oxen in the cattle *scherm* lowed a protest at their untimely awakening.

The red flares of torches gleamed; rays of them entered the Major's prison hut, and by their light the two men could see each other, dimly, as through the murk of fog.

Tomi's teeth chattered with fear.

"They are looking for me," he moaned, "and if they see me here they will guess my purpose, and—" An expressive gesture completed his sentence.

The Major eyed him shrewdly, half suspecting a trap.

But Tomi's expression assured him that, if trap there were, the old man was not party to it; his fear was evidently not simulated.

WITH A sudden spring, the Major grappled with Tomi, slipping his bound hands over the old man's head and shoulders. The two rolled over and over, apparently locked in deadly combat.

"You had risen," the Major said swiftly in Tomi's ear as they struggled, "planning to see that the warriors appointed kept good watch over this hut. You found them asleep—"

"As I knew I would," Tomi commented grimly, "having put sleep medicine in their beer."

"Listen, don't talk," the Major grunted. "You entered the hut to see that I was safe bound and I spring upon you. That is your story. Now call for help."

And Tomi, seeing in the Major's ruse a way out of the predicament in which he found himself, yelled lustily, "To me warriors! The prisoner is escaping."

He and the Major now put more realism into their mock struggle. Warriors came running to them; the hut was filled with the swirl of smoke and the flickering light of the torches.

Rough, strong hands grasped the Major, forcing him to release his hold on Tomi who, scrambling to his feet, turned wrath fully upon the warriors, upbraiding them in a shrill, shrewish voice; explaining how he had come to be in the Major's hut; insisting that, but for his foresight and courage, the white man would have escaped.

"And now," Tomi concluded triumphantly, "tie up this dog so that he can move neither hand nor foot."

Quickly the warriors obeyed and the Major, what with the coils of rope which now swathed his form from head to foot, looked like a monstrous cocoon.

A few minutes later Tomi left the hut, boasting volubly of his prowess. He was very human, was Tomi, and, having made a strong gesture to a memory, he was determined to make what capital he could of the unexpected turn his errand of mercy had taken.

Soon the *kraal* settled down to sleep again. Once again the Major was in darkness.

He considered for a while the things Tomi had said to him, endeavoring to find a reason for the old man's overture of friendship. But, the answer continually eluding him, he philosophically resigned himself until the riddle's answer should present itself.

FOUR DAYS had passed. It was nearing the hour of sunset. Once again, after an interval of many years, the Major and Jim were at the *kraal* of the Chief Magato; were standing in the center of a large clearing before the chief's hut.

Now, as then, a big fire blazed in the center of the clearing and, lining the stockade were massed Magato's warriors. Now, as then, the warriors were singing the praises of their chief—but then the Major's name was coupled with that of Magato's, now the warriors' chant spoke of one they called "Ears and Mouth."

That other time the Major had sat in a place of honor awaiting Magato's appearance before holding court and instructing Magato's people in the way of white man's justice. But now he was an object of ridicule, a prisoner waiting for judgment to be passed upon him.

"No foolish tricks, Jim," he said to the Hottentot. "I will do what talking is required, You will be dumb. You are not to talk or act."

"There will be no need, *Baas*," Jim replied gaily. "Once let Magato hear your name and all this folly will be ended! *Wo-we!* For four days they have kept you shut up, treating you like a mangy dog. But these warriors are young. Maybe they never knew you."

The singing increased in volume. It was accompanied now by a booming noise made by the drumming of spearheads on bullock hide shields.

"Look, *Baas*," Jim exclaimed, capering about excitedly, "Magato comes! and I, I am free, unbound, because they think me mad. Do not forget that, *Baas*, no matter what happens."

The drumming increased its tempo. It sounded louder, louder, ceasing suddenly in one devastating crash as the warriors, brandishing their assegais, shouted a welcome to Magato and the one who was with him.

Then silence.

Strangely excited, the Major watched Magato emerge from his hut and seat himself on a stool which had been placed nearby. A tall, emaciated looking native, his face hideously painted and masked, his ribs outlined with white ash paint, bedecked in the bizarre regalia of a witchdoctor, following closely behind Magato and, when the chief had seated himself, stood directly behind him and, stooping, whispered in his ears.

Magato was very fat, stupendously fat. In the old days his fatness had seemed to lend him an added dignity. But now its constant jelly-like quivering made the Major think that it was the visible expression of the mental sickness which lurked in Magato's mind, a sickness which made him helplessly dependent on the man who stood behind him.

Neither Magato nor the witch-doctor gave any sign that they were aware of the white prisoner. Indeed, it seemed to the Major that Magato studiously refrained from looking in his direction.

Then, without further preamble, the business of the evening began. Magato held court.

HUSBANDS BROUGHT complaints against their wives: wives came begging for protection. Others came with tales of witchcraft, of theft and of black murder.

The sun set; darkness fell.

Disputes were aired concerning the lawful ownership of cattle; intricate points of inheritance; more husbands, more wives.

Hours passed. And still claimants for justice passed before their chief.

But rarely was a case heard to its conclusion. Sometimes, even before the case had been presented, the witchdoctor would bend down and whisper in Magato's ear.

"Enough," that man would then cry. "The 'Ears' have heard. Silence—and the voice will give judgment."

Another consultation with the witchdoctor and then Magato would pronounce judgments which burlesqued justice: Guilty, evidently guilty ones, were rewarded and the innocent punished, condemned to beatings, torture, death.

The night aged. The people no longer lauded the pronouncements of Magato. A resentful murmur arose which would not be quieted, despite the efforts of certain warriors.

At last no more came forward that their wrongs might be adjusted. For a little while there was silence and the Major, realizing that his turn was at hand, tensed slightly.

"To deal with you, white man," Magato said suddenly in a harsh voice, "is easy!" He leaned forward, resting his hands on his fat thighs. "Unbidden you and your black dog came into this country. Your purpose doubtless an evil one, for you lied to Tomi, the man I sent to bring you to this place. Without question you lied, for you claimed to be one who stayed with us long ago."

"I am that one, Magato," the Major said slowly, "and you know I am that one."

"I know you are not that one," Magato insisted. "And even if you were that one, what then? He was no friend of mine. He was no friend of my people. *Wo-we!* He tried to take to himself the place that is mine: he set himself up as a judge over us. He was a liar, practising deceit for his own gain.

"And so I say, if you are indeed that one, then I am glad to welcome you back to my country, back to the vengeance which has been awaiting you."

Magato rose to his feet and shook his clenched fist.

"You evil one," he cried, his face contorted with passionate anger, "this is my day of vengeance. Now listen to the judgment we will pass upon you."

He sank back again on his stool, apparently rendered speechless by his wrath.

The Major breathed hard. The whole affair seemed to him like the phantasy of a nightmare—the silence—the menacing forms of the warriors, their naked bodies tinged, it seemed, with the red glow of the fire—the tips of their upraised spears silvered by the white radiance of a late rising moon—the soft murmurs of women beyond the clearing—Jim's haggard, self-accusing face—the impressive figure of the obese chief, sitting on his judgment seat like a personification of doom—the stooping, sinister figure of the witchdoctor—the "Ears and Mouth," bending down, whispering—

The Major felt totally unconscious of self. It seemed to him, despite the fact that he was one of the central actors, that he was witnessing a drama from some remote height. He wondered, vaguely, why the action halted; wondered if they were awaiting a prompter's cue. He heard himself say, "The night grows cold and I am tired, Magato. Give me leave to depart, to sleep. And, whether I awaken in this world or that of the spirits, what matter?"

The spell was broken, the phantasies dispelled and the Major saw things as they were. His brain worked coolly, efficiently, as he waited to hear the decision of a fat heathen who knew not gratitude.

He looked toward Jim, Faithful Jim who wanted nothing so much as to argue things out with Magato—and Jim would use a forceful argument. As it was, the Hottentot was only restrained by the Major's orders that he must not speak, must not act.

"It is all right, Jim," the Major said to him. "The bitterness has passed. And there is no blame. Nothing is left but good memories."

Jim grinned happily.

The witchdoctor straightened himself; Magato slapped his tremendous thighs with his hands.

"The 'Ear' has heard," he said. "The 'Mouth' gives judgment. Give heed, white man:

"Until the night of the new moon, you shall live. On that night we will send you to the land of the spirits. And—" he smiled grimly—"your leaving will not be a pleasant one."

THAT SAME evening Fane and Bates came to the place where the Major's wagon had crashed into the tree.

Their discovery of the deserted, broken wagon had put Fane into a rare good humor, and neither of the two men were sufficiently bush wise to read the story the spoor had to tell.

"We're getting warm, Tubby," Fane cried exultantly. "We're really on the bloody dude's track at last. An' to think I'd almost decided to give the business up an' start back tomorrow! Hell!"

"All I know is," grumbled Bates, "I wish you hadn't waited till tomorrow before goin' back. I don't like this business, as I've told you before. We're in Magato's country now—an' I like it less. The old blighter's got a bad reputation. Got a nasty way of dealing with visitors. He's not what they call hospitable, by all accounts. I wouldn't be surprised if they've killed the Major."

He shivered and looked around apprehensively.

"Don't be a bloody fool, Tubby. I tell you the Major's a big friend of Magato's. He saved the nigger's life once. So that's that! The Major wouldn't stand by an' let us get beat up by his pals."

"Oh, hell! What's the good of talking. Come on—let's *skoff* an' turn in."

"God! I wouldn't be surprised to find the Major's after old Magato's diamonds. I bet that's it. Come to think of it, I wouldn't be surprised to find he's been digging into them for some time past an' that's how he gets the diamonds he sells. You know, for all his reputation, he ain't what I'd call a real, genuine I.D.B."

"No," Bates agreed bitterly. "It takes skunks like you and me to be that, Fane."

"Anyway," Fane continued, scowling at Bates' interruption, "Whatever the Major's after, we're goin' to share. See?"

"I'd rather be trekkin' back, Fane. I values my life more than a share of what the Major's getting, no matter what it is. However—"

They were eating their evening meal when Tomi's men rushed them, giving them no chance to use their guns and, in less than five minutes, they were roped tightly together.

"Yah!" the little man snorted to Fane. "You know everything, don't you? If you ask me, I'd say they're treating us the same way they treated the Major. Yah! You're goin' to share with him all right!"

FOR THREE days the Major had been confined in a filthy hut about which a strong guard had been set.

He had tried to talk to the men who stood on guard, but they had refused to listen to him. He had flattered the hideous old hag who brought him his daily ration of mealie meal and a small gourd of water, hoping to gain some information from her. But here again he met with no success.

Engulfed in a wall of silence, unarmed, watched by men who never relaxed their vigilance—they bound him hand and foot each night at sundown—he fell into a fit of moody depression.

At first his attitude was one of egotistical despair. He thought of himself as a martyr; as a man who had sacrificed himself for savages who were little better than beasts, who were lower than beasts in their lack of gratitude. It was that lack of gratitude which had hurt him most. Despite his protestations to Jim, he had counted on being warmly received by Magato and his people.

With his awakening on the morning of the third day, his mood suddenly changed. He began to make excuses for Magato.

"Maybe," he drawled, seeking relief from the oppressive silence by speaking his thoughts aloud, "maybe Magato didn't recognize me. I was bally dirty. I'm dirtier now! Hadn't shaved or washed for three or four days. Magato never saw me looking like that in the old days. And I didn't really play fair with the old laddie. I ought to have talked to him like a Dutch uncle instead of actin' like a sulky school-brat.

"Still, that doesn't explain what he said about the man I was. Of course, the fat old tub of lard is gettin' old and it's quite within the well known grounds of reason, that his brain box isn't workin' at top pressure. Yes: I rather fancy that hits the nail on the bally head. But," he laughed ruefully, "that doesn't help me any more than it 'ud help a cat to know that the brat that jabs it with a needle ain't conscious of wrong doing.

"Therefore my old brain had better start working. Yes, indeed. I've never heard of a cat that passively submitted to being torturted by an infant. Most generally, quite ignoring the fact that their torturers were moral minors, as it were, an' therefore not responsible, they scratched like—er— Hades an' got away.

"So then, to consider ways an' means. I could go about this in a much better spirit if I knew what was happening to Jim. Maybe they've killed him. If they have, I don't think I care a great deal what happens to me. Only, before I—

er—shuffled off this mortal coil, I'd want to send the men responsible for it to keep Jim's shade company.

"However, I fancy Jim's very much alive."

FOR THE first time since his capture by Tomi the Major definitely gave himself up to a serious consideration of his predicament, his keen brain forming and rejecting threads which might be woven together and form a rope of escape.

As the hours passed a light began to gleam, an understanding of the real cause of things filtered through the mire of unexplainable happenings and a sure plan formed itself. It needed, now, only a final touch—the keystone, as it were, to the bridge he was building.

He was suddenly disturbed by a violent uproar outside the hut.

He rose to his feet, intending to brave the wrath of the guards by going to the door of the hut in order to discover the cause of the tumult.

And then the door was opened and two men thrust violently into the hut. They sprawled headlong on the floor, almost at the Major's feet.

Then the door was closed again and the three were left alone in the murky gloom of the hut.

For a moment there was silence, broken, at length, by the Major's shout.

"Jim, you bally old heathen!"

"Golly, damme no, yes," Jim replied with a chuckle.

"And who is this other," the Major continued in the vernacular, looking doubtfully toward the third man who sprawled supine just inside the doorway, his naked, bleeding back raw from *sjambok* wounds.

"It is Magato, *Baas*," Jim said.

"Magato!"

"Yah, *Baas*," Jim said impatiently. "Who else could it be?"

The Major seemed not to hear. He was bending over the chief, examining his wounds, swearing softly.

He gently turned the chief over and raised him to a sitting position. Evidently the man was still half-dazed, for he seemed barely conscious of his whereabouts and only stared vacantly before him.

The Major turned to Jim.

"What is the story, Jim?" he asked.

The Hottentot chuckled softly.

"There is little I know, *Baas*. The little I will now tell you. Because they thought me mad but little watch has been kept over me. So, wandering here and there, I found out things, *Baas*. I discovered that the people of this *kraal* were divided against each other. The young men, the warriors, desired to see another chief in Magato's place. But the old ones—they desired to return to the old order of things. But the ones who thought thus, did not cry their thoughts aloud. Nay: they walked in silence as if they feared the warriors. There is not much else I can tell you. But presently, I think, Magato will be able to talk. He will tell you everything.

"There is this, *Baas:* I found it amongst the stuff they had taken from our wagon."

JIM REMOVED his tattered coat and shirt and, fastened about his waist was a cartridge belt to which hung a revolver in its holster. He took it off and gave it to the Major.

The white man's eyes gleamed contentedly.

"Good work, Jim," he said.

"Yah, *Baas*. This, too, I found."

This was the Major's large hunting knife—a knife Jim had always coveted. It was very heavy, but beautifully balanced. Its tempered blade, broad at the hilt and tapering to a needle point, was a good nine inches long.

For a little while the Hottentot was silent. He toyed happily with the knife, juggling with it; throwing it up into the air and catching it between his strong, white teeth. Then, he made a great show of stabbing himself, pressing the spring which released the blade and allowed it to slide up into the haft at the slightest pressure.

"It is great magic, *Baas,*" he said with a grin.

"Hide it and the revolver, Jim. Hide them somewhere in the thatch of the hut. If they keep to their custom, they will come in to bind us when the sun sets. So leave the knife open and in a place where we can get at it after we are bound."

Jim nodded approval and quickly followed his *Baas'* instructions.

As Jim squatted down again beside the Major, Magato said, speaking slowly at first, the words trembling off his lips, "White man, my friend. There is much to say, much to do. But first I must set myself right in your eyes. I had not forgotten you. Nor am I devoid of gratitude. But what I did, I did for my peophe's sake. It would seem, now, that I denied my friend in vain, but let that go. Truly it grieved me to talk as I did the other night. And the knowledge that you could not understand added to my grief."

"I did not understand until this morning," the Major said gently. "And then a glimmer of light came to me. You played a part, doubtless for some good reason?"

"Aye." Magato smiled grimly. "A good reason. Listen; come close that I may talk in a whisper less men hear. I can not move to you, my back is stiff. But not as stiff as my will to avenge the evil that has been worked upon me."

The Major moved so that he was very close to the chief.

"That is better," Magato continued. "Again listen; six moons ago a half-caste came to my country and pleaded for food and shelter. It was given to him. How are we to blame the sins of his father and his mother. So I gave him my protection. He was eaten with a bitterness, my friend, toward all white people. For that he is not to be blamed. His father's was the greater sin. But let that pass. He was clever, this half-caste, and he could perform many miracles—nay, I know they are but tricks—which made him greatly feared by my people. Also, he always carried with him the weapons of a white man.

"I SAY that, by his magic, he made himself feared by the people and I—perhaps I, too, feared him and forgot that his magic was but trickery—made him my chief counsellor.

"And that was the beginning of trouble. He used his wisdom for evil ends. *Wo-we!* He set brother against brother, he divided my people so that he could afterwards use them for his own ends.

"People began to murmur against me. The young men loudly demanded that the half-caste—Hans, is his name—should be chief in my place. But Hans dared not make an open move. He was crafty. He waited until yet others came over to him. To that end, he made me the tool of his evil. At all times, he was the 'Ears and the Mouth.' I was only an empty shell echoing his words. To have refused would have meant death for, you must understand, all the warriors who were loyal to me Hans had sent away from this *kraal.*

"So, secretly, I began to plot and, in order to hide my plottings, I was always harshest to those who were my friends.

"As I saw it, that was the wisest way. Had I done otherwise he might have suspected. When my friends were brought before me for trial, I dealt harshly with them *Wo-we!* I had no friends. I had no kin. It was very hard. My only son I sentenced to die, claiming that he had bewitched me. And he would have died had not the women, led by his wives, rescued him. Aye! They rescued him and took him away from this place of evil. He waits now in a place appointed; in a place where he is gathering together others who remain loyal to me.

"Truly it was hard. But what is the death of a few compared to the death of all my people? And it is to that Hans would have led them. The fool, in his bitterness, boasts that he will wage war on the white men, and the young warriors are eager to baptize their spears. There can be only one end to such folly.

"It was to delay the evil day that I threw filth on you, my friend. Had I not done so, Hans would have killed you because you were a white man. Tonight the women would have rescued you as they rescued my son. Tonight there is to be a beer drink and the women would have beguiled the warriors from their watch. But now—woe is me!"

Magato rocked dolorously back and forth.

"Listen," he continued suddenly. "My hand was forced by the arrival of two white prisoners Tomi had captured. They told Hans that they had followed you and that you were my friend.

"They told him of your cunning and might; told him that the Hottentot was only playing at madness. And so Hans determined to wait no longer. Me he took prisoner

and beat, hoping to get information from me. That failing, he has let it be known that tomorrow night, when the
moon is full, he will put us all to death. But first he will
torture. And that would have been his undoing, could some
of the women have escaped from the *kraal.* They would
have taken word to my son. But Hans is clever. He keeps a
strong guard over them. Further, now that I am a prisoner
and all seems lost, it may be that the women have lost their
spirit and would not go even if the way were open to them."

"Then I must go, Magato, if a way can be found," the
Major said.

"It is not so easy, *Baas,*" Jim interposed. "Best that I go."

"*Tchat!* Supposing it were possible," Magato said, "for
you to get away from this *kraal,* do you think my son and
the warriors with him would listen to you, a Hottentot?"

THE FOLLY would be theirs, Magato," the Major
said curtly. "So, as I have said, I will go as soon as a way
presents itself. Where waits your son?"

"At the *kraal* of Chivamba's—you know it. We hunted
from there in the old days; hunted leopards in the hills."

"There are many caves hidden in those hills," the Major
said, smiling reminiscently.

"Truly. It is in them that the warriors hide now, the
warriors who are still my men. Others join themselves to
my son's party with every passing day. A few more days,
in less than a week, their numbers would be greater than
those who support Hans. But now—now that my hand is
forced—I do not know. Nothing is sure but that the spirits
always fight on the side of the greater number."

The Major ignored that.

"On foot," he muttered, "Chivamba's *kraal* is a forenoon's
trek from here."

"No need to go on foot, *Baas*," Jim put in. "The black horse—*Au-a!* None of the warriors dare go near him— grazes all day just beyond the stockade. At night he goes with the goats into the small *scherm* which is without the stockade. If he were called, he would come to you. The thorn fence would be no bar to him."

The Major nodded.

And then a party of warriors crowded into the hut. It was the hour of sunset and they had come to tie up their prisoners.

They worked clumsily, for, in anticipation of the night's beer drink of celebration, some of them had already been indulging. Presently, their task finished, they would have left the hut, but, aggravated by the curses of Magato and Jim they delayed a little while longer and violently gagged the three men with strips of rag. Then, with much brutal jesting, they departed.

THE SUN set; darkness followed.

The beating of tom-toms sounded and the drunken laughter of men.

Jim strained at his bonds. The warriors had done their work thoroughly yet Jim found, when he afterwards relaxed, that he could move his right hand a little.

He continued his endeavors.

The warriors on guard—he could see them through the open doorway, seated about a fire, their backs to the hut— were muttering resentfully because they could not take part in the beer-drinking.

Later, after an excited discussion, two deserted their posts with promises to bring back beer to the men who stayed. When they returned, carrying a big calabash, they reeled unsteadily.

PRESENTLY, ALL the guards were singing maudlinly and Jim wondered at the beer's potence. He did not know, of course, that the liquor Fane and Bates carried had been poured into it.

And now Jim found that he could release the fingers of his right hand and could just move his legs.

He rolled over and over until he came to the wall of the hut directly under the place where he had hidden the knife and revolver.

He struggled painfully to his feet.

A few moments later, the knife in his hand, he rolled over again to the Major's side. Then, with a grunt of satisfaction, he sawed at his *Baas'* bonds. The operation was a slow one for Jim's hold on the knife was very precarious and he dropped it several times.

At length the Major's hands were free and, taking the knife from Jim, he quickly completed the task. He removed the gag from his mouth, then from Jim's. But, when he was about to cut loose the Hottentot, Jim said:

"No, *Baas*. You must leave Magato and me bound. You must go alone to the *kraal* of Chivamba. It will be easier for one man to escape; you will travel faster alone. And so it will be best that you leave us bound and gagged so that the warriors can not accuse us of helping you and, in their anger, kill us before you return."

The Major nodded agreement.

"I shall go when the moon rises, Jim," he said.

He replaced Jim's gag, patted him on the shoulder, then having buckled his revolver and belt about his waist he sat down at the back of the hut—thinking, planning.

The gloom of the hut lightened. The moon was rising.

The Major crouched down, moving to one side in order to get out of the beam of light which streamed through the doorway of the hut.

He bared his chest and made there an incision with the razor-keen blade of the hunting knife. The blood flowed freely. A little he smeared upon his face then he pressed his shirt against the wound, chuckling softly as the black stain spread.

The moonlight brightened.

With a long, wailing cry the Major leaped to his feet and staggered into the moonlight. The warriors on guard turned slowly, but did not rise. Their legs were weakened by the beer they had drunk; their minds were fogged, their sight bleared.

They saw the white man flourish a long-bladed knife. Their eyes, wide open, filled with fear, saw him stab himself in the chest; they saw the knife enter his flesh; saw him thrust it in—awfully, slowly—up to the hilt and hold it there.

They saw him reel and drop with a thud to the ground. He stared sightlessly up at the roof of the hut; his mouth sagged open. And still they dared not move.

THE TOM-TOMS were beating maddeningly up at the council place. The white light of the moon paled the red flames of the fire and cast an eerie glamor of unreality upon everything.

The dead man groaned. The warriors saw his limbs move. They gasped as he rose to his feet and walked slowly toward them. His left hand, red stained, was stretched out as if he were groping his way through the land of shades: his right still pressed the knife in the wound. He seemed to "flow" over the ground.

They shrank back, avoiding his touch. He came to the fire and halted for a moment in the center of it, turning a grimacing face toward them. The flames leaped up about him and, groaning with fear they shut their eyes, covering their faces with their hands.

When they dared to look up again the "thing" had gone.

And, because fear had closed their ears, they did not hear—it came from the goat *scherm* beyond the *kraal*—a soft, low whistle, a horse's whinny of delight and, a little later, the galloping thud of horse's hoofs.

"It was a spirit," they murmured in awed tones. And none thought of entering the hut; none dared to go to Hans to tell him of the strange things they had seen.

BEFORE SUNRISE next morning the Major returned to the *kraal* of Magato. At his heels ran Jhentsi, Magato's son whom years ago the Major had saved from death. With them were all the warriors who had waited hidden at the caves. It had needed all the Major's eloquence and knowledge of their psychology to persuade them to travel through the night.

"We are not jackals," they said. "Neither are we cowards that we should attack sleeping men. Let us wait until the sun is up. And then you shall see how men can fight."

But that the Major would not have. He knew that once the story of his escape was known to Hans he would prob-ably kill Magato and Jim, would kill all he suspected of being friendly to Magato. Maybe he had already acted, and was on guard. For that reason alone he was in favor of a surprise attack and, finally, to that course he won the warriors' approval.

Silently, now, they swarmed through a gap in the pole stockade and made their way to the hut where Magato and Jim were imprisoned.

No one challenged them for the warriors of the *kraal* were sleeping off the effects of their night's debauch.

Quickly releasing the prisoners they made their way then to the chief's hut.

The ground was littered with drink-soddened sleepers whom Jhentsi's men disarmed and bound, lining them up at one end of the clearing, threatening death to any who dared give alarm.

The east lightened and the Major greeted the rising sun with a shot from his revolver.

A man rushed out of the chief's hut, firing as he ran. One of Jhentsi's men fell, a bullet in his leg—and then the Major fired. The bullet hit the half-caste in the right shoulder; it spun him round like a top and, before he could recover, warriors grappled with him and held him fast.

It was all over. Other warriors staggered from their huts, but none showed fight.

"And now," Magato said grimly, turning to the Major, "I will hold court as I did in the old days. And you shall be at my right hand that I may consult with you. *Wo-we!* These evil ones shall suffer and first—first I deal with Hans."

But the Major shook his head.

"No," he said. "First I must wash and rid me of this beard. And I must dress myself as a white man should be dressed. And I am hungry."

"I am a fool," Magato said. "I should have thought of these things. So it shall be as you say. The evil dogs can wait."

GREATLY RELIEVED the Major turned away and with Jim started a search of the huts, looking for his equipment. His chief object in persuading Magato to postpone the trials was that that man's anger might be allowed to cool; he had no intention of allowing Magato to indulge in an orgy of bloodshed.

In one of the huts he discovered the two men, Fane and Tubby Bates. Both were bound and beside themselves with fear.

"By Jove, dear lads," he drawled as he cut them loose, "and what are you doin' here?"

Tubby was silent, his *only* sensation was one of great relief and gratitude. But Fane snarled:

"I don't know what little game you're playing up here, Major. But I'm betting there's big money in it. So, whatever it is, you can take it from me I'm going to make you share it."

"Fancy that, now," the Major murmured. "You are a greedy bounder. I should have thought you'd experienced quite enough of the things I've been getting. Still, some men are bally gluttons.

"I say: You don't happen to have a monocle with you? No? Too bad. I'm quite lost without one. Never mind—I may find one when I find the rest of my kit. Ta-ta! See you later. Or perhaps you'd like to come along with me. Only, if I were you, I'd get hence as soon as possible. Magato doesn't like you. He thinks you were responsible for his beatin'."

"I'm stayin' near you. Major," Fane growled.

The Major shrugged his shoulders and continued his search.

IT WAS a week later. Once again all was harmonious in the land of Magato. Hans had been expelled from the country, threatened with death should he dare to return; and the men who had followed him were now reconciled to the rule of Magato, their punishment being an order that they were not to possess arms of any sort until a year had passed.

The Major counted it as one of his greatest triumphs to have been able to persuade Magato to so merciful a course.

Fane and Bates had already been escorted out of the country and now the Major, riding his horse ahead of the wagon, came to the borders of the country.

And there he halted to bid good-by to Magato and the host of people who had accompanied him.

"And so," he said, "we again say 'Good by.'"

"Aye," Magato replied. "You leave us—and our hearts go with you. Into the Hottentot's hand I gave a gift this morning. It is for you to do with as you will. 'Tis a measure of our gratitude."

A few minutes later the Major rode away, Jim following. But Magato and his people did not move. For a long time their songs in praise of the Major—they called him the 'Deliverer,' the 'White *Induna*'-echoed across the veld.

"BAAS!" JIM said softly later that afternoon. They had outspanned and made camp on the edge of a large tract of thick bush. *"Baas*—I think they watch us."

"Doubtless, Jim," the Major replied indifferently. "That was to be expected." He was thinking of Fane's vow to have a share in whatever the Major's game might be. "They have watched us ever since we left Magato's country. But what matter? We have nothing of value, and, besides, they lack, I think, the courage to attack us."

"When we sleep, *Baas,* they might find courage."

"True. But still, what would it avail them?"

"You forget Magato's gift, *Baas*."

The Major roused himself and looked curiously at Jim.

"I had. What is it. Go and fetch it."

Jim grinned and going to the wagon took out a calabash which he gave to the Major.

"It is heavy, Jim," the Major muttered and emptied its contents out on to the ground before him.

"By Jove!" he exclaimed excitedly and he ran his fingers through a little pile of glittering stones. "By Jove!" he said again and examined the stones with the assurance of an expert.

"Now," Jim chuckled, "you know the measure of Magato's gratitude, for he has given you his people's treasures."

The Major nodded absently. After a little while he asked, "And you think these are diamonds, Jim?"

"I know they are, *Baas*. They are Magato's diamonds. All save a few which he kept for tradition's sake."

"It is a big gift, Jim," the Major said slowly. "Now get a spade."

Wonderingly Jim went again to the wagon.

"And now what, *Baas*?" he asked.

"Dig a big hole here." The Major pointed to a spot at the foot of a nearby tree.

Still wondering, Jim obeyed.

For a little while the Major sat motionless, staring thoughtfully before him. Then he picked out one of the stones and put in his tunic pocket. The others he returned to the calabash, one by one, counting aloud as he did so."

"Is that deep enough, *Baas*?" Jim asked.

"Yes," the Major said as he carefully put the calabash into the hole and covered it over with the loose dirt. "And now, Jim," he continued when he had destroyed all traces of Jim's handiwork, "we will inspan and trek."

"But, *Baas*—" Jim commenced excitedly, thinking of the men who watched; thinking his *Baas* demented.

"OR MUST I inspan," the Major interrupted. He continued, laughing at Jim's look of despair: "I am not mad, Jim. And you, you have not examined the stones?"

"No, *Baas*. Why?"

"They are not diamonds, Jim. Pretty stones, some of them, but worthless."

"Au-a, Baas! How could that be? They are Magato's treasure. He almost cried like a woman at parting with them. He—"

"And what does Magato know of diamonds, Jim? He values these stones because of the traditions. He thought I would value them because men had come seeking them in the old days. So his gift to me was a big gift. I would return them—even if they had been diamonds I would return them—if I could find a way of doing so that would not give offence. But to return such a gift would only hurt the giver.

"And so—" he patted his pocket—"one stone I have kept to remind me of many things. The rest—" he shrugged his shoulders—"I leave them here for the two men to find. I think that they, fearing a trap, will wait until the morning before they come for them. Yah! Even were the stones diamonds I should not weep if they robbed me of them. The farewell songs of Magato's people still ring in my ears. They cannot rob me of that. So—inspan, Jim."